Born in 1916, **Mark Hebden** wrote many fictional crime books. He was both a sailor and an airman – during the Second World War he served with two air forces and two navies – and also a journalist, a travel courier, a cartoonist and a history teacher. After turning to writing full time, he created a sequence of crime novels centred around the quirky fictional character Chief Inspector Pel. Hebden is a master of his genre, and his writing is as timeless as it is versatile and entertaining.

BY THE SAME AUTHOR
ALL PUBLISHED BY HOUSE OF STRATUS

The Dark Side of the Island
Death Set to Music
The Errant Knights
Eyewitness
A Killer For the Chairman
League of Eighty-nine
Mask of Violence
Pel Among the Pueblos
Pel and the Bombers
Pel and the Faceless Corpse
Pel and the Missing Persons
Pel and the Paris Mob
Pel and the Party Spirit
Pel and the Picture of Innocence
Pel and the Pirates
Pel and the Predators
Pel and the Promised Land
Pel and the Prowler
Pel and the Sepulchre Job
Pel and the Staghound
Pel Is Puzzled
Pel Under Pressure
Portrait in a Dusty Frame
A Pride of Dolphins
What Changed Charley Farthing

MARK HEBDEN

This edition published in 2001 by House of Stratus, an imprint of Stratus Books Ltd., 21 Beeching Park, Kelly Bray, Cornwall, PL17 8QS, UK.

www.houseofstratus.com

Typeset, printed and bound by House of Stratus.

A catalogue record for this book is available from the British Library and the Library of Congress.

ISBN 1-84232-902-2

Though lovers of Burgundy might decide that they have recognised the city in these pages, in fact it is intended to be fictitious.

one

It didn't look very lethal. There was remarkably little look of menace about the thing. It was small – tiny, really – slender, white and harmless-looking.

Chief Inspector Evariste Clovis Désiré Pel, of the Brigade Criminelle of the Police Judiciaire of the Republic of France, held it carefully between his fingers and stared at it morosely. Uneasily he looked at his second in command, Inspector Daniel Darcy, who was sitting across the desk from him, and then at the head of the sergeants' room, Sergeant Jean-Luc Nosjean, who, one of these days, would be an inspector himself if Pel had anything to do with it.

He gazed at the small white object again. It was a killer, as well he knew. He'd studied the reports. Though it looked so innocent, it had an insidious ability to destroy.

'It's a wonder the Russians don't get everybody at it,' he said slowly. 'Then, when we're all flat on our backs, send in the tanks.'

He stared again at the small object in his hand, his expression one of anger, then he sighed, put it in his mouth and, applying a match, drew the smoke down to his socks. For the life of him, he could never understand why he couldn't give them up.

'Do you think,' he asked, 'that it's cowardice and lack of moral fibre?'

Darcy shrugged. 'It doesn't worry me all that much,' he said cheerfully, leaning back and drawing on his own cigarette as if it had never had the power to put him on his back with bronchitis, heart failure, cancer or any of the other associated ailments.

Unlike Pel, who worried constantly about his vices, Darcy had always been able to conduct his with dignity.

'In fact,' he was saying, 'when I travel by train I invariably head for the smoking section. That's where you meet people of compassion and humility. In the non-smoking section the air's clean all right but it's heavy with self-righteousness.'

'You don't believe that, do you?'

'We smokers are becoming an elite group.'

Pel looked at Nosjean, the third member of the group. 'Why do you smoke?'

Nosjean grinned, taking his cue from Darcy. 'Why not?' he said. 'If there's going to be a nuclear war.

'We all have a reason,' Darcy said.

'I certainly do,' Pel admitted gloomily. 'It's because I can't stop.' He studied his cigarette again. 'I've often wondered if I'd do better sticking a dozen in my mouth at once, lighting them all together, smoking them at full speed, and then forgetting them for the rest of the day. While it might reduce the number in the end, though, I have a suspicion it would kill me more quickly.'

'You look well enough at the moment, Patron.'

Pel disagreed. He felt he had a cold coming on and, as he well knew, *his* germs were different from everybody else's. They were big and hairy, he felt, and probably had fangs and claws. So they couldn't miss the point, he coughed a few times.

'You sound like Mimi in the last act of *Bohème,*' Darcy grinned. 'Perhaps you should try Lourdes. They're supposed to be able to cure anything.'

'Except crime,' Nosjean pointed out. 'They have a crime rate that's double the average.'

Never a man with a high threshold of tolerance, Pel scowled, feeling the levity had gone far enough. He removed the cigarette from his mouth and studied it again, a small man with intense dark eyes, spectacles on the end of his nose and thinning hair that lay over his head like wet seaweed across a rock. The occasion was his daily conference. Every morning he and Darcy held an informal chat on the subject of what the department was handling at the moment. Sometimes it included every crime in the calendar and then, with Pel sour at the encroachment of evil across the daily life of his beloved Burgundy, every member of his department was involved – even Sergeant Misset, who was known to be either stupid or suffering from a case of terminal inertia and who, if Pel could have had his way, would have been back directing traffic round the Porte Guillaume at the top of the Rue de la Liberté. Today, because there was remarkably little happening, the conference consisted only of Pel, Darcy and Nosjean and, since there was little else to occupy their attention, they had got on to Pel's inability to stop smoking.

They had covered everything else first, the state of the crime statistics, the fact that the authorities in Paris – in fact, Paris in general – had no idea how the provinces thought, the coming election.

With only a week or two to go, the political campaign was beginning to gather force and at that moment, in the street outside the Hôtel de Police, a van with a loudspeaker was roaring away, the metallic tones loud enough to make the windows rattle. Just the thing for committing a murder, Pel thought sourly. You could let off a sub-machine gun and it wouldn't be heard above that lot. It was a wonder criminals hadn't thought of it.

The city walls were daubed with posters in a variety of colours – where possible over the opposition's – all of them portraying politicians wearing beaming smiles to indicate how much they loved children, dogs and going to church. No wonder, Pel thought, that they had come to be regarded with a contemptuous attitude of dismissal. In addition to informing the country at large what was being said in the Assembly, clever newspapers these days also took care to run a funny column mocking the men who said it.

Sourly he studied Darcy. He was quite certain that, despite his indifference to the dangers of using cigarettes, if he'd wanted to, Darcy could have stopped smoking in an instant, while he, who was convinced that at any moment he could drop dead of heart failure, was totally incapable of doing a thing about it.

'Things are slack,' he said.

'There's been another break-in at the supermarket at Talant,' Darcy said with a grin.

Pel shrugged. There was always another break-in at the supermarket at Talant. They had break-ins the way dogs had fleas.

'Who this time?'

'Kids,' Darcy said. 'The management renewed the alarms on the doors and windows when we complained after the last break-in, so they got in through the skylight. They were caught because they didn't know how to get out again.'

Pel nodded and looked at Nosjean. 'What about your art theft?' he asked.

Nosjean, who looked like the young Napoleon leading his troops across the bridge at Lodi, was a bit of an expert on art and antiques, chiefly because he had a girl friend, Marie-Joséphine Lehmann, who worked at the Galeries Lafayette and knew a lot about it. Nosjean had plenty of girl friends because he was good-looking, intelligent, ambitious and obviously had potential. Mostly they looked like Charlotte Rampling, because Nosjean had always had a thing about Charlotte Rampling, and Marie-Joséphine Lehmann was one of them. But there had been a succession of others in between, one or two who didn't look like Charlotte Rampling, one even who looked like Catherine Deneuve, and at the moment it was a lady estate agent who worked at

Agence Immobilière Lafaye. She was a year or two older than Nosjean and he had a feeling that the affair wasn't coming to fruition. The lady estate agent seemed to think more of selling houses than she did of Nosjean and seemed to find it difficult to take time off to see him.

He thrust her from his mind and looked up. 'I'm a bit worried, Patron,' he said.

'Why? The picture was stolen, wasn't it?'

'Yes, it was. A Vlaminck – *Landscape with Houses*. Claude Barclay provided it with one or two others to decorate the hall of the Hôtel du Grand Cerf at Lorne when it reopened after modernisation.'

'Showing off again, was he?'

'He can afford to, Patron. He's a member of the National Assembly who'll get re-elected next month whatever happens to anybody else, and he's got a lot of money. He's also an architect who's been involved in some pretty big contracts. That new centre at Lake Souillat, for instance. That must have brought him in a bit in fees. The new buildings at the Collège Privé de l'Est at Noray. It's a big complex and very up to date.'

Pel sniffed. Though he'd never met Barclay, he'd long since decided he didn't like him. He didn't like *any* politicians, as a matter of fact – or, come to that, anybody who was wealthier or better-looking than he was.

'They have huge fees there,' Darcy said. 'For backward sons of the forward-moving wealthy. To bring them up to the right standard for going into Daddy's business and eventually taking it over without ruining it.'

'Girls, too,' Nosjean said. 'They learn very important things: How to arrange the cutlery on the dining table, the right number of guests to invite, how to chat up Hubby's colleagues.'

'All right!' Pel slapped a hand down on the desk. There was only one person allowed to be sarcastic in Pel's team and at the moment it was getting out of control. 'Let's get back to business. Are you listening?'

'Both ears,' Darcy said and Pel scowled again.

Darcy and Nosjean grinned at each other. Nosjean tried to explain. 'Barclay's a financier, too,' he said. 'And he's got money in the hotel so it seems fair enough that he should provide half a dozen pictures from his collection to make the place look tasteful.'

'So what's the trouble?' Pel asked. 'This type, Guiho, appears in a uniform with a cap and shiny buttons as if he's an attendant and, in front of everybody, as bold as brass, calmly walks up to the picture, removes it from the wall, remarking to the watching crowd as he does so that it has to be taken away for repairs, and quietly walks off with it. But he's identified, caught at home the next day, the picture's returned, he'll get a spell in 72, Rue d'Auxonne, by which delightful if obscure name we choose to call our prison, and that's that.'

'Not quite, Patron,' Nosjean persisted.

'There are problems? Inform me.'

'Well, Professor Grandjean, of the Fine Arts Department at the University, happened to be there at the time. He's an admirer of Vlaminck and has one of his paintings himself, and he'd just been looking at the picture before it was removed. He's also an uncle of Mijo Lehmann and he happened to discuss it with her. She passed what he said on to me.'

Pel was pleased to see that the relationship between Nosjean and Marie-Joséphine Lehmann was still standing on its legs, however tottery they might be. He was a romantic at heart, believed in true love and approved of Mijo Lehmann.

'So?' he asked. 'What comments did he make?'

'He had reason – and now so have I – to believe that the picture might not be a Vlaminck at all.'

'Something else?'

'A fake.'

'Ah!'

Pel sat back, crushed out his cigarette and, without even noticing it, lit another one immediately. The moment he put the match out he realised what he'd done but, being on the mean side – careful, he preferred to call it – he decided it couldn't be wasted (no good Burgundian wasted things) so he sat back and decided he might as well enjoy it.

'Does Deputy Barclay know about this?' he asked.

'I spoke to him on the telephone.'

'What did he say?'

'He said it *wasn't* a fake. He sounded a bit indignant.'

'But Professor Grandjean's certain?'

'Pretty certain, Patron. He didn't put it to all the tests the experts use, of course, but you know what they're like. They have a gut feeling about things and they're not often wrong. He suggested it should be properly tested.'

'Have you asked Barclay about this?'

'Not yet, Patron.'

'Perhaps you'd better.'

'Yes, perhaps I had,' Nosjean agreed. 'But I've been wondering how to set about it. I've had dealings with a few people who own paintings and I've come to the conclusion that most of those who've been bamboozled over them don't like admitting it. Especially the self-important ones.'

Pel waved the matter aside. Nobody had been hurt. Nothing had been lost. And if a wealthy politician had been diddled out of a little of his money because he was too pompous to admit to a lack of knowledge, that was his business. There was no rush. Especially with Deputy Barclay. If the painting was indeed a fake, then certainly a crime had been committed somewhere, but it seemed to be one that would keep for a day or two.

'I'll leave it with you,' he said. 'Tomorrow's Saturday and I'm going to Bois Haut for the weekend. There's a family party on. My wife's relations like to have them from time to time. It's at her uncle's estate.' He pulled a face because he didn't expect to enjoy himself. 'Still the weather's good and there's nothing demanding our attention.'

The party started on the Friday evening as Pel and his wife appeared, to be greeted by bent and elderly relations and their spouses who were all gathered at the home of Uncle Georges-Louis in the forest, all full of life despite their age. They represented only a small proportion of Madame's family because there were plenty more – scattered all over France, all wealthy and all eager to leave their money to her when they died.

Since marrying Madame, the money problems that had darkened Pel's days from the moment he had started earning his living as a young cop had faded from the memory. A policeman's salary never allowed for a life of sybaritic luxury and what he had tried to stash away in the bank for his old age had never seemed to be enough, so he derived a lot of comfort these days from the fact that Madame Pel seemed to have the ability to conjure money out of thin air. She ran a hairdressing salon in the Rue de la Liberté which was the envy of the best in Paris and had recently opened a boutique next door so that, after spending a fortune on having their hair done, her clients could now spend another on buying clothes.

The relations were all obviously looking forward to the party and were delighted to see each other, but as soon as they assembled for dinner the table resounded to argument. Nobody was angry. It was just that the family liked arguing and, with the election due, they were at it hammer and tongs. Before they rose to go to bed, it was decided that, before the local guests arrived the following day, they would all go for a walk together. It involved a long and noisy argument about which part of the estate they should explore but they were all up bright and early the following morning. When Pel crossed the courtyard at 7a.m. towards the woods that surrounded the house, they were at it again over breakfast. At least, he thought, they showed no signs of dropping dead, which was something, because when Pel had been courting Madame they had always chosen the time when he had a date with her to disappear from the scene so that she was always having to vanish into the wild blue yonder to attend a funeral, a wake or the reading of a will.

As he entered the woods, he bumped into another of the relations, a plump cheerful man called Cousin Roger, who came from Lyons and had a plump cheerful wife. He grinned at Pel.

'Have you come here for what I've come for?' he asked.

'I've come to do my breathing exercises,' Pel pointed out stiffly.

'That's what I call it,' Cousin Roger said. 'Actually, I've come for a quick drag.'

For the first time, Pel felt warmth for the family. At least one of them showed signs of being human. He accepted a cigarette with gratitude.

Cousin Roger gestured towards the house. 'They're like a lot of mad hamsters,' he said.

It was true the argument was coming noisily from every window.

'It sounds like an Italian street riot,' Cousin Roger went on. 'Are you looking forward to this walk they're going to take?'

'No,' Pel admitted.

'Me neither. Walking makes my feet ache. We'd better walk together.'

Lying back on a grassy bank under a sky as blue as it could only be blue in Burgundy, they studied the leaves and watched the smoke curling up.

'Great ones for parties, this family,' Cousin Roger commented. 'You're a cop, aren't you?'

'Yes.' Pel waited for the usual silence that followed such an announcement. People tended to sneer at cops because they stood up to be shot at by terrorists or have their heads broken by rioting students, even, since they were paid so little, because they were always assumed to be corrupt.

It didn't come.

'I always fancied being a cop,' Cousin Roger said wistfully. 'Instead I became an accountant. It bores me silly. Should I have heard of you?'

'Perhaps,' Pel conceded.

'Pel, Pel – ' Cousin Roger frowned ' – got you! You're becoming quite well-known. Evariste Clovis Désiré Pel.'

Pel had been enjoying the admiration. Now he frowned. He had been blessed at birth with a label that was enough to make a man worry rats and, because he'd not been old enough at the time to object, it had become a source of playground hilarity at school and acute embarrassment while chasing girls as a young man. His wife had cottoned on to the fact within weeks of their marriage and had settled for calling him simply 'Pel'. At least, you couldn't muck about with that.

Cousin Roger turned his head to study his companion.

'Live around here?' he asked.

'Leu.'

'Funny, that.' The conversation was quiet and undemanding and went with the weather, the smell of grass and the hum of bees. 'We live at Lieu, near Lyons.'

'Isn't Lyons where there's some fuss going on at the hospital?'

'Fiddling. Somebody's been at it.' Roger drew a deep breath. 'Gather everybody from Paris to Marseilles is coming this afternoon. Even Claude Barclay. He has a house here somewhere. Met him?'

'No.'

'He's a big shot round our way, too. Has an apartment in the city. Lot of interest in business there. We act as his accountants. His house here's just over the hill, I believe. Cost a lot of money. Great one for charities, too. Welfare homes for old soldiers. He was one himself. He did well in Indo-China in the Fifties. Junior minister in the government. Keen on education, believes in straight-up, true-blue youngsters. He'll have no problem getting re-elected for Yorinne next month.'

Pel shrugged. 'I gather the seat's so safe he doesn't have to do any canvassing.'

'Good job. He bores the pants off most people.'

Cousin Roger sat up and carefully stubbed out his cigarette. There was no one in sight. 'I think,' he suggested, 'that perhaps we ought to join the others. Are you busy just now?'

'No,' Pel said. 'Things are pretty quiet. Nothing much's happening.'

Pel had often been wrong and he was wrong now because, even as he followed Cousin Roger into the sunshine and the waist-high grass, things had already started happening.

In the woods outside the village of Suchey not ten kilometres away, two small boys were looking for bait for a fishing expedition they were planning for the following day at the dam of a farmer called Gaubert. The dam was situated out of sight of the farm and the two boys had taken fat perch out of it on more than one occasion.

They were always careful, of course, to leave their bicycles where they couldn't be seen but were nevertheless handy for a quick getaway in the event of the farmer appearing in any of the neighbouring fields. Since Farmer Gaubert had stocked the dam with perch for the benefit of himself and his sons who also liked fishing, it was as well to be prepared and Jean-Pierre Deniaud and Paul Guyot had worked hard at their scheme. Like many small boys, they already had the makings of expert con men and knew exactly what to do.

The bait they were after was maggots, the larvae of flies that laid their eggs on the carcasses of dead animals, and they were hoping to find, as they had on other occasions, the body of a dead pigeon or a dead rabbit.

'Keep your eyes open,' Paul Guyot said. 'They're hard to spot in the undergrowth.'

'You think I'm blind, copain?' Jean-Pierre Deniaud jeered. 'I've been hunting bait as long as you have.'

'And keep your eyes open for Gaubert, too,' Paul warned. 'He's not all that old and he moves fast.'

'He's got nothing on us.' Jean-Pierre grinned. 'The rods are with the bikes and there's no sign of what we're doing. We're simply walking through the woods.'

'It's private property, all the same. Don't forget that.'

For a long time they pushed through the ferns and brambles and fallen trees, then Paul shouted.

'Hé! Jean-Pierre! Here! I've got something!'

There was no sign of the body of a rabbit or a pigeon but there were certainly maggots – a seething mass of them on a mound of rough sods of turf loosely covered with beech cuttings a few feet from the footpath.

'Mother of God,' Jean-Pierre said. 'Thousands of them!' They started to pull the beech cuttings aside, and then the turf. 'Whatever it is,' Jean-Pierre observed, 'it's big. And it stinks.' 'Perhaps a cow. Perhaps Gaubert had to kill one. Broken leg. Something like that.'

Paul shrugged. 'Shouldn't think so. Dead cows get sold for dog meat or cat meat.'

'Not if they're diseased, mon brave. Perhaps it's a dog. Too old to work any more. You wouldn't sell a dog to – hé!'

Paul looked up.

Jean-Pierre had suddenly fallen silent. 'Paul,' he said. 'Come over on this side.'

Paul rose from where he was scooping maggots and soft turned earth into a jam jar and moved towards his friend.

'What's that?' Jean-Pierre said, pointing.

There was a long silence before Paul replied. 'It's somebody's arm. You can see the fingers. I think we'd better shove off.'

'We ought to tell the police,' Jean-Pierre urged. 'That's a man. Or a woman. Or something.'

'I'm not going to tell the police,' Paul insisted. 'They'll want to know what we were doing here.

'We were walking.'

'*And* collecting maggots. *Why* were we collecting maggots?'

'We're interested in maggots, that's all. We're entomologists.'

'They'd only have to ask around to know we're not. What they'd find out would be that we like fishing, and that Gaubert's dam's just over the hill. He'd murder us.'

'Not if the police were in on it. He wouldn't dare. I'm going to report it.'

'It's tricky.'

Jean-Pierre frowned. 'Not half as tricky as not reporting it,' he said.

two

The party at Bois Haut started at midday with drinks in the courtyard. Just outside, beyond the *pigeonnier*, tables were set in the sunshine for fifty guests.

'They're coming from Paris, Lyons and Marseilles,' Madame Pel said cheerfully. 'Even Great-Aunt Béatrix, who hasn't moved from home for years.'

By the time the fiftieth guest – the Maire of Mergneu – had arrived, Pel was already wondering how soon they could decently depart. From time to time he slipped into the trees with Cousin Roger to smoke a quick cigarette. Not because it would have offended anyone – everybody else was smoking like factory chimneys – but they'd both promised their wives they'd try harder to give it up.

Around 4p.m. when lunch finished and the flow of wine diminished to a trickle, one or two children belonging to locals were riding bicycles – brought along, with one eye to possible boredom, in the back of cars. Among them were the infants of the Maire of Mergneu, a young army officer, and a woman teacher Uncle Georges-Louis has his eye on. The old men were playing cards in the shade and on the boules court a mixed game involving what appeared to be four or five thousand arguing people was in progress.

Madame touched Pel's arm. She had wisely made no attempt to draw him into the family conversation and now she put her hand in his.

'Aren't you enjoying yourself?' she asked.

Pel sniffed. 'The children are interesting,' he allowed.

'We can leave after lunch tomorrow. Besides, they'll all be going to bed early. They tire easily at their age.'

As she drifted away, Cousin Roger appeared from the boules court. He had been going hard at the wine.

'The best player of the lot's the Maire's wife.' He indicated the large earrings she wore. 'I think it's the radar screens in her ears. She uses them to get the range.' He gestured at a tall man who had arrived too late for the pre-lunch drinks and missed being introduced. He wore a grey suit with a blue tie and a pink shirt, and had the regulation inch of cuff showing. His shoes were immaculate and his hair looked as if he visited his barber once a week. He was shaved to the bone and was handsome and slim. Pel, who was anything but tall, far from handsome and inclined to a pot belly, disliked him on sight.

'Got the chic type?' Cousin Roger asked. 'It's Claude Barclay. Deputy Barclay himself, Member for Yorinne and national hero. It's in all the books. Called with his class to the colours, ended up as a young officer in Indo-China and when the Vietcong besieged Dien Bien Phu he was one of the few who came out with some honour.' He pulled a face. 'He gets his name and face in the papers a lot.'

'He probably makes sure he does,' Pel suggested.

Cousin Roger nodded. 'Goes in for impassioned speeches. I heard him once. I reckon he could make a visit from a plumber sound earthshaking. I've never really liked him much.' His speculative glance was inclined to be a little tipsy and his comments unconsidered. 'He looks shifty.'

Pel warmed to him again. Barclay, in fact, looked anything but shifty. But that was the sort of opinion bigots were made of and Pel saw he would have to admit Cousin Roger into the Society of Bigots, of which he was president, secretary and sole member. Cousin Roger seemed to have the right instincts.

'He goes in for pictures,' he was saying now. 'Renoir, Manet and that lot. Kids' comics are about the limit of my appreciation of art. Still, it must be nice to own a lot of valuable daubs. I think that's why he's a friend of Georges-Louis.' Cousin Roger was clearly not intending to give much away in the manner of warmth. 'I hear he picks his brain on what to buy.'

Pel smiled. 'Perhaps he ought to listen more carefully,' he said. 'I heard recently he picked a dud.'

By the time evening arrived and the locals had departed, lethargy was setting in. It was pretty inevitable, considering the amount of food that had been eaten, the wine that had been drunk, and the temperature of the day, and Pel was just wondering if they couldn't go to bed when his wife announced that they'd been invited to drinks at Courtois-Saint-Seine. Pel didn't fancy drinks anywhere except in his own home, but he didn't object. To anyone else he would have objected at the top of his voice but he was prepared to accept – occasionally, anyway – that his wife had a right to be considered in the scheme of things from time to time.

'What's at Courtois-Saint-Seine?' he asked cautiously.

'Claude Barclay's home. He has a big house there. It's twelfth century.'

Pel wasn't very keen on the twelfth century. It took him all his time to cope with the twentieth.

'He's converted and modernised it,' Madame encouraged, wary of the look in his eye. 'He's an architect, of course, as well as a financier. And there are some superb paintings.'

The whole tribe of them set off in motor cars through the low knuckled hills of the Plateau de Langres, to draw up in the courtyard of Barclay's home at Courtois. It wasn't a château but it certainly wasn't just a house. The main street of the village had come into being in the days when the grain of the district had been carried away in carts by teams of horses and was wide enough for six pairs of Percherons or a mule train to turn with ease. The house, which had probably been built by some wealthy medieval grain merchant, looked as if it had been fortified to withstand the attacks of robber barons.

The street was virtually empty, though there were a couple of old men sitting on chairs outside a bar down the road, and a voice, appearing through an open window somewhere in an item from *Gems from the Operas,* rose to a high-pitched level – dead on note, however – and made all the heads turn.

'Madame Boileau,' Uncle Georges-Louis said. 'Practising. She used to be on the stage.' He gestured vaguely. 'Lives over there.'

'There'll be drinks,' Barclay was saying as they moved into the courtyard. 'Served by my good Gefray.'

He gestured at a manservant in a white coat who appeared as they approached what appeared to be the main door, a huge square affair of heavy oak studded with bronze. Barclay gestured, however, at a smaller door set in the base of what had once been a turret and as they passed through it he spoke to the manservant and the door was closed behind them and the huge bolts of square wrought-iron were slid home.

'Frightened we'll steal the silver,' Cousin Roger whispered, and his wife hurriedly shushed him to silence.

They were shown into a long room which seemed to be solid brown stone dimly lit by hidden lights. Although it was not yet dark, all the shutters were closed and bolted.

'Trying to simulate the atmosphere of a siege,' Roger observed and again his wife hastened to shush him to silence.

The manservant appeared with bottles and glasses, followed by a maid with a tray of delicacies. The young man was tall, dark and handsome and the girl was blonde and pretty.

'Monsieur Barclay not only likes to be surrounded by beautiful paintings,' Cousin Roger observed, 'he also likes to be surrounded by beautiful people.'

'Where's his wife?' Madame Pel asked.

'He doesn't have one. He's a bachelor.'

'Ah!'

'But not for the reason you're thinking. There've been plenty of women in his life. Especially when he was younger and had just come home from Indo-China.'

More interested in architecture than Pel, Madame drifted off and for a moment he was alone.

Somewhere ahead of him, Barclay was extolling the joys of owning valuable paintings, to 'oohs' and 'ahs' from the women whose eyes were more on Barclay than on the pictures and, for the most part, indifferent silence from the men. So far there had been too much of Barclay and too little of his wine and, after trailing round what seemed about fourteen storeys and being shown into at least a couple of hundred rooms, all dimly lit to show twelfth century living with twentieth century décor, Pel began to grow bored and managed to slip back to the hall. He had intended going outside for a quick cigarette but all the doors and windows on the ground floor seemed to be still locked and bolted.

'Frightened we might escape.' Cousin Roger appeared alongside him.

Just above their heads, at the top of the stairs they could hear Barclay still explaining the virtues of his home and, by inference, as he dwelt on the improvements he had made, of himself. Two more bored men drifted down to the wine bottles and Pel stared through the windows at the assembled cars outside. It pleased him, remembering they belonged to Madame's relations who had no one to leave their money to but Madame, to notice that they were all large and expensive.

'I think,' Cousin Roger said, 'that we should bully someone into giving us a drink.'

Seeming to know a trick or two, he took the manservant to one side. 'You'll be the good Gefray,' he said.

The manservant nodded and smiled.

'Then how about a drink? Architecture's thirsty stuff and I'm sure your boss wouldn't wish me to suffer.'

Gefray had had orders not to dispense the drinks without the presence of Barclay, but Cousin Roger slipped him twenty francs and a bottle was opened. For a while they managed to enjoy themselves.

Cousin Roger nodded at an attractive blonde woman in a yellow dress that accentuated her figure and showed off her bronzed skin. She wasn't one of the party and seemed close enough to Barclay to be intriguing.

'Who's that?' he asked Gefray.

'Madame Pouyet, Monsieur.'

'Sister?'

'Er – no, sir.'

'Cousin?'

'Not exactly, Monsieur.'

'No relation?'

'No, Monsieur.'

Roger turned to Pel. 'That seems to make her his girl friend,' he said softly. He eyed the woman. 'Well, she's worth having as a girl friend, I suppose, if you like that sort.'

The sun was beginning to grow golden as the telephone rang. An admirer no doubt, for Claude Barclay, Pel thought. To his surprise, the manservant, who answered it, turned to him.

'Inspector Pel, I think,' he said.

'Chief Inspector,' Pel said stiffly.

'It's for you.'

Pel was surprised. Nobody could have known where he was. It was the weekend and, apart from unusual circumstances, Pel wasn't on duty at weekends. Weekend duties were for lesser mortals who had to sit by the telephone, reading the weekend papers and catching up on odd bits of clerical work.

He picked up the instrument, staring at it as if he expected it to bite him. 'Pel,' he said cautiously.

'Patron.' Immediately he recognised the voice of Darcy. 'I rang Bois Haut. They said you were at this number.'

'What's the trouble?'

'A body, Patron. Turned up by a couple of kids in the woods near Suchey. It's been there some time. De Troq's gone out with Aimedieu. Doc Minet's just telephoned. He says it looks like murder.'

'Do we know who it is?'

'No idea yet. Everybody's out there. Photography. The Lab boys. I've informed the Palais de Justice. Judge Brisard's next for call so he should be on his way. We can handle it.'

'I'll come.

'It's not necessary, Patron. I was only informing you.'

Pel cocked his head. Barclay was still droning away to the huddle of admiring women upstairs.

'Makes no difference,' he said. 'I'm on my way.'

Anything was preferable to Barclay and his house.

three

Darcy was waiting in the office when Pel arrived. 'De Troq' and Aimedieu have reported in,' he said. 'I've also told Bardolle to go along. He was born in the country and a countryman's views could be useful. He might spot something.'

He held out a packet of Gauloises. Pel eyed it warily but helped himself nevertheless. Darcy had his lighter out before he could change his mind and, stuffing his pockets with notebooks, pens, pencils and cigarettes as if there were no tomorrow, Pel followed him through the door.

'Inform me,' he said.

Behind the driving wheel, heading out of the city in the warm summer evening, Darcy gestured. 'Two kids,' he said. 'Fell into the police station at Suchey and said there was a body buried in the woods.'

'What were they doing in the woods?'

Darcy smiled, showing his splendid white teeth. Darcy's teeth were magnificent and looked as if, should you get in their way, they would snap your head off – literally. 'They said they were walking. But there's a dam out there full of perch – '

'How do you know?'

'It was there when *I* was a kid. They were hunting for bait. That's how they found the maggots. I think there were rather more than they expected.'

The sun was still visible when they reached the wood. Screens and tapes had been rigged and, under a battery of lights, Doc Minet had made a start on the scientific disinterment of the body. Photography had finished. They had been taking pictures with their polaroids from every angle and every stage as Doc Minet removed the layers of twigs, soil, leaves and dirt. As Pel appeared, Darcy spoke to Inspector Pomereu, of Traffic, whose men were putting up barriers at the side of the road.

'Judge Brisard not here yet?' he asked. 'He should be, by now. A juge d'instruction's supposed to see the body in situ.'

'I saw him leaving the Hôtel de Police,' Pomereu said. 'It was probably before you telephoned, though.'

Minet was just removing the last of the twigs and the sprays of beechwood. The body was only lightly covered and it didn't take him long.

'It wasn't done here.' He gestured at the neighbouring trees. 'There are no beech trees around here.'

Pel turned to Bardolle who was standing nearby, huge and thickset, like a patient bull mastiff.

'There are no beech trees in this wood at all, Patron.' His heavy voice echoed among the undergrowth.

Pel nodded and bent for a closer look. The air which had been full of the hum of disturbed flies, had quietened as the sun disappeared and the shadows took over, but the stench was enough for everybody to work with handkerchiefs to their noses.

The body was that of a man, fully clothed and lying on his back.

Doc Minet looked up. 'It's murder,' he said bluntly.

'You're sure?'

'Suicides don't cover themselves with turf and beech twigs.'

'Accident, perhaps? Somebody caused his death, panicked and covered him up?'

'Not a hope.'

'There's no sign of a weapon,' Bardolle pointed out.

'There probably won't be one,' Doc Minet said.

'Why not?'

'Because of the state of decomposition, I decided I'd better examine him where he is. There's blood in the voice box. The small bones of the larynx are crushed. Because of the decomposition, I could pick them out.'

'Strangled?'

'Not a constriction. A blow.'

'On the throat? What sort? A punch? A kick?'

'How about a blow with the fist? Or a karate chop? That could have done it.'

'Could a woman have done it?'

'A lot of women learn it these days,' Darcy said.

'It's possible.' Minet rose and dusted off the knees of his trousers. 'I'll have him up and taken to the lab. I can examine him better there. Any sign of Brisard?'

Darcy frowned. 'He's probably making life miserable for some poor con somewhere,' he said. Judge Brisard was not popular with the Police Judiciaire.

Minet shrugged. 'Well, I'm not going to wait long. I might find other injuries. If there are none, then I'd say the blow to the windpipe was definitely the cause of death. It would render him unconscious and he'd inhale the blood and choke. He'd die in a few minutes.'

'Could it possibly have been an accident? A branch that swung back and hit him?'

'Not a chance.'

'No chance he could have done it himself?'

'Not a hope. That's the sort of injury that's done with the heel of the hand. You try and hit yourself across the throat with the heel of your hand. It's not possible.'

'Who is he? Any indication?'

Bardolle shook his head. 'None, Patron. I've tried his pockets but they've been turned out.' His thick finger indicated the lining of one of the jacket pockets among the scattered leaves.

'How long has he been here? Or – the same question – how long has he been dead?'

Minet pulled a face. 'It's too late to measure loss of body temperature,' he said. 'And rigor mortis has been and gone long since. The body's disintegrating. Another week or so in this heat and he'd be unrecognisable.'

'He looks a big type,' Darcy observed. 'Can you tell us anything else, Doc?'

Minet shrugged. 'Big hands,' he said. 'Strong. So he wasn't a clerk or anything of that nature. He's tall – around 190 centimetres – and well developed. But gone to seed. I'd say he was a bit of an athlete in his time.'

'Age?'

'Hard to say. Decomposition's pretty extensive. Say around fifty. Perhaps a bit more or a bit less. There's one other thing which should make him not too difficult to identify.' He indicated the right arm, lying among the disturbed earth. 'He probably broke his arm at some time during his career. It's set crookedly.'

Pel glanced about him. The sun had gone completely now, the shadows deepening, the lights round the screen the only bright spot among the trees. The hum of flies had stopped as the light had vanished, and the laboratory men, who had been searching the undergrowth, had straightened up, unable to search any more.

'Right,' he said. 'We'll call it off until daylight, and tackle it again tomorrow.'

'I'll get in touch with Missing Persons,' Darcy said. 'They might have somebody who matches his description.'

'Try round the local stations, too. If he's local, it might save time.'

As Darcy moved away, Pel turned back to Minet. 'How long has he been there? Six or eight weeks?'

Minet's smile came again. 'Oh, mon Dieu, no,' he said. 'Nine or ten days, that's all – certainly not more than twelve.' He gestured as Pel stared in disbelief and indicated the maggots. 'Those little chaps are surprisingly informative. It's amazing how quickly they eat up the flesh. I've seen a body reduced to this state in a matter of ten days. It's fairly safe to assume these are the larvae of the bluebottle *Calliphora erythrocephalus.* They tell us the time of death.'

'They do?'

'Roughly, anyway. The eggs are laid in daylight in warm weather. A blowfly wouldn't dream of laying eggs in the dark or the cold, and any self-respecting entomologist could establish, by observation of the various stages of development, just when it happened.' Minet indicated the body. 'These are mature, nice and fat and a bit lazy. They're third-stage unpupated maggots, and I estimate they were laid nine or ten days ago. Allowing a little extra time, in case the bluebottles didn't find the body immediately, let's say death occurred on the 16th or 17th of the month.'

Inevitably the newspapermen had heard what had happened by the time Pel returned to the Hôtel de Police, and three of them – Fiabon, of *France Dimanche,* Henriot, of *Le Bien Public,* the local rag, and Sarrazin, the freelance – were waiting in the corridor.

'Heard you'd found a stiff, Chief,' Sarrazin said.

'*How* did you hear?' Pel had long suspected Sergeant Misset, of his squad, of making money by passing on titbits of news to the press. Misset was growing fat and lazy and he was always in need of cash for his growing family and the girls he constantly chased, and Pel was longing to catch him.

If Sarrazin had received information, however, he was giving nothing away. 'Heard everybody was out, Chief,' he said. 'It indicated something. Made a few enquiries and found the blood wagon had gone from the Lab. That usually indicates a stiff. And not just an accident either, because they don't handle accidents.'

It was hard to catch Sarrazin out, and it seemed to Pel best to admit what was going on. They'd be happy to use a 'Have you seen this man?' sort of story if nothing else, because everything was grist to the mill. They might even pick up something. French newspapers had a nasty habit of making wild guesses that were sometimes embarrassing, either to the police, the victim's family, or themselves, but just occasionally they came up with information.

He told them what he knew. 'A body's been found in the woods at Suchey,' he admitted. 'A man. We have no name and no details yet. A big man. Around a hundred and ninety centimetres. If anyone has anyone missing of that type, they should communicate with us.'

'Is it murder, Patron?'

'It's murder.'

They went away, satisfied, and Pel headed for his office. In the corridor he bumped into Nosjean who was heading for the sergeants' room, his nose in a file.

'Patron!'

'Nosjean!'

'You look preoccupied, Patron.'

'Come to that, so do you.

Nosjean frowned. 'I have a problem, Patron.'

'What sort of problem?'

'This art thing. You remember, of course, that Professor Grandjean and Mijo Lehmann both felt that Deputy Barclay's Vlaminck was a fake.'

Pel gestured. 'We have a murder on our hands,' he pointed out. 'I don't think one fake picture matters much at the moment.'

'Perhaps *one* doesn't, Patron,' Nosjean agreed. 'But another one's come up.

'Another what?'

'Another fake.'

Pel directed Nosjean inside his office. 'Inform me,' he said.

For a moment Nosjean considered how to start. 'The manager of the Banque des Fermiers de l'Est at Givry telephoned me yesterday,' he said. 'He wanted our help.'

'At a weekend?'

'He thought it might be important. It concerned a painting, and, since I was already involved with one, I went to see him at his home. He thinks they're in trouble.'

'Somebody been robbing them?'

'In a way, probably. A type called Jacques Chevrier, who's a fabric designer living at Givry, needed to raise a loan to improve his house, which is a new acquisition. He approached the Banque des Fermiers de l'Est. The manager wasn't against the idea because Chevrier's credit's good, but he needed a collateral and Chevrier offered a picture he possessed, a Rembrandt called *Soldier With Helmet* which it was decided the bank should hold until the loan was paid off. The painting's only small – thirty-six centimetres by forty-two – but it looked good and Chevrier had had it looked at by an expert called Professor Solecin, of the Musée Fervier, near Lyons. He had the verification, all the provenance that was necessary for it, and the painting was valued at 750,000 francs. It was stuck in the vault, Chevrier got his loan and everybody was quite happy – Chevrier because he'd got the money and the bank because they had a picture which they felt was worth ten times what they'd loaned to Chevrier.'

'There's a "but", of course.'

'Of course, Patron. On the bank's inspecting staff from Paris there's a man who's keen on art and makes a point of visiting galleries and studying art generally in an amateur sort of way. He doesn't class himself as an expert but over the years he's learned a lot about it. When he heard of the bank's painting, because he likes paintings and because Rembrandt happens to be a favourite of his, he asked to see it. They fished it out for him. He took a good look at it and then another. After about three good looks, he began to have doubts about its authenticity and said so. The bank was worried because it could hardly demand its loan back. But it got a couple of real experts in to have a look at it. They were unbiased and both professionals. One was a professor of Fine Art from Marseilles, the other a retired professor of Fine Art from Paris.'

'And?'

'They took about two minutes to decide the painting was a dud. They had no knowledge of a *Soldier With Helmet* in the Rembrandt *raisonné*, and it seems catalogues are pretty extensive these days. And, anyway, they didn't think it was even a very good Rembrandt or even Rembrandt school, pupil of Rembrandt or what have you. They decided it was a deliberate fake.'

Pel said nothing but Nosjean knew he had captured his attention.

He went on quickly. 'The bank manager informed Chevrier, the owner, who was horrified. He swore he didn't know and wasn't an expert anyway. He thought quite simply that he'd got a bargain, a lost master, and he agreed immediately to them testing it. It *was* a fake. It's supposed to be a Rembrandt of the late period but the style's all wrong.'

'How do you know?'

'Mijo said so. She had a look at it, too.'

'Ah!'

'It also contains colours Rembrandt could never have heard of, colours which were discovered long after 1669 when he died. One's a cadmium red, and cadmium wasn't discovered until 1817. And there's a Brunswick green, which contains lead chromate pigments, and is also a colour which was produced for the first time long after Rembrandt died. The whites show traces of titanium. This is a modern painting, Patron, and not one for a discerning collector either. The bank manager's been worrying about it ever since. Yesterday he felt he ought to report it.'

'Do we know where this Chevrier bought the painting?'

'He bought it from a man called Cubescu, who's a Rumanian expatriate living in Avignon. He's a geologist.'

Pel studied Nosjean thoughtfully. He was a handsome young man who was maturing well. Pel had a suspicion he would never make a top policeman because, though he was cleverer than Darcy, he lacked Darcy's ruthlessness. Nevertheless, having trained him from the day when he had been a very modest young detective complaining about his expenses and the lack of time off, Pel had a soft spot for him.

'How are things with you and Marie-Joséphine Lehmann?' he asked.

Nosjean blushed. It always pleased Pel to discover there were still young men who could blush. 'Still all right, Patron,' he said.

'Then how about taking her to Avignon', Pel suggested, 'and going to see this Cubescu? She's a bit of an expert and she might spot something you might have missed.'

four

Doc Minet was the first to arrive the following day. Pel spared him a thin smile but as his face came unglued he knew that, despite the cold he'd feared coming to nothing, his sunny temper wouldn't last long and it was therefore best to get it out of the way so that he could forget the pleasantries and concentrate on his work.

Minet took the chair at the other side of Pel's desk and offered a cigarette.

Grimly, Pel shook his head. 'I'm trying to cut them down,' he said. 'I thought you were, too,' he added as if Minet was a traitor.

'I was.' Doc Minet, who was round and friendly, grinned at him. 'I was a chain smoker. Sometimes, in my job, it's necessary. But I gave it up. But it was hard work and I didn't enjoy it and I decided it was better to suffer from the effects of smoking than from remorse at the sin of it.' He blew out smoke – another, Pel thought bitterly, who could happily transgress without any sign of doubt.

'Our friend in the woods at Suchey,' Minet began. 'I've been having a look at him. It's much as I thought. Eight to ten days ago, I'd say. But there's not much we can tell from the body. It's too far gone.' He paused to explain. 'Decomposition usually starts about forty-eight hours after death following the disappearance of rigor mortis. Putrefaction is caused by bacteria moving from the intestines and spreading through the body by way of the blood vessels. You know all this, of course, but I'll tell you again. Gross disfiguration arrives usually after three weeks and liquefaction sets in after four weeks. In this weather, it all speeds up and if you'd left him much longer there wouldn't have been much for us to work on.'

'However – ' Doc Minet seemed to be enjoying his grisly diatribe ' – the internal organs collapse at a different rate, and the tendons and fibrous tissues are the last to go. Heat advances the growth of bacteria, which is why our friend in the wood was in such a mess. So – what did I find out? Nothing much more than I'd already guessed. What I said yesterday stands. There are no other wounds. He was hit across the throat either with a narrow blunt instrument, the heel of the hand in a karate chop, or by a kick while he was on the ground. Age: As I said. Around fifty-odd. Big chap. When the body was stretched out it measured one-eighty-five centimetres. Teeth had been attended to in the past – well attended to – but neglected in recent years. Left arm broken at some time. There's a scar, so something must have hit it with some force. Tattoo on left forearm – a number, 179, garlanded with a wreath. It's quite clear. It looks like some sort of badge and seems to indicate what he'd once been, even if he still wasn't when he died.'

'What's that supposed to mean?'

'I think he'd been a soldier. He's a big chap and I imagine he was in good condition physically. Straight – no sign of stooping. Teeth well attended to – while in the army, for instance – but neglected after he left it. Arm broken. By a bullet or something while on active service? Tattoo – that's a thing soldiers go in for – 179, garlanded like a badge. The number of his regiment?'

'It's a start,' Pel admitted. 'Anything else?'

'Prélat's hoping to get a fingerprint. If he does and our friend has a record, we have him. Leguyader's going through his clothes now. He should be here at any moment.'

In fact, Leguyader appeared as Doc Minet left. Leguyader was head of the Forensic Laboratory and he and Pel had been conducting a private vendetta for years. Leguyader liked to announce either that he had found nothing – which was no help at all to Pel – or that he had found a vital clue so that he could boast that it was he, not Pel, who had solved the mystery. This time it was the former.

'Nothing important,' he said, poking his head round the door. 'Grey suit. Not expensive. Someone had been through his pockets.' He smiled. 'Tailor's tab on the jacket. Bomli, of Lyons. It won't be much help. Bomli is a department store. They sell hundreds of inexpensive grey suits every year.'

As the door closed, Pel rose, clutching the *Liste des Avocats et Juristes Français,* which lay on his desk. Immediately the door closed, it opened again and Darcy appeared. He looked startled.

'You about to hurl that at me, Patron?' he asked.

'Not you. That lunatic, Leguyader.'

'Ah!' Darcy understood at once because the Hôtel de Police had been taking bets for years on which of the two would be the first to crack under the strain and murder the other. 'What's he got on our friend?'

'Nothing. Just a tailor's tag on the jacket. Bomli, a department store in Lyons. That won't tell us much.' Pel paused, tossed the *List of Advocates and Barristers* on to his desk, lit a cigarette hurriedly to calm himself and looked again at Darcy. 'What have you found?'

'With luck, our friend in the woods.'

'What!'

'Name of Jules Arri.'

'How did you perform that miracle?'

'Not quite a miracle, Patron. Not yet. I'm not certain even, but I got in touch with Missing Persons and they said they'd had a report from Brigadier Foulet, who runs the station at Valoreille about a type called Jules Arri, who was reported missing about a week ago. He's a bachelor, it seems, and looks after himself. But a couple of old dears – ' Darcy glanced at his notebook ' – name of Yvonne and Yvette Ponsardin – go in to clean the house for him. They hadn't seen him for a couple of days and saw that his bed hadn't been slept in. They occasionally prepare food for him but a casserole they left hadn't been touched so they thought something might have happened to him and reported it to Brigadier Foulet. He took a look round and passed it on to Missing Persons.'

'Why did these two women think something might have happened to him? Couldn't he be visiting relatives?'

'They don't think he has any. Besides, he's a very correct sort of chap, it seems. Quiet. Keeps to himself. Good at looking after himself. Mends his own clothes. Keeps the house clean. Never fails to let them know if he's going away. Very much a man of routine.'

'As an ex-soldier might be?'

Darcy's eyebrows rose. 'Have you got something, too, Patron?' Pel told him what Doc Minet had found. 'Where does this Jules Arri work?'

'Foulet doesn't know. But he said he didn't seem to lack money. He thought he had some sort of small private income.'

'Such as an army pension?'

Darcy smiled. 'Patron, I think we might have found him.'

'*I* think it might be time to go to Valoreille to see what we can find.'

Valoreille was only a few kilometres from the city, a village of grey stones and ancient beams tucked away among the first hills to the north. Brigadier Foulet, who was in his office going through papers, leapt to his feet at once as he saw Pel.

He was young, ambitious and clearly eager to please. He had shown admirable sense in reporting the absence of Jules Arri so quickly, but he knew very little about him because he was a newcomer to the village. However, he suspected that Minet's guess that Arri was an ex-soldier was probably correct.

'Walked very straight, sir,' he said. 'Kept himself to himself. Very self-dependent.'

It wasn't difficult to establish that Arri *had* been a soldier, because an enquiry at the post office revealed that he was in the habit of collecting an army pension there once a month.

'I think he must have been a regular non-commissioned officer,' the postmaster said. 'I was a regular myself and I get an army pension, too, and his was a lot bigger than mine. I worked it out that he was probably a sergeant and that he'd done his full time.'

'Did he ever talk about himself?'

'Never. I sometimes tried. Two old soldiers sort of thing. But he never said much.'

'Did he go in the local bar?'

The postmaster stared at his fingers for a while then he shook his head. 'Once or twice when he first arrived, I gather. But never since.'

'Somebody upset him?'

'I don't think so. He just stopped, that's all. He was friendly enough, but then it stopped.'

'That's odd, isn't it?'

'It is a bit. Old soldiers like talking. Especially about themselves and what they've seen and done.'

'Ever difficult? Any complaints?'

'Never. He was always polite. Always said good morning. But that was it. Nothing more.'

They enquired round the shops and found that Jules Arri rarely did any shopping in the village, not even at the *épicerie* where they might have expected him to have bought food.

'Let's have a look at his home.'

Arri lived in a small cottage on the edge of the village, one of two standing close together. The garden was well-tended and the house well-painted, all indications of a man brought up to routine, self-respect and cleanliness. As they halted outside, a small round woman with straggly grey hair and a torn pinafore appeared from next door with a key. Just behind her appeared another woman who might almost have been her shadow.

'I did the cleaning,' the first woman said. 'I'm Yvonne Ponsardin.'

'Madame?'

'Mademoiselle.'

'And I'm Yvette,' the other woman said. 'Also Ponsardin. I'm her sister.'

'We never married.'

'Nobody asked us.'

Pel backed away a little. 'You knew Monsieur Arri?' he asked.

'We cleaned for him,' Yvonne Ponsardin said. 'I did it one day… '

'And I,' Yvette Ponsardin chimed in, 'did it the next.'

'Except, of course, when there was anything special to do.'

'Then we both did it.'

It was like a cross-talk act.

'Did you know him well?'

'No.'

'He didn't talk much and kept himself to himself.'

Pel frowned. 'Seems to be a bit of a mystery man, this Arri,' he commented to Darcy. He turned to Yvonne Ponsardin. 'Was there *anybody* who knew anything about him?'

'Shouldn't think so,' she said. 'I know he came from Champagne, because he told us so.'

'About five years ago,' Yvette Ponsardin added. 'He bought the cottage outright. He wasn't an old man.'

'In the prime of life, I'd say.'

'An army pension's hardly enough to live on, on its own,' Pel pointed out. 'So he must have worked. Where? Do you know?'

'No idea.'

'We only know he went out every evening.'

'Night-watchman, was he?'

'We don't think so.'

'If he went out at night he might have been,' Pel said.

'He could have been a croupier at a gambling saloon,' Yvonne offered. 'I expect he got around a bit.'

'Perhaps,' her sister suggested, 'he was a bouncer at a night club. A heavy. Perhaps he was with the gangs.'

'We don't have any gangs here,' Pel said.

'No. But they turn up now and then, don't they?' The old ladies read their newspapers, it seemed.

'What time did he leave home?'

'Six o'clock to six-thirty.'

'We usually saw him drive off as we were sitting down to our meal.'

'What about coming back?'

'Early morning. We never saw him.'

'But his car was always back when we got up.'

'So he *could* have been a night watchman.'

'He *could* have been a gangster.'

There were no photographs, nothing to indicate relatives, nothing even to indicate what Arri did in his spare time, though Darcy turned out two or three books that were mildly pornographic from the back of the wardrobe.

'Doesn't mean a thing, of course,' he observed. 'I suppose he had to have something to amuse him.' He moved the clothes about and eventually turned to Pel. 'Seen this, Patron? A uniform. It wouldn't fit our boy but I expect he left the army some 37 years ago and put a bit of weight on.' He touched the stripes on the sleeves. 'Sergeant. 179th Regiment.'

'We'd better check with the regimental historian,' Pel suggested. He turned to the two women. 'Did you know he'd been in the army? Did he talk about it?'

'Never. But we guessed.'

'Did you do anything else for him, apart from cleaning the house?'

'Occasionally we cooked a casserole and left it for him.'

'Did he cook himself?'

'We never saw any dirty pans. And he never bought food in the village. Just petrol for his car.'

Jules Arri seemed to be a blank. His home left a picture of a large, self-dependent, faceless man whom nobody knew. There was nothing in the drawers or cupboards that revealed anything at all. Pel removed a plate from the kitchen cupboard. It had a pattern of gilt and rose. 'Nice plate,' he pointed out. 'Especially for a bachelor.' He glanced at Mademoiselle Yvonne. 'This came from a very expensive dinner set. Are there any more?'

They found six of the plates, all different sizes and patterns but all expensive-looking and all chipped. Pel stared at them, frowning. 'What did he do all day?' he asked.

Mademoiselle Yvonne shrugged. 'In summer he worked in the garden a bit.'

'So where did these plates come from?'

'Bought cheap, Patron?' Darcy asked. 'Damaged lot?'

'An old soldier?' Pel ran a finger over a minute chip along the edge of a rose and gold plate and handed it to Darcy. 'Let's have it checked. We might find out why *he* has them.'

The two old women, who were muttering in a corner, came to life suddenly. 'Sometimes,' Yvonne said, 'there were plastic boxes which had contained cooked food. As if he bought it somewhere ready-cooked and brought it home.'

'He liked his wine, too,' her sister agreed. 'We saw the bottles when he put the dustbin out for collection.'

Darcy, who had been sniffing around outside, put his head round the door. 'Have a look at this, Patron,' he suggested.

By the back door, the dustbin was full to overflowing. Cats had obviously been around because some of the contents were scattered. But what interested Pel were the bottles standing alongside. There were two large champagne bottles, a Mumm and a Piper Heidsick, as well as five empty wine bottles, all of excellent quality.

'Expensive taste for an ex-sergeant,' Darcy commented. 'And if these are what he's drunk since the dustbin was last emptied, he's shoving it away a bit. It must have cost him a fortune.' He turned to the two women. 'Did he have a car?'

'Yes. It was usually in the garage but it's not there now.'

'What sort was it?'

'It was grey.'

'With four wheels.'

'Can you describe it?'

'Yes. It was grey with four wheels.'

'With a bit of a dent at the back. It wasn't new.'

'But it wasn't old either.'

'Did he appear to have money?'

'He banked with Crédit Agricolaire just along the street. They might know.'

The clerk at Crédit Agricolaire was a young man with long hair and an immaculate suit that made Pel feel disreputable. He also had a stubborn streak and considered the affairs of Jules Arri of no account to anyone but Jules Arri and the bank.

Pel didn't hesitate. 'Get the manager,' he said.

'He's just gone out for a coffee.'

'Where?'

'The bar next door.'

'Get him.'

The manager arrived in a lather of indignation. 'You've no right to do this,' he snapped.

Pel flipped his identity card at him. 'Police Judiciaire,' he said. 'I have every right. I want information on one of your customers.'

The manager looked worried, then he gestured at a small glass-surrounded cubicle. 'In here,' he said. He turned to the clerk. 'Let's have Monsieur Arri's statement, Edouard.'

The statement showed that Arri possessed a not insubstantial sum of money.

'It's a good account,' the manager said. 'He puts it away regularly and rarely draws it out. Just a couple of times a year. When he goes on holiday, I suppose.'

'How did he pay it in? By cheque?'

'No. Always cash. Once a fortnight.'

'Did he ever tell you where it came from?'

'We don't ask. It's none of our business.'

'Didn't you ever chat with him?'

'He didn't encourage chatting. We normally know about our customers – where they work, what their affairs are, what their families consist of. It's impossible not to. When you see them almost every week, sometimes more, inevitably you mention the weather, ask how they are. It leads to small confidences. You learn their background.'

'But with Arri, never?'

'Never. Nothing. He said good morning and that was all. You might ask at the garage opposite. I've seen him buying petrol. Perhaps they know.'

They did.

They knew not only the make of Arri's car, they also knew the number, 1111-AR-41.

The garage proprietor gestured at a Peugeot 205 standing on the forecourt. 'Like that, it was,' he said. 'And in damn good condition. That's for sale. Fancy buying it?'

'Not at the moment.' Pel glanced about him. 'Not big, this car of his, Daniel,' he said to Darcy. 'But in good shape. Like his house. Simple. Not short of money but not flashy either, so it doesn't sound as if he's in some sort of racket. Probably just adding to his pension with some job that sounds as if might be a night-watchman or security guard.'

The garage proprietor couldn't help on that score. He had no idea what Arri had done with his evenings, though he'd heard stories that he ran a gambling club.

'I didn't believe them,' he admitted. 'There aren't any round here. We don't go in for them. I haven't seen him around lately, mind – or his car. Not for a week or so, I should say. Perhaps longer.'

Pel nodded and glanced at Darcy. 'That's just about the time Doc Minet says he's been dead. I think, Daniel we're going to have to find this car and then find out where it went to of an evening.' He gestured to Foulet. 'Telephone Inspector Pomereu of Traffic,' he said. 'Give them the number and the description and tell them to keep a look out for it.'

They returned to the Hôtel de Police eager to put out a description of Arri and his car, only to find that the car had already turned up and was at that moment under guard. It had been spotted in the car park of a supermarket at Varagne which, of course, was as big as the Parc des Princes and just the place to leave a car if you wanted to lose it for a few days.

'It's been there all the time,' Pomereu said.

There was no car park attendant but there were always cars there, sometimes overnight, and the old man who wandered round the area collecting trolleys had noticed the Peugeot 205, Number 1111-AR-41. Realising it had been there over a week, he had wondered if it had been stolen and telephoned the local police. The local sous-brigadier, doing a check, had just been brusquely informed that Brigadier Foulet, of Valoreille, had telephoned a minute or two before to say that it was a car Pel was seeking and that he'd better put a guard on the vehicle at once. Pomereu looked triumphant.

'It's the one you're looking for, isn't it?' he said.

'Yes, it is. Let's have Fingerprints go over it for dabs.'

'Already being done,' Pomereu said. 'In the meantime, I'll check with Records to see if we can find the owner.'

Pel sighed. 'I'm not so sure it's necessary now,' he said slowly. 'I think we know.'

five

Sitting at his desk, Nosjean stared at the papers in front of him. The lady estate agent had seemed more than ever indifferent lately.

Of course, he admitted to himself, there was always the possibility that she didn't want to see him. After two evenings out together, perhaps she'd decided he wasn't what she was seeking.

With the sun on his face, Nosjean could see his reflection in the window, because beyond it was the roof of the General Hospital and it acted like a mirror. Staring at himself, Nosjean decided he looked normal enough. Thin intelligent face. Honest. Good-looking in an earnest sort of way. What was wrong with him? Impulsively he picked up the telephone and dialled the number of the Agence Immobilière Lafaye.

'Mademoiselle Julie Colin,' he said.

There was a couple of clicks then the voice of Julie Colin came on the line.

'Jean-Luc Nosjean here.'

'Oh, hello,' she said. 'How nice to hear from you. Where've you been?'

Sulking, Nosjean thought bitterly. 'Busy,' he said. 'Look, I'm free tonight. I'm on an art enquiry and it leaves the evenings free. It isn't one of those cases when you have to be on duty all hours. How about a meal together?'

There was a long silence. 'Oh, merde,' she said. 'I can't. I have this man to see.'

'Which man?'

'He's from Paris. He's interested in one of our properties. It's a big deal. I have to have dinner with him.'

'To sell him a house?'

He heard her laugh. 'I'm what's known as an asset to the office. They say I'm attractive enough to sell houses that people don't want to buy. It's something the Old Man fixed up. He thinks I'll sell the house just by putting on my best smile.'

Nosjean sighed. She could have sold *him* a house with her best smile, he had to admit.

'Right,' he said. 'How about tomorrow?'

There was another long silence. 'My mother's coming over from Bordeaux.'

'Can't you put her off?'

'Have you ever tried putting your mother off?'

Nosjean had to admit he hadn't and wouldn't like to. He had a mother who thought the world of him, and three sisters who thought because he was a policeman he was James Bond or someone, and kept buying him what they liked to think was suitable equipment or clothing for a secret agent – thermal underwear for the long winter nights when he was trailing Russian spies, a compass for his car in case he got lost and had to find his way home by the stars. Any time now they'd be buying him a laser gun or a heat-seeking rocket.

'No,' he agreed. 'I haven't tried to put my mother off.'

'I can't even get in touch with her. She left Bordeaux to spend the night with an old friend who lives in the country and doesn't believe in telephones. She's a poetess or something. I can't contact her until I face her on the station when she arrives.'

'When *will* you be free?'

'When she goes home.'

'When will that be?'

'I wish I knew.'

It sounded like the usual brush-off. I'm seeing mother. I have to see a client. Any day now she'd be telling him she had to wash her hair.

'Oh, well,' he said. 'Never mind. I'll try again later.'

He put the telephone down, deciding it wasn't worth the effort and that he'd better do as Pel suggested and try Mijo Lehmann and get her to go to Avignon with him to have a look at the Rumanian, Cubescu, who'd sold Chevrier his dud painting. He knew she would. Though he'd stood her up more than once she always seemed willing to come back for more. It was one of the aspects of Nosjean's life, he decided. The women he wanted to see didn't want to see him; and the ones he didn't particularly want to see were always more than willing to wait. There had been one who'd waited for him for three years until she'd suddenly grown tired and decided it was easier to marry someone with a nine-to-five job who was better paid and wasn't in danger of getting shot at by some criminal type, and had got herself hitched to a tax inspector.

It was hard to say whether Nosjean's trip to Avignon was a success or not. It had not been hard to find Cubescu, a small man with bright black eyes whose house was full of paintings. He said he was actually a volcanologist, a student of volcanoes, and one room was full from floor to ceiling of pictures of volcanoes erupting. To Nosjean it was like being in Hell.

He was cheerful, friendly and willing to answer questions, but when Nosjean asked him about the disputed *Soldier With Helmet,* the property of Jacques Chevrier, he shook his head. 'It's no longer in my possession,' he insisted. 'I sold it.'

'I know,' Nosjean said. 'To a man called Chevrier. For what sum?'

'Three hundred thousand francs.'

'Have you a valuation or documents to say it's worth that much?'

Cubescu's eyes lit up. 'I have a photocopy. Chevrier has the original, of course. He asked for it because he wanted to raise a loan on the picture.'

'He did.'

'I'm pleased.'

'Unfortunately, it now seems the bank thinks it made a mistake. It's not genuine.'

Cubescu's jaw dropped. 'But it *must* be genuine. I only sold it because I was making a good profit and Chevrier was very keen to have it. I had a valuation on it from a professor of Fine Art.'

'Can I see it?'

'But of course.

The letter had an embossed heading 'Professor Yves-Pol Solecin, formerly curator of the Fervier Museum of Art, Lyons.' It stated, 'This painting is full of the magnificent energy and character of Rembrandt van Rijn (1606-1669), the great Dutch master of the 17th century. Rembrandt felt in nature the expressive qualities of a subject and had the mental power to give him dominion over nature, something which enabled him to isolate and extract the inmost essence of his subject. The outstanding characteristic of oil paint is the texture and the force of the modelling, and Rembrandt set out to make full use of them. After many years he became the supreme master.'

'It says a lot about Rembrandt,' Nosjean pointed out. 'But not a lot about the painting.'

A slightly agitated Cubescu produced another document which stated that the work had previously been verified by one Jerôme Sède, Professor of Fine Art, of Metz. The authentication of Professor Solecin, dated seven months before, valued the painting at 200,000 francs.

'It seemed a reasonable figure,' Cubescu said. 'I had no reason to assume it was anything but genuine.'

'How did you get this authentication?'

'I was told about this Professor Solecin. I was told he would give an authentication on works of art at a very reasonable price.'

'Is that usual? The cheapness?'

'Well, he was pretty old.'

'Who told you about him?'

'I heard of a man called Riault and telephoned him. He recommended him.'

'And the painting? Where did you get that?'

'Jean-Philippe Roth. He has galleries in your city. Just behind the Rue de la Liberté.'

Nosjean seemed to be getting somewhere at last, especially that night when Mijo Lehmann, who had been checking the galleries, met him at the hotel where they were staying. They ate at a good restaurant, exchanged ideas and discoveries, held hands over the table and drank a little too much wine.

As Nosjean undressed in his room he wondered if Mijo Lehmann was expecting him to make a foray down the corridor after the lights went out. Was it possible, he wondered. Nosjean was a well-brought up young man with a great respect for the opposite sex because of his three older sisters who had made sure he didn't go off the straight and narrow. It was different these days, through, and he accepted that girls seemed to expect that sort of thing. Yet, if Mijo Lehmann didn't, it could ruin a beautiful friendship. It seemed to call for courage and a touch of *élan*. On the other hand, Nosjean's mind was full of the dire warnings of his sisters.

Though the situation seemed to demand a show of spirit, Nosjean reluctantly came to the conclusion that the spirit of Jean-Luc Nosjean wasn't quite the spirit that had made France great. He thought about it a lot, feeling the situation required a considerable amount of delicacy, and was just on the point of falling asleep when he suddenly decided to gird up his loins and have a bash. Heading down the corridor, he scratched at Mijo Lehmann's door.

There was no reply and, deciding he was making a fool of himself, he was just about to turn away when he heard the bolt withdrawn. His heart thumped and as the door opened he saw Mijo's face staring sleepily at him.

'I thought you were never coming,' she said.

It had been a long night and, feeling twice the man he had been, Nosjean drove back at his usual lunatic speed, Mijo Lehmann asleep beside him with her head on his shoulder. His chest swelled with pride. Nosjean wasn't a promiscuous young man but he also wasn't a virgin and he was feeling proud of himself. He had always thought of Mijo Lehmann, with her brains, her skill with antiques, the salary she commanded at the gallery where she worked, as being quite beyond him, but she had fallen into his arms, all warm with the scent of perfume and soft flesh, and stumbled with him to the bed. He could see it leading to better and more wonderful occasions.

Then he shifted uncomfortably in his seat. Did she expect marriage? Nosjean wasn't sure he wanted wedlock. He was too young to die and he had an uncle whose wife had always been held up in the family as an example of what could happen to a marriage. She had gone for the bottle, had men friends and had eventually hit her husband over the head with a kitchen stool and kicked him out of the house. She might well even have been the reason why Nosjean's sisters had never married.

On the other hand, he couldn't imagine Mijo Lehmann going for the bottle or hitting him with the kitchen stool. Especially after last night when she'd been all softness and warmth and murmured endearments. As they turned off the motorway into the city, he decided to take a chance and let things follow their own course. Mijo Lehmann had an apartment and he enjoyed her company. Whatever happened, it surely couldn't be too bad.

Jean-Philippe Roth was in his gallery talking to a customer when Nosjean arrived. He had dropped Mijo at the end of the street where her apartment was situated. 'I'll expect you,' she had said quietly.

Roth was contemplating a single painting set on an easel below a strong light. Nosjean was not an expert but he had learned a lot about art and the painting seemed to be an interior in the manner of Jan Steen.

'We have only the picture to go on,' Roth was saying. 'And, of course, there are always doubts. But there are little touches' – a limp hand fluttered over the painting – 'here and here – which you as an expert must recognise. That figure there on the right, for instance. It could well be Steen himself and we know a lot of artists went in for self-portraiture when they were short of models. It came into my hands from Lombards' in Paris. I paid 25,000 for it, though there was no proof, so I examined it carefully and decided to take a chance. But I can't tell you if it's a genuine Steen.' Roth stared at the canvas. 'Of course, there is this little group here. Very interesting, that.'

The plump pink-faced man who was examining the picture with him smiled. 'You were always on the cautious side, Roth,' he said. 'The brushwork round those trees very much suggests Steen to me.'

'Or a pupil, of course.'

'A pupil?' The plump man stared at the canvas and shook his head. 'Not a chance!'

'I can find no mention in the catalogues of any picture at all like this.' Roth shrugged. 'But, let's face it, in those days people were never very accurate.'

'I think I'm going to back my own judgement.' The plump man made up his mind. 'Put it aside for me.'

When the business was finished and the pink-faced man had gone, Roth turned to Nosjean who had been waiting quietly in the background. When Nosjean produced his identity card with its red, white and blue strip, Roth stepped back and Nosjean noticed he looked nervous.

As Nosjean knew, Roth was careful never to sell fakes as authenticated works of art, but he was also not averse to encouraging buyers to believe they were genuine by suggestion. As Nosjean had just seen, his line was always 'Well, this isn't authenticated, but it looks sound to me.'

'Surely you don't think – ?' he began.

Nosjean smiled and gestured at the painting. 'That? I'm not interested in that. I'm interested in a painting called *Soldier With Helmet*. A Rembrandt. I believe you sold it to a man called Cubescu. Can you tell me about it?'

Roth looked relieved. 'Of course. Perhaps you've seen a photo of it. No? Well, no matter. It's a handsome picture. Not to be confused with another I've seen like it, called *Farmer with Sickle.*'

'Oh? Where?'

'At the home of a man called Riault. It was very similar. In fact, I suspected it was a copy, with the soldier's helmet changed to a hat, and the sword to a sickle. That sort of thing's done sometimes by copyists. So they can put them out as originals.'

'And this one we're talking about? The helmet one.'

'I sold it to this type called Cubescu. For 150,000.'

'Was that its value?'

Roth shrugged. 'I thought it was fair. I didn't say it was a Rembrandt.'

'But, like the Steen, you suggested it might be?'

'In this case, not even that.'

'Have you seen it since?'

'As a matter of fact, I have – or one like it. That was in Riault's home, too. He valued it at 1,800,000 francs. He'd had it verified as a genuine Rembrandt.'

'Was it?'

Roth pulled a face and shrugged again.

'Who'd verified it?'

'An expert. I'm not involved, of course. I'm a straightforward dealer. I don't deal in fakes. I buy paintings, have them cleaned and restored and sell them again. If people choose to think they've found a bargain, that's their affair. You could see Charles Vacchi. He's bought from me and he'll verify what I say. He's *Vacchi et Bonet.* Actually the firm's just Vacchi nowadays. Bonet's retired. Vacchi has a large collection. You won't find it easy, of course. He's busy and a very wealthy man and he doesn't give interviews all that easily.' Roth smiled. 'Models himself on something out of *Dallas,* I think. Tough. Very macho. He has the paintings in his office to impress his customers.'

'And?'

'I believe *he* bought a painting called *Farmer with Sickle.*'

'What was the name of this expert who verified Riault's picture?'

'Professor Solecin. Curator of the Fervier Museum at Lyons.'

Same Professor Solecin, Nosjean noticed. This was becoming interesting.

It was hard to arrange an interview with Vacchi. His secretary was all for putting Nosjean off but Nosjean was insistent.

'Tell Monsieur Vacchi that I'm making a police enquiry and that refusal to assist the police can be interpreted as an *unwillingness* to assist, and that can be assumed to be caused by a variety of reasons, none of which would seem good.'

There was a long silence and the secretary looked nervous. 'I'm supposed to protect him,' she said.

'Not from the police,' Nosjean snapped.

There was a long silence while the secretary disappeared.

'Monsieur Vacchi will see you now,' she said as she returned.

Vacchi was waiting by his desk as Nosjean opened the door. He was a tall, grey-haired, hard-faced man in a suit that looked as if it had been built round him. He clearly didn't like having to give an interview and was obviously used to having his own way.

'I understand you've been bullying my secretary,' he snapped.

'Hardly bullying,' Nosjean said calmly. 'Just pointing out that I'm a policeman investigating a fraud and that I have reason to believe you can help me sort it out.'

'I don't go in for frauds. Sit down. What do you want?'

The room, Nosjean noticed, was full of paintings. He recognised none of them but he noticed the style of Van Gogh, Picasso and several others.

'I'm making enquiries into a series of art sales,' he said.

'I can't help you. I don't sell paintings.'

Nosjean gestured at the walls. 'You buy them, Monsieur Vacchi.'

Vacchi frowned. 'So how does that help you?'

'I believe you buy these paintings to improve your office.'

'It's necessary to make it look important and cheerful. Clients judge a businessman by his taste. They also judge his success by his possessions. That's why I run an English Rolls Royce.'

'I see. Where do you buy your paintings?'

'Through a man called Riault. He's a lawyer really and does it as a sideline. He's cheaper than the galleries and he seems able to make more finds. Paintings of value that interest me. Claude Barclay, the Deputy for Yorinne – you'll know of him; he's a great collector – is a friend of mine and recommended him.'

'Does Riault provide provenances, verifications and authentications?'

'Always. He has a man called Solecin. He's a professor of Fine Art who was formerly a curator of the Fervier Museum of Art near Lyons.'

'Do you buy originals?'

Vacchi looked indignant. 'My paintings are *all* originals,' he snapped. 'I pick them up here and there and have them restored. I get them through Riault who finds them in all sorts of weird places. They're all verified by an expert, of course, but they usually need work on them to give them back their original beauty because they're often dirty, scratched or faded through neglect.' Vacchi gestured at the paintings on the wall. 'These, as you can see, look at their best.'

'Indeed they do. Who did the restoration work? Do you know?'

'I leave it with Riault to arrange it. He uses a man called Ugo Luca. He's an Italian, I think.' Vacchi was looking at his watch impatiently. 'These are trivial questions. Do they affect my paintings?'

'They might,' Nosjean admitted.

'Is there anything else?'

'Nothing, Monsieur,' Nosjean said. 'You've been most helpful.'

Vacchi grunted. 'A waste of my time,' he growled. 'Your questions could have been answered for you by Riault or Luca.'

Nosjean smiled. 'I prefer', he said, 'to have them answered by you, Monsieur Vacchi, because I have reason to suspect that there is something very odd about this man Solecin whom Riault uses for the verification of the paintings he sells.'

Vacchi gave a sour smile. 'I think, young man,' he said, 'that you'll find you're very wrong so I should be very careful of any accusations you might make. Deputy Barclay has a name for honesty and straightforwardness and, as a junior minister in the government, he would hardly recommend someone dubious to an old friend.'

No, Nosjean thought as he headed for the door. But, on the other hand, Barclay might also have been taken in by friend Riault, whoever he was. He had clearly been taken in by *somebody* over a Vlaminck and he might well have been taken in over other things, too.

It might be well worth seeing Claude Barclay. On the pavement outside, Nosjean looked at his watch. It was late and Mijo Lehmann had said she'd wait at her flat for him. He remembered the previous night with a little shudder of pleasure. In the big bed they had done unmentionable things that had left him feeling he had been wasting his time for years over all those other girls like the estate agent and the librarian and the girl who worked in a travel agency, simply because they looked like Charlotte Rampling. For years he'd had a thing about girls who looked like Charlotte Rampling but he felt he'd got over it now and Mijo Lehmann was worth ten of them. He had never realised she was as enthusiastic as she had been, always assuming that with her knowledge of antiques, she was cool and self-possessed. And – the thought gave him some pleasure – *she* looked like Charlotte Rampling, too! He felt a little tremor of what he had to admit looked remarkably like lust run through him and decided that perhaps he could leave Deputy Barclay and his picture until the following day.

While Nosjean had been busy with the paintings, Darcy had been on the telephone to the War Ministry about Jules Arri, and they had put him in touch with the regimental historian of the 179th Regiment of the Line, currently billeted in one of the big yellow barrack blocks at Metz. The regimental historian, an ex-major called Leroux, ran a small museum there and he was more than willing to help.

Well, Darcy thought, Metz wasn't all that far away. Only far enough to leave him worn out for his date in the evening. As Darcy left the city heading east and north, Pel was with the Chief. The Chief was angry.

'Judge Brisard complains that the body at Suchey was removed before he arrived,' he was saying 'And that, as you know, is not the usual practice. The juge d'instruction should see it in situ.'

Pel's hackles rose. Brisard, he felt, was a powerful argument for euthanasia. He was all for a heart attack crippling him for a while. Nothing permanent. Just something to stop his pious rattle.

'The body remained exactly where it was found until as late as possible,' he rapped back. 'The Palais de Justice was informed immediately the message about the discovery came in. Doctor Minet was there when I arrived and everybody else arrived about the same time. Judge Brisard had ample time to visit the scene of the crime before the body was removed.'

The Chief frowned. 'He says his department wasn't informed,' he growled.

Pel scowled. He didn't have a lot of time for the Palais de Justice where, he considered, they spent all their time thinking up ways to advance their own ends at the expense of the police. And Brisard was an old enemy. Tall, pear-shaped, setting himself up as the acme of righteousness with a deep love for his family – though Pel knew very well that he had a woman in Beaune who was the widow of a police officer – he and Pel had hated each other from the moment they had met.

The Chief knew all about the feud and for a lot of it blamed Pel with his eccentricities and inexplicable dislikes – though, it had to be admitted, he disliked Brisard even more. If he could have got rid of Brisard he would happily have done so for a bit of peace, because he had no intention of getting rid of Pel. For all his irritability, his eccentricity and bigotry, Pel was the most valuable member of his staff and the Chief intended keeping him until he retired or descended into senility. All the same, he thought, the little bugger had to be brought up sharp at times because he always liked to work without a juge d'instruction looking over his shoulder which, as he well knew, was not permitted by the system.

'It'll have to go in your file,' he said.

Pel was quite indifferent. Complaints dropped into Pel's file like confetti at a wedding, but it didn't stop him doing his job and the Chief mostly took no notice of them or immediately countered them by putting in commendations to balance them.

'All right,' he said. 'Let's forget that now.'

Pel nodded, but he was spiteful enough to decide to do nothing of the sort. If Brisard wanted war, he thought, he could have it. He knew the message *had* been passed on and that somehow he'd find proof. He drew a deep breath and turned to the case of Jules Arri.

'We've established his identity,' he said. 'Now we have to establish where he went to at night. We have his car but there were no useful fingerprints on it and I'm having it returned to the spot in the supermarket car park where it was found with a notice on it, "Have you seen the owner of this vehicle?" We'll also have it photographed; with the number prominent, and let the press have it. They'll be on to it like a lot of vultures and it will give them something to write about and keep them out of our hair for a bit. I'll have a word with Sarrazin, the freelance, because what he does the others always do, too. Same sort of thing. "Have you seen the owner of this car? Did you see it on or around the 16th of the month and, if so, where?" Somebody may have noticed what he did when he left it.'

Somebody had.

When he returned to his office, Inspector Pomereu was waiting for him. Pomereu was a humourless individual but he ran Traffic efficiently. Not, Pel thought contemptuously, that it required more than a third-rate brain to run Traffic. You only had to know the difference between right and left and be able to wave your arms. Anybody could keep vehicles moving and hand out parking tickets.

Pomereu was not in a very good temper and he was quick to notice Pel's scowl. 'Something troubling you?' he asked sarcastically.

'That ass, Brisard.'

Pomereu brightened up. He'd had a few passages of arms with Brisard himself. 'What's he complaining about this time?'

'He says his department wasn't informed about Arri. They were. He just failed to turn up. I expect he was somewhere he shouldn't be.'

'He tries it on,' Pomereu agreed. 'It's a pity his right arm can't drop off.'

Pel brightened. He hadn't realised Pomereu's dislike of Brisard was as strong as his own. 'Or that he could be paralysed all down one side,' he suggested.

Pomereu grinned. It was unusual in Pomereu, whose pale face was normally totally without expression. For the first time since he'd known him, Pel warmed to him and for a while they contemplated with pleasure the things that might happen to Judge Brisard. Then Pomereu remembered why he was there.

'We've found someone who noticed Arri's car,' he said.

'Who?'

'The attendant of the car park in the Place de la Liberation, opposite the Palais des Ducs.'

'Here, in the city?' Pel had been expecting someone from Varagne.

'It's the only Palais des Ducs I know,' Pomereu said. 'He's pretty indignant. He says it shouldn't have been in the supermarket car park at Varagne. It should have been in his car park outside the Palais des Ducs.'

Pel looked puzzled and Pomereu explained.

'There's no full-time attendant,' he said. 'Just an old boy who goes round from time to time to make sure people who park their cars there are doing their stuff. It's a pay-and-display park with a machine on the wall by the bar-tabac. You put your money in, receive a ticket and stick it on the windscreen of your car. The attendant wanders round to make sure nobody's in there without paying. He's often noticed the Peugeot 1111-AR-41 there, but always only for a short while.'

'Why only for a short while?'

'The regulations don't come into force until 8a.m. which is when the attendant comes on duty and they finish at 7p.m. when he goes off. He's noticed the car often but it always arrived just as he was packing up to go home and disappeared just as he was coming on in the morning. So Arri never needed a ticket, because none's required to park there during the evening and night.'

'Go on.'

Pomereu made himself comfortable on the corner of Pel's desk. Apparently Arri had arrived every evening about the time the car park emptied, and reappeared to collect his car just about the time it opened the following morning. Then, it seemed, he went into the bar nearby which opened at 6.30, took a café rhum, ate a roll and finally drove off. 'Mind you,' Pomereu said, 'the old boy admits there were occasional short periods when the car didn't stay there overnight. When, he thought, Arri must have been on holiday from whatever job it was he did.'

'What *did* he do? Does he know?'

'No. He didn't talk much.'

'Not even to the proprietor of the bar where he bought his coffee and rolls?'

'He seems to have been a bit tight-lipped.'

'Does your car park attendant know where he went after he left the car in the evening or where he'd come from when he returned?'

'He says no. Arri never spoke to him: simply nodded good evening and good morning.'

Pel frowned. 'He seems to be a laconic type, this Arri,' he said. 'We'll see the proprietor of the bar; he should know something.'

But he didn't.

He was no more help than the car park attendant. Sergeant Lagé, who was growing slow and deliberate as he neared the age of retirement, was offered a cup of coffee because he'd been around a long time and was known by everybody in the city as a fair and responsible cop, but there was no information for him.

'Same as the car park attendant, Patron,' he reported to Pel. 'He never spoke. The first few times – about five years ago, they reckon – he asked for a coffee with rum and a roll and butter, but after that they got used to him and he didn't bother to ask. They just handed it over, and he took it, sat down at a table with a newspaper, got rid of it, got up, nodded and left.'

'Every morning?'

'Every morning.'

'Had they no idea where he came from? Or where he went to?'

'Apparently he never spoke to anyone.'

'Where did he buy his paper?'

'The tabac next door. It's part of the same premises. Always the same one – *Le Bien Public.* He also bought cigarettes – one pack of Gauloises – and occasionally fuel for his lighter.'

'Man of routine, eh?'

'Seems to be. They knew him and just handed the paper over. Then he went next door, to the bar, looked at the front page over his coffee and roll and left.'

'Never saying a word?'

'Never more than just "Thank you".'

'Didn't anybody ever notice where he went when he left his car in the evening, or where he came from when he arrived to pick it up?'

Lagé had the answer. The bar had usually just opened when he arrived in the morning, he said, and the owner, who stood outside when it was fine to have his first cigarette of the day, used to see him turn into the Rue de la Liberté from the Rue de Bourg, then walk down to the Place de la Liberation and into the newsagent's. By the time he reached the bar, his coffee, rum and roll were on the counter waiting for him.

Pel frowned. 'Rue de Bourg,' he mused. He crossed to the wall and studied the map there. 'The Rue de Bourg leads to the station, the General Hospital, the canal port, the Lycée, the Arsenal, and the Zone Industrielle.'

Lagé managed a smile. 'It also leads to the Hôtel de Police, Patron,' he said. 'Here.'

Pel treated him to an icy look. Pel's sense of humour usually lasted until his first cigarette, by which time it had all been expended. 'He doesn't work here,' he said. 'But he might work at the station, the hospital, the port, the Lycée, the Arsenal, or anywhere in the Zone Industrielle. As a night-watchman.'

Lagé frowned. 'So why didn't he leave his car in the car park where he worked, Patron? Those places all have them.'

That was a puzzler, to be sure.

'That's something that will be explained when we learn where he worked. You've got a job, Lagé. Find out. Try that area first.'

Pel watched Lagé leave. Lagé was no longer young and he was slow but he was a hard worker and was willing to help others, something of which Misset, who wasn't, was always quick to take advantage. Lagé never jibbed at long slow enquiries and he was painstaking. It was an ideal job for him because what he lacked in imagination or inspiration he made up for in dogged concentration. If Arri had worked in the area he seemed to have worked in, then Lagé could be trusted to find out where.

Darcy arrived back from Metz in the early evening just as Pel was about to leave.

'We've got a picture, Patron. The regimental historian found it for me.'

'In uniform? Complete with képi? It'll be hard to recognise him as a civilian.'

Darcy grinned, showing his splendid white snappers. 'No, Patron. Not in uniform. No képi. Not a single brass button. Standing with the regimental rugby team. He played with them for years, and, after he grew too old, he acted as trainer-coach. Very respected.'

He had been fishing in his brief case as he spoke and he laid on Pel's desk a photograph of a group of men in shorts and shirts, all heavily built and looking the essence of determination. 'That's him,' Darcy said. 'On the right. In trousers.'

Arri had been a good-looking man, tall, strong, and with a ruggedly handsome face.

'Is it like him as he was just before he died?' Pel asked.

'They said so, Patron. He'd been to regimental reunions and I gather he hadn't changed much. However, for confirmation, I came back via Valoreille – it's not far out of the way – and showed it to those two old Ponsardin biddies. They picked him out at once. So did Brigadier Foulet and the type at the garage. I think we can use it.'

'Right. Lagé has a lead to where he might have worked. But it might not come off because he seems to have been a secretive type.'

'That's what Major Leroux said. A bit of a loner. A good soldier but not the chummy type.'

'Right, then. Let's have the picture copied and get the boys showing it round. They might turn him up.'

Darcy paused. 'Patron,' he said. 'There's another line on him I found. He was wounded at Dien Bien Phu, and Claude Barclay was his officer.'

'The Deputy for Yorinne?'

'The very same. He was alongside him when he was hit and risked his life to drag him to shelter. He got him aboard one of the last planes out so that he survived. If he hadn't he might have died. Major Leroux told me all this. It's in the regimental history. Barclay was captured, in fact, but he escaped and got to the coast and finally to Saigon. The Major had an idea that Barclay might eventually have found Arri a job here somewhere.'

'It might save us a lot of time,' Pel said, 'if we found out where. Get in touch with Barclay. He might be at Courtois or he might be at his office here.'

But Barclay was not available. He had gone to Paris and wasn't expected back until late. 'He'll be in his office tomorrow,' Darcy said.

'Right.' Pel rose, took the cigarette Darcy offered and headed for the door. 'How about a beer in the Bar Transvaal? I think we're making progress. We'll see him tomorrow.'

Pel was barely awake when the telephone went the following morning. He was unshaven, in his dressing gown, his hair standing on end, staring at his stomach in the bathroom mirror and wondering where it had come from.

His wife regarded him with a smile. 'Something wrong, Pel?' she asked gently.

Pel studied his face. 'I've decided it's never going to improve much,' he said. 'The lines are deeper every day. They're no longer just on the surface. They go right through to the back of my head.'

As his wife laughed, the telephone went and he snatched it up. It was Darcy and Pel knew at once that something had happened.

'Sorry to disturb you, Patron,' he said. 'We've got trouble.'

'Let's have it.'

'A kidnapping.'

'A *what?*'

'A kidnapping.'

'That's what I thought you said.' Pel's eyebrows rose. He'd been involved in most things but kidnapping wasn't normally part of the Burgundian scene. 'Who've we lost? The Baron de Mougy's son? His wife? Somebody with money, I expect.'

'Somebody with money all right, Patron. But it's not a child or a wife. It's Barclay. Deputy for Yorinne and junior minister. They collared him as he arrived at his office half an hour ago.'

six

Darcy was on the telephone when Pel arrived at the Hôtel de Police but he put the instrument down immediately he saw his superior.

'That was Aimedieu,' he said. 'I sent him out to Barclay's home as soon as I heard, to get some idea of that end.'

'You'd no need to bother,' Pel rapped. 'You'll remember I had a conducted tour of the place only a couple of nights ago. Inform me.'

'He left his house at Courtois at 7.30 by car – a big grey Merc. He's got an office in the Place Saint-Julien and he always arrives early. But this morning he arrived particularly early – eight o'clock. The Place Saint-Julien's full of offices and at that time it's fairly empty. It seems there was a car parked either side of the entrance to his office and another one across the other side of the square, all with drivers, and at the end a motor cyclist who was obviously the look-out.'

'Have we numbers or descriptions?'

'Very insubstantial, Patron. There was just room for Barclay to park right outside his office entrance and that's what he did. As he arrived in the Rue Saint-Julien leading into the square, the motor cyclist, wearing a black visored crash helmet – so he couldn't be recognised, I suppose – started up his machine, did a complete circle and disappeared down the Rue Armand-Duvalier. He was obviously giving the sign to his pals that Barclay was on his way. As far as I can make out, the car at the opposite side of the square started its engine and, as Barclay slipped into the choice spot outside his office, it crossed the square at full speed and pulled up alongside. With the two other cars on either side of the entrance, one in front, one behind, it was impossible to drive away. The drivers of the cars parked outside his office got out, dragged him from his car, pushed him into the car from across the square, and then all three men drove off with him, leaving his Merc with the engine still running. His brief case went with him. According to one of the eyewitnesses, it looked full and heavy.'

Pel frowned. 'What about these cars?'

'The one from the other side of the square which took him away was a Citroën CX. The other two were a Peugeot 309 and a small Fiat.'

'Witnesses?'

'Caretaker of Barclay's office. There's a long hall and he was at the other end of it. All he saw was a scuffle. He's an old man and didn't hurry to get involved. He saw men, heard a lot of doors slamming and engines roaring, then there was nothing but Barclay's Merc with the engine still running outside the door.'

'Was he the only one?'

'No. Two others. One of them, Jacqueline Duhamel, is a typist in the office of Mansoni-Littel, solicitors, opposite. She had a lot of typing to do last night, it seems – stuff on the dictaphone – but she had a date and got permission to come in early this morning instead. She'd just arrived and was adjusting her make-up with a hand mirror at the window of her office on the second floor where the light's good. She saw the whole thing. She was so startled, she was a bit vague at first, but she's bright and, after thinking about it, she was able to give a fairly clear description. She knows about cars too, it seems, and she recognised every one of them. Not that it'll make a lot of difference. I suppose they were all stolen.'

'And the other witness?'

'An old touch who's the concierge for Number 15, Rue Armand-Duvalier. She was heading for the bakers' in the Rue Saint-Julien for a baguette for breakfast. She'd just reached the Rue Saint-Julien exit from the square when she saw Barclay's Merc arrive. It came rather fast and she had to nip smartly on to the sidewalk, so she turned to tell Barclay what she thought of him and as she did so, she saw what happened. She's seventy, though, knows nothing about cars and doesn't think very fast. But her idea of what happened tallies with the description by Jacqueline Duhamel, so I think we've got it right.'

'Who's been informed?'

'The Chief, of course. Forensic, in case they can pick anything up. Fingerprints, in case anything was left on Barclay's car. Judge Polverari, who's already on his way to the Place Saint-Julien. The Chief said he'd see you here. At the moment De Troq's out there with Lacocq and Morell. Nosjean's still busy with the art thing.'

Pel frowned. 'He insists Barclay's picture was a fake,' he remembered. 'Think there's any connection?'

'Patron, artists don't go in for kidnap. Neither do art dealers, critics or experts. Kidnap's the work of people after money from a ransom, terrorists who want something from the government, or gangsters who've got something against the victim.'

'Which is this?'

Darcy shrugged. 'Money for ransom, I reckon,' he said. 'Barclay's a do-gooder and people don't kidnap do-gooders. He's known for his work for charity, for art galleries, museums, orphans and ex-soldiers. That sort of thing. And he's popular and not involved in anything controversial. Who'd want to kidnap him for that? Terrorists? He's only a junior minister. He has no influence with the President. It's got to be for money. Kidnapping's a growth industry these days.'

'*If* it's for money that means the gangs.'

'Maurice Tagliatti or Pépé le Cornet?'

'They're not the only ones these days. There are a few others coming up, ambitious types who think those two are growing a bit long in the tooth. We'd better contact them to see if they know anything.'

While they were talking, the Chief appeared. He was a large man with a red face, shoulders like a drayhorse and big fists which, in his youth, had helped to make him a champion boxer. He came in, in his usual fashion, flinging the door back and slamming it against the wall as though he were trying to tear it off its hinges.

He didn't speak but simply jerked his head in the direction of his office. Pel and Darcy followed and waited until the Chief had circled his office a couple of times, a little like a bull trying to decide which side of a china shop to attack, and then sat at his desk. Reaching down, he fished out three glasses and a brandy bottle. The red in his face deepened until he looked as if, gently blown on, he would burst into flames.

'This seems to call for a drink to steady our nerves,' he said. 'Pouring it will give us time to adjust.'

When they'd all drunk, he looked at Pel. Pel gestured at Darcy, who told him what he'd told Pel.

'That's all we know?'

'At the moment, sir.'

'Any theories?'

'Terrorists?' Darcy said. 'Barclay's not important enough. If terrorists had wanted to collar somebody, there are plenty with more influence than he has. It must be for money. I expect we'll be getting a ransom demand before long. Or, at least, his family will.'

'He doesn't have a family,' Pel said. 'He's a bachelor. Or that's what I was told the other night.'

The Chief's head jerked round. 'The other night?'

'I was having a conducted tour – with about twenty-four other people – round his house at Courtois.' As Pel explained the circumstances, the Chief frowned.

'I think we'd better keep quiet about that,' he suggested. 'It would look bad if we admitted it. You know what the Press would make of it. *'PJ officer was with kidnap victim.' 'Why didn't he realise?' 'Are the police blind?'* We'll let it lie for the time being. What do you know about him?'

'Nothing,' Pel said. 'Except that he's a crashing bore, collects paintings, and is given to ruining splendid old houses.'

'Women?'

'Just a girl friend.'

'You're sure she's a girl friend? Was she good-looking?'

'She was *very* good-looking.'

The Chief frowned, poured them all another brandy and considered. 'We'll have to inform Paris, of course,' he said. 'The man's the Deputy for the Yorinne district. A representative of the people. And with an election due. The fact that he was self-satisfied, given to ruining houses and a crashing bore has nothing to do with it. Most representatives of the people are self-satisfied crashing bores. But the man was a member of the government. We shall have to inform the DST.'

The Direction de la Surveillance du Térritoire, who were responsible for security and the safety of the people's representatives, were housed in Paris and, part of the country's counter-espionage service, were in close contact with the West German Bundesnachrichtendienst, Scotland Yard in London, and the security forces of most other countries.

'They'll clutter the place up.'

The Chief glanced quickly at Pel. He knew what he was thinking: Paris invariably got in the way of the provincial and city police organisations and he felt much the same about them as Pel. But there was no getting round it. The kidnapped man was a junior minister and *might* have had access to secrets which could be obtained from him by pressure.

'I'll attend to it,' he said. 'We can't leave them in the dark. They know things we don't and, if it comes to a siege or anything like that, they have sophisticated devices we shan't get until the year 2000. There's one thing: If we get him back, it'll win a few sympathy votes from his constituents.'

'And if we don't,' he added, 'it'll mean a by-election.'

Jacqueline Duhamel was a pert little creature with black hair cut in a smooth bob and a figure that held Darcy's eyes longer than it should. She immediately obviously recognised Darcy as a man with an interest in girls and responded by studying him. He was worth studying. He was handsome, with square white teeth like gravestones, and he was always dressed as if he were about to go to a levée at the Elysée Palace, with a tall white collar that sawed at his ears and an immaculate suit that made Pel's look as if it had been cast off by a tramp.

With the permission of Jacqueline Duhamel's boss, they interviewed her alone in her office and one of the other girls brought in coffee.

'You didn't notice any of the car numbers?' Pel asked.

'No.' Jacqueline Duhamel shook her head. 'It happened too quickly. But I did notice that the motorbike was red – they all seem to be red these days, don't they? – red for danger, I suppose, and that the rider had a black visor so I couldn't see his face.'

'You saw none of the men from the cars?'

'They all wore hats so that their faces were shaded, and I was above them so I couldn't see them properly. They were all dressed in suits, too – so they'd look like businessmen waiting to go into the offices when they opened, I suppose. There are always a lot about around that time in this square because it's full of solicitors' offices.'

'Nothing special about any of these men?'

'Nothing I noticed. Grey and blue suits.'

'The cars. What colour were they?'

'The Citroën that took him away was grey. They make a lot of grey ones. Monsieur Barclay's Merc was grey. They do, too. The Peugeot was beige and the Fiat, which was smaller, was red. That was parked on the Rue Saint-Julien side of the door. The Peugeot was parked on the Rue Armand-Duvalier side. There was a good space between them, big enough for Monsieur Barclay's car, but it was blocked by a Renault van that was parked between the other two cars but not against the pavement. There was a man in it in a white coat, looking at a list, as if he were delivering something.'

Pel glanced at Darcy. 'That's the first we've heard of this van,' he said.

Jacqueline Duhamel smiled. 'I've really only remembered it since Inspector Darcy saw me earlier. I've made a plan.'

She laid a sheet of typing paper on the table between them, a neatly worked-out indication of the positions of all the cars involved.

'I think,' she said, 'that the gap outside the door was left deliberately and the van was there to make sure nobody slipped into it because that's where they wanted Monsieur Barclay's car to be – between the other cars, so he couldn't get away.'

'You obviously use your eyes and your head,' Darcy said and she blushed with pleasure. 'Why do you think that?'

'Because when the motor cyclist started up and circled to go down the Rue Armand-Duvalier, the van started up too. I saw the driver drop his list quickly. He'd been looking back down the Rue Saint-Julien as if he were waiting, but when the motor cycle started up, he began jumping about in a hurry and the van moved off after the motor cyclist. Immediately. But as soon as Monsieur Barclay's car appeared, the car at the other side of the square – the Citroën – started up, too, and as Monsieur Barclay slipped into place between the Peugeot and the Fiat outside the door, it crossed the square and stopped alongside him, so that he couldn't get away.'

'You're sure about these cars?'

'Yes. Certain. I'm thinking of buying a car, my first, so I look at them a lot. I expect what I'll buy will be small – I couldn't afford anything bigger – but it's nice to look at the big ones now and then and daydream, isn't it?'

She gave a wide smile but Pel noticed that it was directed at Darcy not himself.

The other two witnesses, the caretaker who had seen the scuffle by the doorway and the old woman heading for the confectioner's, were able to add nothing.

As they left, Pel gestured. 'We'd better ask,' he said, 'if anyone's seen these cars that were used or reported them stolen.'

There was no need. The owner of the red Fiat, an indignant Algerian living near the Zone Industrielle, had telephoned with the news of the loss of his car before they returned to the Hôtel de Police. His car, he said – Number 741-BC-21 – had been stolen from the street outside the apartment where he lived. Even as Inspector Pomereu of Traffic passed the information on to Pel's department, another telephone call came – from a doctor who had lost his Peugeot. It was beige, brand new, and fast. He offered its number and wanted to know what the hell the police were doing to allow the car of a busy doctor to be stolen from outside his house.

'Was it locked?' Pomereu asked.

'Of course not. It was outside my house.'

Pomereu didn't argue but he allowed himself a small dry smile.

The third car turned up late in the afternoon even before it had been reported missing. One of Pomereu's men from Traffic noticed it parked badly, its rear end sticking out into the road, in the Rue Alphonse-Rémé. The driver of a small Renault was trying to park behind it but it was difficult because the Citroën was a big car and the projecting rear end was making it awkward to reverse into the only spare parking place in the street.

'You'd think people would take the trouble to park properly, wouldn't you?' the owner of the Renault said bitterly to Pomereu's man. 'People like that should be fined for obstruction.'

Pomereu's man thought so, too, and decided to have a look at the Citroën. He had been on duty all day and hadn't received anything beyond the briefest description of the stolen cars but he remembered one of them was a Citroën CX. This one looked as if it had been abandoned in a hurry and, while it might only have been taken by joyriders late at night,

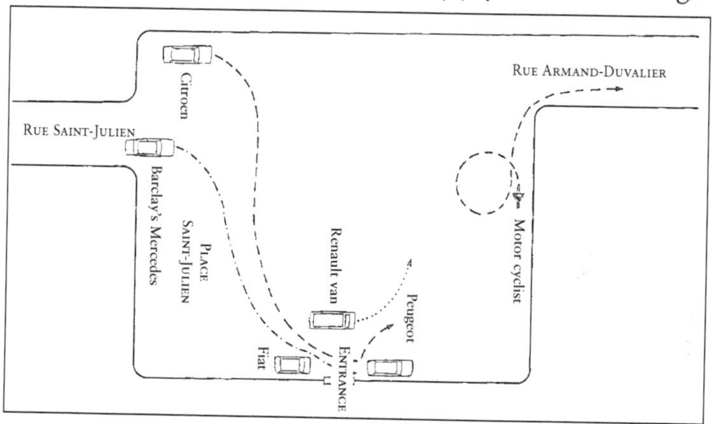

it might also have been used for something else.

He walked slowly round the Citroën. It appeared to be empty but there was a briefcase on the back shelf, which was unusual because stolen cars were usually rifled before they were left. Trying the driver's door, he found it unlocked but there was no key in the ignition. The other doors were also unlocked and that seemed very suspicious. The briefcase contained papers and sales pamphlets referring to eletronic devices and computers and seemed quite important.

His call brought Sergeant Bardolle to the scene within ten minutes. 'It answers the description of a CX that was used to take away Barclay,' he reported.

Within a quarter of an hour the keys had been found in the gutter not far away and Prélat of Fingerprints was there with one of his men dusting it for dabs. There were plenty but they were the same as those they found on the briefcase, which had a name on the inside, Roland Ennaert, Apartment C, 15, Rue Souf.

A quarter of an hour later, another of Pel's men, Sergeant Brochard, was outside Apartment C. Roland Ennaert was a Belgian electronics engineer working at Groupe Electrogène Karzinski in the Industrial Zone, a slim handsome young man with pink cheeks and a mandarin moustache. He took a long time to answer the door and when he appeared he seemed to have just got out of bed, because his hair was on end, he was unshaven and he wore a shirt and trousers which appeared to have been donned in a hurry. On his feet were bedroom slippers.

He listened politely to Brochard. 'Yes,' he said. 'I've got a Citroën CX with that number. I bought it last summer. Why?'

'We have reason to believe your car was used in the kidnap of Deputy Claude Barclay. Perhaps you've heard it on the radio?'

Ennaert frowned. 'I saw it on the early television. But it can't be *my* car. Mine's still in the garage.'

'Which is where, Monsieur?'

'Round the back of the building. There are half a dozen lock-ups for the people with apartments.'

'Are you sure it's still there, Monsieur?'

'Yes. I haven't been out today – I have a long weekend – but I can see the garage from the kitchen window and the lock's secure on the hasp.'

'Would you mind accompanying me to the garage just to check, Monsieur?'

'It seems stupid when I can see from the kitchen that the door's still locked.'

'Nevertheless, sir... '

'Well, I – I'm a bit busy... '

Just what he was busy at seemed to be indicated when a petulant female voice called from somewhere inside the apartment. 'What's keeping you, Rolot?'

Ennaert looked at Brochard with a helpless you-see-what-the-situation-is expression.

Brochard was unmoved. 'I'm afraid I shall have to insist, sir.'

Ennaert pulled a face and turned back into the apartment. There was a hasty whispered conversation before he reappeared. 'This way,' he said. 'By the back door.'

He led the way downstairs and along a corridor into an open space at the back of the block where a line of garages with red doors stood, all with large and expensive-looking locks on the hasps. As Ennaert fished for his keys, Brochard, who was considered in the sergeants' room to be a bit of a humorist with a sense of mischief, put a hand on his arm. 'Allow me, sir,' he said.

'You've got a key?'

'Sort of.'

Taking out a penknife, Brochard opened the device like a spike intended for cleaning pipes.

'You'll not get it open with that,' Ennaert said confidently.

Almost before he had finished speaking, Brochard had the lock unfastened. Ennaert stared.

'Mother of God,' he said. 'That's a lot of good, isn't it? It cost a bomb, too!'

'It *is* possible to get good locks, Monsieur,' Brochard said cheerfully. 'If you like, I can give you the name of one or two.'

Panicking suddenly at the thought that his expensive lock could be opened so easily, Ennaert was dragging at the doors.

Inside was a used tyre, an empty petrol can, a carton of pamphlets from his business, and a dead sparrow.

'It's gone,' Ennaert said.

Brochard smiled politely. 'I thought it might have, Monsieur,' he said.

Already telephone messages were jamming the lines and telex messages were being delivered to security officers at airports and harbours. The city airfield was surrounded and police cars were receiving a constant flow of instructions.

'It looks to me', Pel said to Darcy, 'as if it were a well-planned affair. I think we've got a job for Traffic. Get Pomereu in.'

Pomereu entered warily, as if he suspected a lot of work was about to drop on him. Pel explained.

'This kidnap,' he said. 'It was all over within half a minute. We've got all the vehicles but the van, so get your boys asking around. We want it.' He turned to Darcy. 'More important, we want the men who were driving them. They'd obviously worked the thing out carefully. They'd obviously watched Barclay's movements. They might even have known them beforehand, which probably indicates a contact in one of those buildings in the square, perhaps in his own office.'

'Shouldn't think so,' Darcy said. 'Those I spoke to seemed to think the world of him. The women were at swooning point, in fact. He's too good-looking. We have one thing, though. The driver's seat of the Citroën that took him away was pushed back as far as it would go but the owner didn't use it in that position. That seems to indicate that whoever drove it was a tall man.'

Pel nodded. 'Not much,' he said, 'but it's something. Let's get going.'

As they rose, Pomereu picked up his cap and headed for the door. Then he stopped. 'Oh,' he said. 'Something I forgot.' He fished in his pocket and laid a sheet of paper on

Pel's desk. 'It was among the other parking tickets. They all come through my office. This one might interest you.'

As the door closed behind him, Pel picked up the parking ticket, studied it for a moment, then he slipped it into his pocket.

'Secret assignation, Patron?' Darcy asked.

'You might call it that,' Pel said. 'In the meantime, let's have a closer look at Barclay. Perhaps he was involved with more than we realise. He was a bit of a linguist, I believe, and the government doesn't always use named officials to do its dirty work abroad. Perhaps he was involved with something that isn't generally known. I expect our Paris friends can supply the answer to that. They have the "in" to the men in the know in the government. Meanwhile, I'll slip out to Courtois and see if Aimedieu's discovered anything of note.'

Aimedieu seemed bewildered. By the time Pel arrived with Judge Polverari he had been at Barclay's home since early morning and he was growing bored. He had called out the local police who were guarding the only unlocked entrance, and he had talked to the staff – Gefray, the manservant, a gardener, a cook and the maid – and had produced nothing. In addition to his profession as an architect, his dealings as a financier, and his work as a member of the Assembly and a junior member of the government, Barclay had been involved with charity work for hospitals and museums, to whom he was always lending paintings; with homes for ex-servicemen and children; and with a fund, which was still functioning, set up for the relief of disasters such as the Mexican earthquake and the African famine. Not only did he appear to be a solid do-gooder, but, as Pel knew, he was the sort of man that women never failed to notice and also still had clinging to him the remnants of a youthful heroism.

He walked round the hall of the old house. Standing under a great iron chandelier converted to carry electric light bulbs, he stared at the walls. The windows were all open now and the door stood wide, letting in the sunshine.

'You remember me?' he asked Gefray, the manservant. 'I was here the other night with the party from Bois Haut that Monsieur Barclay brought.'

'I remember you, Monsieur,' Gefray said. 'I have a good memory for guests' faces. And, of course, I've seen your photograph in the newspapers from time to time.'

Pel was surprised he could recognise anything from those. Most of them made him look as if he'd been struck by lightning.

'That night', he said, 'all the doors and windows on the ground floor were locked and bolted when we were inside – I suspect at Monsieur Barclay's orders. I saw him speak to you and the door was secured.'

'That's right, Monsieur.'

'Was it his habit always to have the doors locked and bolted?' Polverari asked.

'At night, sir, yes.'

'Even with guests in the house?'

'In recent weeks, Monsieur.'

'Why?'

'The general atmosphere of violence, I suspect, Monsieur. It's something everybody goes in for these days, I imagine. There's also the election due.'

Pel could hardly find fault with anyone who made his job easier by taking precautions. He stared about him. 'With the doors and the ground floor windows bolted and barred, it wouldn't be possible to get in, would it?'

'No, Monsieur. This house was built in the twelfth century and in those times big houses like this were virtual fortresses. The Dukes of Burgundy and their supporters were at war against the Kings of France at the time. There was a lot of treachery and they took care to make sure their homes were secure against assassins. The ground floor windows are five or six metres above the ground.'

'Has Monsieur Barclay been afraid of intruders?'

'Everybody is these days, Monsieur.'

'I'm not thinking of burglars. He's been kidnapped.'

Gefray considered and shook his head. 'I don't know, Monsieur.'

'Would you say Monsieur Barclay was a nervous type?'

'No, Monsieur. Far from it. He'd been a soldier. And a brave one, too. Until recently, he was often out at night. He had friends. He had admirers... '

'Women?'

'Yes.'

'Know any of them?'

'Some, Monsieur. It's only recently he's started to have the place so carefully closed.'

'As if he thought something might *be about to happen?*'

'Since you mention it, Monsieur, though it didn't occur to me before, yes, I think that might be the case.'

'Even as if he thought that what happened today might have been about to happen at any time?'

'I hadn't thought of it like that, Monsieur.'

'Did he talk to you much?'

'Not a great deal, Monsieur.'

'He never mentioned his fears to you?'

'No. Never.'

'To your knowledge, did he have any enemies?'

'I know of none, Monsieur.'

They seemed to be getting nowhere. Fast.

seven

Breakfast time at Pel's home usually started with a stroll round the garden. Until his marriage he had never had a garden, unless you could call a green pocket handkerchief behind the house he'd owned in the Rue Martin-de-Noinville a garden. You could hardly have called it a house, in fact, because it had always been a little tight round the hips. Pel had lived there for some time, his housekeeper, Madame Routy, who had ruled the place, keeping him well in subjection, cooking appalling meals, helping herself to his brandy and spending most of her time watching television. The only good thing which had come out of the relationship was Pel's friendship with Madame Routy's nephew, Didier Darras, now a police cadet and part of Pel's office staff in place of one Cadet Martin, who had handled letters, studied the newspapers and fetched the beer and sandwiches when necessary but was now, a fully-fledged cop, out on the streets, combating the crime wave on his own.

On his marriage, it had seemed to Pel that his new wife had committed the blunder of her life in taking Madame Routy on with Pel, but to his surprise, she had had Madame Routy eating out of her hand in less than a week, cooking splendid meals and watching the television only after working hours in the little flatlet she occupied at the back of the splendid new house at Leu.

The disappearance of Didier Darras from the scene had also been more than adjusted by the arrival of Yves Pasquier, aged nine, at the house next door. Pel liked to hold conversations through the hedge with his new neighbour and he was determined not to be stirred out of his routine. He had been at the Hôtel de Police until midnight the day before and he knew he was likely to be there until after midnight again. Darcy had slept on a camp bed in his office, holding the fort. Always regarding himself as Pel's protector, he had insisted on Pel going home, so there was no point in panicking to get the office. It was going to be a long enough day as it was, and his daily conversation with Yves Pasquier would help steady the world a little on its axis.

It seemed that Yves Pasquier enjoyed the conversations, too, because whenever the weather was fit, he always seemed to be there before disappearing to school. He was there now, accompanied by his dog, a black mongrel devoid of shape but so plentifully endowed with hair it was impossible to tell which end was which. Only the fact that it sat on one end indicated that the other end was the end that might bite.

'A man got shot in Paris yesterday,' he informed Pel as they met.

'People often get shot in Paris,' Pel agreed. 'It's an occupational hazard with people who live in Paris.'

'When people get shot they go "aaaagh!", don't they?'

'Only on television or in children's comics.'

Yves Pasquier considered this for a time then he looked up. 'There was a kidnapping yesterday, too,' he said. 'Here. Type called Barclay.'

'So I heard.'

'I read it in the paper. Are you handling it?'

'These things usually fall into my lap.'

'Was it spies?'

'It seems unlikely.'

'But that's why they usually kidnap people, isn't it?'

'I'm sure there are other reasons.'

'They usually demand the release of spies from the other side, don't they?'

'Which other side?'

'Russia. America.'

'I thought the Americans were on our side.'

'England, then. They've never been on our side.' Yves Pasquier considered. 'Perhaps they're going to blow up the world.'

'Who?'

'The kidnappers.'

'There wouldn't be much point in kidnapping anybody if they were going to blow up the world.'

'No, I suppose not. But I was watching this video about this man who wanted to rule the world and threatened to blow it up if they didn't let him. He'd got masses of plutonium buried in an abandoned coal mine.'

'Did he succeed?'

'No, they stopped him just in time.'

Pel nodded sagely. 'On television they usually do.'

He could see his wife waving, so the conversation came to an end and Pel went indoors. Madame Routy poured coffee for them both and Pel did his usual balancing act of trying to spread jam on a croissant with a spoon as he held it in his hand. Finishing his meal, he rose, wiped his mouth and headed for the door.

'I might be late,' he said. 'The kidnapping's altered a few timetables.'

'I heard,' Madame Routy offered, 'that it's Red terrorists.'

Pel gave her a look that wouldn't have shamed a frozen food plant. '*I* heard,' he said, 'that it's a gang who want to blow up the world.'

His wife didn't have to guess very hard to know where that one had come from and she laughed. Madame Routy glared. As Pel headed for the front door, she handed him his briefcase as if she hoped it contained a bomb which would explode as soon as he was safely away from the house. There was little love lost between Madame Routy and Pel. Indeed there never had been. For the sake of Madame Pel they had endeavoured at first on Pel's marriage to live at peace with one another, but it hadn't worked and now they enjoyed their enmity as much as ever, while Madame Pel, realising in her subtle way that it kept them busy and happy, allowed them to enjoy it, merely stopping Madame Routy from shoving her oar in too often and gently chiding Pel in her quietly humorous manner when he was in danger of becoming too rude.

He drove down the hill into the city without incident – unless you could call narrowly missing an eight-wheeled truck as he joined the main road an incident. From the movements of the truck driver's mouth he had discovered something that a lot of people had known for a long time – that Pel was not a good driver.

'You deserve to be écraséd,' he roared. 'Flattened! I've a good mind to report you to the flics.'

It wouldn't have done him a lot of good, Pel thought sourly. The flics knew he was a poor driver, too.

The election campaign was beginning to hot up, he noticed as he drove into the city, and posters carrying the pictures of candidates were appearing everywhere, where possible pasted over those of the opposition – a case of last come, best served. Teeth were more than ever in evidence in flashing smiles, though some of the candidates preferred to show themselves as earnest-minded individuals with the weight of the Republic firmly on their shoulders and presented grim visages to the voting public. Party colours were also well in evidence with huge placards full of party propaganda or abuse. Country people being slower to anger or delight, the villages were fairly subdued, as they always were, but the city was hard at it despite the early hour, with loudspeaker vans already on the streets making the morning hideous with their clamour.

The office seemed to be full of people when Pel arrived, all of them apparently arguing about the election. Most of them disappeared abruptly as Pel's face appeared round the door – especially those like Misset, who was always skilful at looking busy until you really studied him and found he wasn't. As he appeared in his office, Claudie Darel, the only woman member of his team, dropped his letters on his desk. She was followed by Police Cadet Didier Darras.

Pel looked up. He still hadn't got used to seeing Didier there and in uniform. Since Didier's mother had an ageing father who sometimes demanded her attention, Didier had often turned up at Pel's house for a snack from his aunt, Madame Routy. He and Pel had become good friends because they both enjoyed boules and fishing and loathed television and had often taken great delight in waiting for Aunt Routy to cook one of the appalling meals she had cooked in those days and then disappearing into the blue to eat out so that she had to polish off the disaster herself. Not long before, Didier Darras had announced he wanted to be a cop and, through Pel's string-pulling, had finally taken the place of the recently departed Cadet Martin. Getting him into uniform was something Pel was proud of and he had already started putting ideas into the mind of Yves Pasquier.

'How are things going?' he asked as the boy placed the newspapers on his desk.

Didier shrugged and, worried that he might be disillusioned with police work, Pel probed.

Didier shrugged again. 'It's not the work,' he said. 'That's all right. It's Louise Bray.'

Louise Bray had been his steady girl friend ever since she had first hit him over the head with her doll.

'What's wrong with Louise Bray?'

'She's started going to discos with Martin.'

'Cadet Martin?'

'He's a cop now.'

Pel frowned. Martin had been known to turn heads before. 'How did she meet him?'

'I introduced them.'

'That was foolish. Martin's a handsome lad. Think they've got something going?'

'It's beginning to look like it.'

'What do you intend to do about it?'

Didier shrugged again. 'I could shoot him,' he said. 'They're teaching me to handle a gun at the armoury. But I don't suppose I will.'

'It would certainly lose you Louise Bray.'

'I wasn't thinking of her. I was thinking I'd lose my job.'

As the door closed, Pel reached for the newspapers. Barclay's kidnapping was plastered over every front page. *Le Monde,* being *Le Monde,* had devoted no more than two columns at the top, but that was star billing from *Le Monde.* 'Minister Kidnapped', it said. The other papers were less restrained and La *Torche* seemed to have thrown its head back and let out a wild howl of indignation.

'Government Compromised,' it yelled. 'Kidnapped Minister Knew All the Secrets.' It devoted the whole of the front page to the kidnapping – it was difficult to devote more because little was known and, anyway, headlines usually occupied most of *La Torche's* front page, but there was also a whole page inside with pictures, telling the reading public what a fine man Barclay was, of his interest in arts, the various charities he supported, the buildings he had designed, his heroism as a young officer in Indo-China. The pictures seemed to indicate they were right, and showed Barclay holding his head up in a heroic attitude, his mane of grey hair ruffled by the breeze, the very acme of good looks, courage and integrity. Inevitably, however, they couldn't resist the urge to stir things up with suggestions that security hadn't been tight enough and that the police had fallen down on the job of protecting members of the government.

As Pel tossed the papers aside, the telephone went. It was the Chief. He sounded nervous. 'The DST will be arriving any minute,' he confirmed. 'They telephoned half an hour ago to say they were on their way.'

As Pel put the telephone down, Lagé appeared. 'Jules Arri, Patron,' he said. 'No luck so far. I've contacted every firm I can think of who might have a night-watchman in the area off the Rue de Bourg. Nobody knows him. I've got the photographs now, too, but nobody recognised them. Nobody's ever seen him. He's been spotted walking down the Rue de la Liberté but that's all. I'm wondering if, after he parked his car, somebody picked him up. That does happen. People share cars and the cost of petrol to go to work.'

'They don't seem to have shared Arri's car. That was always in the Place de la Liberation.'

'Perhaps they had an arrangement and Arri did the paying while the other type did the driving. Perhaps he didn't like driving. I'm still asking. I've got Lacocq and Morell showing the photographs on the buses. They're running at that time in the morning and somebody might have spotted him getting off one. I'm also trying taxis. I'll pick him up eventually, Patron.'

As Lagé vanished, Darcy appeared. He looked spotless and shaved to the bone, his collar gleaming, his clothes uncreased, as if he were about to take a girl out to dinner. Pel couldn't believe he'd slept on a camp bed in the office all night. If Pel had slept on a camp bed in the office, he'd have looked like something the cat had dragged in.

Darcy didn't waste time. 'Pomereu, of Traffic,' he said. 'He's reported that all the missing vehicles have now turned up. The van was found on a feeder road to the motorway at Chimeray. There were no fingerprints. Prélat's been at it ever since dawn. It was well worked over. We're obviously dealing with professionals.'

'What about the rest of the boys?'

'I've got De Troq', Lagé and Bardolle asking questions in the Place Saint-Julien area. Brochard's seeing Ennaert, the owner of the Citroën, again and asking questions round the Rue Souf to see who knew it would be in its garage. I've heard that the DST boys are on their way from Paris.'

'So have I, God help us. Under the circumstances, you'd better take over the Arri file because I've not the slightest doubt they'll want the red carpet out and all the top brass dancing attendance on them. Perhaps, even, you'd better get De Troq' on to it, too; then, if they expect *you* to be involved as well, he can look after Arri.' Pel looked hard at Darcy. 'It's going to be hell,' he said.

The DST men arrived late in the morning, blank-faced men who gave remarkably little away. There were six of them, four in a big Peugeot who were obviously the dogsbodies and did all the hard work, and two others in a Citroën who were clearly the men who did the thinking, the co-ordinating and the making of decisions.

'Lamiel.' The speaker was a tall thin man in a grey suit with grey hair, and a frozen grey face that made him look like a corpse due for interment. 'Jean-Pierre Lamiel.' He gestured at his companion, a shorter thickset man with his hair cut en brosse. 'Thomas. Armand Thomas.'

There was no indication of what rank they held, even if they held any rank at all, Or whether they were police or army or secret service, but they immediately called a conference which Pel and Darcy were requested to attend.

'A statement will have to be issued, of course,' Lamiel said at once.

'Why?' Pel asked.

Lamiel gave him a cold look, as if he were something he'd picked up on his shoe. 'Because a statement *must* be made. Barclay's a member of the government.'

'A junior minister.'

'He might have known things.' Lamiel looked sourly at Pel. 'Besides, he spoke out very strongly at that conference on terrorism in Paris.'

'So did a dozen others.'

Lamiel frowned. 'Indeed. But they'll be thinking of reprisals. They always do. And perhaps Barclay was the one most available and most vulnerable. We'll find out. We'll be working together.'

'With whom in charge?' Pel asked.

The Chief held his breath. He had a great regard for Pel but he could never trust him to hold his tongue.

'It's all rather delicate,' Lamiel said. 'This is your area. We're visitors and we try not to put the local forces' backs up. But... '

But, Pel thought, supplying the qualification he knew was on its way, the DST would be running the show and everybody else would be taking orders from them.

It didn't come out quite like that but that was what it meant. 'It's only a question of drawing lines', Lamiel said, 'and, after all, terrorism makes it very clear that sometimes toes have to be trodden on. It's unreasonable, even sheer bad management, to allow the other side to seize the initiative with the sort of international organisation they always have with all its bang-up-to-date devices, while we...'

'How do we know they're terrorists?' Pel asked. 'How do we know they have an organisation behind them with up-to-date devices?'

'The kidnap of a junior minister by terrorists *is* an international incident.'

'If it *is* terrorists,' Pel went on, plugging away at his theme. 'We've no proof yet and the chance of being kidnapped has lately become a daily risk with the rich.'

'I think you'll find that where a member of the government's involved,' Lamiel snapped, 'it'll turn out to be terrorists or activists of some sort. Especially with an election due. What messages have been received?'

'None.'

'None at all? Who's claimed responsibility?'

'Nobody.'

'No demands for a ransom or the release of hostages?'

'No.'

'There must be some.'

The Chief suppressed a smile. Good old Pel, he thought. Trust the little bugger to hold his own. There were times when the Chief found Pel a pain in the backside, especially when he was standing up for his rights or for his beloved Burgundy, but at least he never let anybody ride roughshod over him. He had been watching Pel for years now conducting his vendetta with Brisard, and there were times when he would happily have encased them both in a concrete block and dropped them in one of the lakes in the nearby Jura. But – and it was a big but – if nobody pushed Pel around, sure enough nobody would be pushing the Chief around. All the same, he thought warily, these men from Paris had a lot of power and it would pay to tread cautiously.

'No fingerprints?' Lamiel was asking.

'None. Fingerprints say they were using gloves.'

'Obviously professionals.'

'That's what we decided.'

'And that indicates a well-organised gang. Still, let's not get hysterical.' Pel gave Lamiel a look of sheer disbelief. He was the last person in the world to lose his cool. 'I shall be going back to Paris soon, but I'll be leaving Thomas here to keep an eye on things... '

'Will he want accommodation?' the Chief asked. 'We can provide it.'

'We prefer to find our own.' Lamiel's words were a snub and the Chief recognised them as such and was once more all for letting Pel have his head.

Lamiel placed a card on the table. 'That number will contact me. Or if not me, then Thomas.'

'At once?' Pel asked.

'At once.'

Pel didn't believe him. Nobody was *that* clever, or that available.

'I expect some sort of message will come before long. When it does, we'll be able to analyse the paper, the writing or – if it's a typewriter – the type. We'll be putting on a cinema show for your people. We've got a lot of film of known terrorists and dissidents so we'll let your boys have a look at them.' Lamiel's smile was forced. 'It all adds to the gaiety of nations.'

And, Pel thought, to the gloom of the local cops.

eight

Nosjean had a lot of useful contacts, one of them a man called Jean Aubineau, who was the manager of the insurance company, Assurances Mutuelles, near the Porte Guillaume. They had had a good working arrangement since Nosjean had been instrumental in breaking a big car insurance fraud which had done the city insurance companies out of a great deal of money.

Nosjean was still a little bemused by what had happened with Mijo Lehmann in the hotel at Avignon. It had not been planned – it had just happened – but his life seemed to have changed quite considerably as a result. Suddenly it seemed to have some meaning. Going to Mijo Lehmann's apartment, he had found a meal waiting for him and a bottle of wine on the table.

'We can afford it,' she had said.

'We', he had noticed, as if she expected him to stay there. He shied a little at the thought of it but after spending the night in her bed he was feeling much more relaxed about it. She had assured him she didn't want to tie him down – though he knew she did – and he had started to make plans to move his belongings and give up his own apartment. He knew it was the first step and that things could happen along the way, but Nosjean had suddenly thrown caution to the winds. Why not, he had thought. He was only young once and he felt he could keep it quiet from his sisters.

He was still a little broody when he called in at Aubineau's office. There was a girl in there who looked like Charlotte Rampling he'd been eyeing some time before. He saw now, as she showed him into Aubineau's office, that she was only a pale shadow of Charlotte Rampling and obviously only half as intelligent as Mijo Lehmann. With a sigh, he accepted he was smitten at last.

But Nosjean was a good policeman and didn't allow extraneous things like girls to stand in his way. His eye well on the ball, he put to Aubineau an idea that had occurred to him. Explaining the case he was on, he asked if there had been any cases of insurance paid out for lost paintings.

Aubineau's eyebrows shot up. 'How did you know?'

'I didn't. Are there?'

'Yes. One a couple of months ago. Type called Yvon Macus. He's not with us. He's with Gau Assurances, but of course, we all know what goes on. It was in *Le Bien Public.*'

Sure enough, when Nosjean went round to the newspaper office, there it was in the file, the story of two old masters being lost in a fire that had destroyed a house. There was even a picture of the owner, Yvon Macus, who looked a pretty shifty sort of individual – though that might have been the newspaper photograph, of course. You could never believe what you saw in a newspaper.

'Thank God they were insured,' Yvon Macus was stated to have said.

It might, Nosjean thought, be a good idea to see Yvon Macus. Especially as the Hôtel de Police had been in a constant uproar since the kidnapping of Barclay. With the arrival of the DST men, the Chief and Pel were going about with faces like thunder and everyone else from Darcy down to young Didier Darras was flapping around in a panic. The DST people had stirred up a hornets' nest and Nosjean, thankfully not involved, had no wish to be part of it. An hour or two outside the office, as things got wound up for the day, seemed to be a good idea.

Yvon Macus appeared to be bearing up well. The photograph hadn't lied and he looked as shifty in the flesh as he did on paper.

'They were worth a lot of money,' he said. 'Fortunately I insured them.'

'When?'

'Six months before.'

'Just in time,' Nosjean said. 'You were lucky.'

Macus smiled. 'You're telling me I was.'

'For how much?'

'Half a million, the two.'

'Has the insurance company paid up?'

'Not yet. I'm expecting their cheque any time.'

'They were genuine, of course?'

Macus looked shocked. 'Mother of God, nobody's arguing about that, are they?'

'Didn't the insurance company?'

'Why should they? I had authentications for both of them. They accepted them without question.'

'What were they?'

'There was a Rembrandt – ' another Rembrandt, Nosjean noticed ' – and a Van Gogh.' And, Nosjean thought, Van Gogh, with all that thick paint, wasn't all that difficult for a good painter to copy. Just get the brightest paints you could find, slap them on with a shovel and you've got a Van Gogh. Doubtless there was more to it than that but it was a noticeable fact that there seemed to be more fake Van Goghs about than any others.

'Do you have the authentications here?'

Macus gestured. 'Oh, yes, of course. I photocopied them for the insurance company.'

He took Nosjean into his study and fished in a drawer. Producing a leather document case, he pulled out two papers. One referred to a painting called *Man in Yellow Trousers* by Rembrandt and the other to a Van Gogh called *Cornfield at*

Arles. They both said much the same thing, that the painting
in question accorded with all the known grandeur and style of Rembrandt – or Van Gogh – then there was a fulsome sentence or two about the artist's skill and a suggestion that they had been painted during the artist's great period. They were roughly the same, the words differing only slightly and they had a familiar ring to them. Nosjean wasn't surprised to see they were signed by his old friend, Professor Solecin, of the Musée Fervier in Lyons. It seemed to be time to see Professor Solecin.

First, though, it seemed a good idea to contact Gau Assurances. Sure enough, they told him on the telephone, they were preparing to cough up. They had no reason to doubt the authentication.

'I think they do it on a computer,' Nosjean observed to Sergeant De Troquereau as he sat in the sergeants' room, also keeping quietly out of the way of the panic created by Lamiel.

De Troq', who as well as being a cop was also a baron, even if a poverty-stricken baron, was reading the documents of the Arri case which Darcy had turned over to him. Being a baron, he knew a bit about art – until his family had gone bust, there had been quite a lot of it around the family home – and he listened with interest.

'If the computer says it's right', De Troq' agreed, 'they drop to their knees, touch their forehead on the ground and pay up. I once wrote an article on the de Troquereaus for a magazine and they paid twice. When I wrote and told them, they told me not to worry, it was too difficult to sort it out when the computer got the name wrong – or the operator programmed it wrongly or something – and it was easier to pay a second time. In the end I kept both sums.'

Nosjean grinned. 'Think our own computer might show if our friend, Yvon Macus, has a record?'

'Perhaps you ought to give it a go.'

Nosjean did and to his delight he found that Macus did have a record. He was shown to have been involved in a blaze at Riom in the Auvergne where he had opened a gift shop which had caught fire. He had claimed a figure of 50,000 francs for his stock but the insurance company hadn't paid up. Apparently he hadn't argued.

Wondering why, Nosjean telephoned Clermont Ferrand where the police knew all about Macus. It seemed he had had other little fires here and there before and the insurance company in Clermont Ferrand which had dealt with this one clearly had a computer which worked.

Nosjean decided he had stumbled on something important.

'This is big,' he told De Troq'.

'Crime often is,' De Troq' agreed.

'Unfortunately, you can't tell the goodies from the baddies. Some are cheating, some just want a picture because they like pictures, and some, if they're important like Vacchi or Barclay, refuse to press charges because, if they do, they might be shown to have behaved stupidly, which is bad for their image. The rest are all small time dealers and gallery owners who specialise in junk.' He paused. 'As well as a copyist somewhere who makes the pictures and some old boy who knows a bit about it to write authentications which sound good but are really valueless.'

De Troq' smiled. 'I reckon', he said, 'that you've been playing at it up to now. You've brushed the fringe of it but not gone deeply into any of the cases we've come up with. So why not pick on one and chase it right back. See if any of the names you've bumped into pop up more than once. If they do, offer it to the courts. It ought to be enough to frighten the rest off.'

'For a bit anyway.'

'For a bit,' De Troq' agreed. 'But long enough for the police to turn their attention to other less important things like rape, arson, murder, terrorism and kidnapping.'

When Lamiel had disappeared about his business and the Chief was seeing him off the premises with a brandy, Pel waited in his office, knowing Darcy would be along eventually.

He wasn't sure what to make of Lamiel. Terrorism could be seen differently by different people. When Europe had been occupied by the Nazis, the use of terrorism against them had been applauded, and even De Gaulle – admittedly safe in England – had accepted Churchill's dictum that Europe should be 'set ablaze'. But anti-terrorism was a difficult job because the man who was a terrorist in one country was a freedom fighter in another, and those whom the French considered important were doubtless well down the list in other countries. It was a pity they couldn't all get together and do with them what countries had done with pirates in the eighteenth century and condemn the lot – not only the terrorists, but those who hid them, lent them money and succoured them when they were hurt.

Unfortunately, there was a lot of talk these days about human rights and the efforts to silence the freedom-loving people of the world. Pel was inclined to think that fire should be fought with fire because a man dead in the street was still dead, no matter who had killed him or for whatever reason, but these days force begat force, violence begat violence, destruction begat destruction, and even the anti-terrorist business seemed to have got a little out of control in recent years with the anti-squads sometimes as dangerous as the terrorists themselves. Enormous sums of money were being spent on things that seemed well able to feed and sustain themselves, and without doubt people were occasionally taken for a ride by ambitious politicians, civil servants, soldiers and policemen making good jobs for themselves out of the misery.

Opening the day's newspapers to see what the press had on the case, he saw the appropriate items had been ringed in coloured pencil by Didier. It was something started by Cadet Martin, who had behaved as if he were the editor of *Le Monde,* and it had been inherited by the new incumbent.

France Soir was now suggesting Barclay had been involved in behind-the-scenes work and was trying to make out he was the *éminence grise* behind the President. *France Dimanche* had gone overboard even more completely and was suggesting he hadn't been kidnapped at all but had quietly disappeared on government business of a secret nature. They quoted Antoine de Saint-Exupéry and the Englishman, Lawrence of Arabia, both of whom, they suggested, had not died but had vanished quietly to carry on underground activities abroad. *Le Bien Public,* being local, country and conservative, simply reported the facts.

Lamiel returned late in the afternoon and immediately called a conference. While he had been away, his deputy, Thomas, had seized a group of offices for their special use and had installed their own clerks, typewriters, telex machines and telephones, some of them with direct lines to Paris. It had meant several of the inhabitants of the Hôtel de Police having to move out, and the grumbles could be heard almost to the Palais des Ducs.

Lamiel looked tired. There had been a bomb incident in Paris where the front window of the Air France office had been blown in, and several passers-by cut by flying glass. Lamiel's presence had been needed and, though he didn't like him, Pel had to feel a certain amount of sympathy for him.

Lamiel opened the conference by saying he had been meeting with his superiors and other important personages in Paris. He made it sound as if he'd had a heart-to-heart with the President, and had them sitting in rows in the lecture room listening to him like a lot of schoolboys.

'With the election due,' he pointed out, 'any hint of scandal would be seized on by one side or the other, so we must walk warily, giving no one the opportunity to accuse us of bias.'

Or, Pel thought cynically, Lamiel would be replaced by someone more favourable – either to a returned government or to the opposition when they got in. Politicians had long memories and were a spiteful lot on the whole.

'It's obvious', Lamiel was saying now, 'that this is a case that's going to take some breaking. For some reason best known to themselves, the kidnappers aren't yet ready to claim responsibility.' He gestured. 'We've therefore produced photographs of known dissidents and had them printed in large numbers. We'd like your people to show them around. If anybody thinks he knows any of them, we'll find them. They must be here somewhere. They wouldn't pull off a job like this from a base in Paris. It's too far away.'

'Two hours in a fast car down the motorway,' Pel observed.

Lamiel ignored the comment. 'Terrorists', he went on, 'operate in small groups. I suspect they've snatched Barclay either for what he knows or because they think the government will pay to have him back. However, he's also a businessman, so they could have snatched him for another reason. So, when we do hear from them, I don't expect their demands to be moderate. It'll be money, an exchange of hostages, or something like that. After all, two hundred representatives of more than twenty revolutionary organisations were present at a recent planning conference in Tripoli. Mustafa Murad, believed to be behind the Rome and Vienna airport bombings, was there. As was George Habash, of the Popular Front for the Liberation of Palestine, responsible for the hi-jackings of the Seventies, and Ahmed Jibril, of the PFLP General Command, who heads the anti-Arafat Palestinian rebels. Principal targets for the new campaign –' Lamiel paused dramatically '– Israel and America, but

European countries, chiefly France and Britain, were also discussed. Is Barclay a Jew, by the way?'

Lamiel spoke harshly as if he didn't have much time for Jews, and the Chief responded sharply. 'No,' he snapped. 'He isn't a Jew.'

Lamiel nodded. 'Then perhaps it isn't the Jew-Arab thing,' he said. 'Perhaps it's Italian. The Red Brigade. Or German. The remains of the Baader-Meinhof lot. It might even be for money because they have to fund their operations somehow. We even have a list of a few of our own people we might safely look at. Joseph Furet, for example, leader of the Groupe Revanche Française. It has a lot of support from Right Wing deputies, and we've discovered that Barclay once accused them of resembling Nazis and Furet threatened to remove him from the political scene. We shall have to look into him.'

He paused and gestured with a sheet of paper. 'There's also a group here round a man called Kiczmyrczik, a Pole, who I understand arrived in France forty years ago. His hatred then was for Russia. Nowadays it's for anything and everything.'

'He's harmless,' Darcy said. 'He was investigated in 1982. There was nothing on him.'

Lamiel seemed to resent the interruption. 'He has friends who visit him, I'm told.'

'Jan Michelowski,' Darcy said. 'Stanislaus Wyspianski. Both Poles. And a man called Nadasy-Crasco, a Czech. They're all geriatrics. They talk a lot but that's all.'

'I'll decide that,' Lamiel snapped.

He turned to the blackboard. 'Finally,' he said, 'there are various freedom movements, and people like that don't hesitate to use terrorism and kidnapping as weapons. After all, what is terrorism but a way of drawing attention to their cause? Their whole aim is to show that the State can't protect its citizens. After all, if it can't protect its known figureheads, it obviously can't protect the rank and file.'

A screen was wheeled in and the lights dimmed. Immediately photographs began to flash on the screen, faces in crowds, faces in groups, faces alone; Arab faces, German, French, Irish and Italian faces. Names were rapped out like gunshots.

'Those which have been circled are the people we're interested in,' Lamiel pointed out harshly. 'Anybody recognise any of them?'

Nobody did.

'We'll have them passed out to your boys, of course,' Lamiel went on. 'We need a face. One would do, because we know who're connected and one face would lead us to others. These people are all in the terrorist thing up to their necks.'

'Suppose,' the Chief said, 'this is nothing like that?'

Lamiel turned and smiled. 'It must be,' he said. 'What else could it be?' He gestured at the screen. 'Just one thing. If your men spot any of these characters, they must make no move. They're to report to us. We don't want them alerting, or they might kill in a panic. Remember what happened to Aldo Moro. On the other hand, we don't want comments made in the House of Assembly about us treating these people gently.'

Lamiel was lecturing them as if he, not the Chief, ran the area. Pel listened silently as the harsh voice continued. It sounded like a football commentator's voice on television – excited, working up a tension to thrill the viewers – or that of one of the TV pundits, the great men who persuaded people to appear on their chat shows and then proceeded to insult them with all sorts of unbelievable suggestions.

'Have we checked for letter bombs?' Lamiel asked. 'There may be some. Poisoned sweets? We know of a group involved in the indoctrination of students, so we must check at the university.'

He speculated, theorised, offered opinions, showed outrage, asked for calmness, and produced veiled hints of worse to come.

Pel interrupted. 'I've been making a few enquiries... '

'Then – ' Lamiel swung round and stared at him ' – I'd prefer that you stopped.'

It was entirely unexpected and came abruptly enough to be insulting. Lamiel made no attempt to soften the decision and Pel sat up, red-faced. 'Why?' he demanded.

'We've been to Barclay's home. We've questioned the manservant.'

'So have I.'

'So we discovered.' Lamiel gave Pel a sour look. 'It would probably help if we didn't duplicate.'

Pel's face grew angry. Holy Mother of God, he was thinking, he had done all the obvious things, yet this gadget from Paris was accusing him of duplicating the things he had done long after Pel had finished with them! Afterwards, he decided, he'd have a few words to say.

He didn't get the chance. Lamiel finished what he had to offer, nodded at Thomas, his deputy, and swept from the room. As Pel rose, the Chief touched him on the arm and jerked his head. In his office he offered him brandy. Pel stared at it warily. Brandy in the Chief's office usually meant bad news. It was worse than he'd expected.

'You're off the case,' the Chief said.

Pel glared, angry enough to bite the heads off nails. 'I've already been making enquiries,' he said.

'Then you'd better stop. Lamiel doesn't want you.'

'Why not?'

The Chief sighed. He knew it was going to be difficult. It always was with Pel. He had a measure of sympathy for him but, after all, he felt, he'd asked for it in a way.

'That business of you being at Barclay's house,' he said. 'They think it looks bad.'

'But I'd never met the damned man before that night!'

'They won't take anybody's word on that. Neither will the media. So be careful what you say to the press. Remember they can do whatever they want with whatever you say and, what's more, even if you reply, they always have the last word, because they're the ones who control the last word.'

Pel was silent for a long time, his mind working briskly. 'I'll turn over the file at once,' he said.

'I knew you would,' the Chief pointed out. 'But Lamiel said they wouldn't be needing it.'

Pel's eyebrows shot up. 'They're that clever?'

'They've got all the details.'

'There are a few more I've found.'

The Chief gestured. 'Then, for God's sake, keep them to yourself.'

'Do I keep you informed?'

The Chief shied away like a startled foal. 'I don't want to know,' he said. 'If anybody asks me what's going on, I want to be able to say I haven't the foggiest. These boys are powerful and they keep their own counsel about what they're up to. I'm not an ambitious man, probably not even a clever one. But I've kept my nose clean up to now and that's how I want it until I retire. Let them work on their own if they want to. Give them the file up to today and put in a letter offering further help if they wish it. They won't, of course, but it'll cover you.'

'What about Darcy?'

'Darcy's working with them, in charge of our own people.'

Pel shrugged. He knew where Darcy's loyalties would lie.

'Stick to the Arri case,' the Chief advised. 'That's safe.'

'Who do I have?'

'Who do you want?'

'Darcy's not available. Nosjean's already fully occupied. Who else are they taking?'

The Chief sighed. 'Officially, everybody. But we can keep one or two back for you.'

'Right. If I need him, I'll use Aimedieu. Otherwise, I'll have Lagé and perhaps Claudie Darel. She's bright. If necessary I can add young Didier Darras. He's no fool.'

'Will that be enough?' the Chief asked.

Pel's face was expressionless. 'It'll have to be, won't it?' he said.

nine

Lamiel might have been slow to let people know what he was doing, but clearly he – or someone – wasn't so slow about letting them know what Pel was not doing.

The press had the story the following day. It had even pushed the government's fears for its majority off the front page.

Madame had brought home a copy of La *Torche* for Pel to see. It was one of the so-called crusading rags, loud-mouthed and large-headlined, enjoying what it called 'hitting hard' at wrong-doers. Many of their wrongdoers turned out to be not half so wrong as they made out and they were involved in a dozen libel actions a year. But headlines were headlines and people who read their accusations didn't always manage to read the apologies they were forced to print.

It carried banner headlines. 'Head Cop Taken off Kidnap Case.' 'Night-time Party With Missing Man.'

Pel flung it across the kitchen. Madame Routy picked it up and even had the grace, which surprised Pel, to look upset and say she was sorry.

'Name of God,' Pel snorted. 'They make it sound like an orgy!'

'It was my fault,' his wife said unhappily. 'I persuaded you to go. I know you didn't want to.'

Pel patted her hand. 'It's nothing,' he said. He reached for the magazine again. 'Let's have another look at it.'

It looked no better at second glance. 'Chief Inspector Evariste Clovis Désiré Pel', it said – they'd even got his names – 'until yesterday investigating the disappearance of the Deputy for Yorinne, has been removed from the case. He was recently a guest at the missing man's home. There were numerous guests, some of them women, at a party which went on to almost midnight.'

'Dancing about in our birthday suits, I suppose,' Pel growled.

'I'll not have that magazine in the house again,' Madame said.

'It's a good idea not to have *any* magazine in the house,' Pel agreed. 'Cancel the lot and buy an extra bottle of brandy with the money.'

Madame Routy was waiting at the front door as usual with Pel's briefcase. For once she handled it gently instead of slamming it into his arms, and he realised with amazement that she thought more of him than he'd realised. Perhaps she always had, and just enjoyed a good fight. He promised himself he'd try not to be rude to her in future. He knew he'd never manage it – come to that, neither would she! – but it was nice to think about it.

Claudie Darel gave him what he took to be a sympathetic look as he entered his office. So did Didier Darras as he put the papers on the table in front of him.

'There are a lot of stories about you, sir,' he said. 'But I didn't mark them.'

'Why not?'

'I thought this time you might not want to see them.'

Pel managed a twisted smile. 'To be a cop, mon brave,' he said, 'you've got to be tougher than that. You have to learn to take everything those idiots say about you without complaining.'

Somebody had obviously contacted the Chief to let him know Pel had arrived because almost immediately he slammed the door back as if trying to tear the wall down.

'It's what I expected,' he said. 'It's a case of not being able to touch pitch without being defiled.'

Pel looked up. 'Somebody been touching pitch?' he asked mildly.

The Chief was disconcerted. 'You know what I mean,' he said. 'You must have seen the story in *La Torche.*'

'Quite a few people have hurried to bring it to my attention. However, I'm pleased to say an equal number have tried to hide it from me. It shows hope. Perhaps I'll sue *La Torche.*'

'You'd never win.'

'No,' Pel agreed. 'But it'd be nice to tell them what I think of them. I think I'll take the day off and go and see the editor. I'll take my gun with me.'

'For God's sake… ' the Chief said, alarmed.

'I don't mean it,' Pel pointed out. 'But it would be nice, wouldn't it, to see him dive for safety under his desk. They're very good at dishing this stuff out, but they're not so good at taking it. You know the saying: "Secure from warfare, they're passionate for war." And I know that one about if you eat with the Devil you should use a long spoon.'

'I'm right behind you, Pel.'

Pel looked at the Chief, wondering if he was. Like everyone else, the Chief had to look after his own job and if it came to the crunch, also like everyone else, he'd probably back off. Pel wasn't being disloyal, and he didn't think the Chief was being disloyal. He was being realistic and he knew that was how the Chief would have to treat it, too.

'What's my position then?' he asked.

'No different. You haven't been suspended. You're just not handling the Barclay kidnapping, that's all. Everything else stays as it was.'

'Suppose I come up with something?' Pel asked. 'Because after this lot, Lamiel will get nothing from me.'

The Chief swallowed. Despite his shows of temper, he was a peace-loving man and he didn't like vendettas. 'Let me know,' he said. 'I'll handle it.'

As the Chief left, the telephone went. To Pel's surprise it was Sarrazin. He was just about to slam the instrument down again in disgust when Sarrazin, almost as if he guessed what he was about to do, shouted.

'Chief!' he said. 'Hang on! It wasn't any of us!'

Pel calmed. 'Who was it?'

'Type called Félix Ailon. Paris man.'

'Where did he get the story?'

'God knows, Patron. None of us have got it. I saw Henriot and Fiabon and Ducrot, of *Paris Soir,* and we're all in trouble because we *haven't* got it. Even if we *had* got it, we wouldn't have written it like that.'

'It's nice to know. Where did Ailon get it?'

'Some type from Paris. Know who it is?'

Pel knew what Sarrazin, despite the genuineness of the call, was doing now. He was trying to find out who the spokesman was so he could make contact himself.

'No idea,' he said.

'Chief – ' Sarrazin's voice became wheedling ' – I suppose you couldn't give us some *real* gen on what happened, could you?'

Pel studied the telephone for a moment, then quietly placed it in its cradle.

When he looked up, Judge Brisard was just closing the door behind him.

'Come in,' he snapped.

Brisard had a smug look of triumph on his face and Pel guessed he'd seen the story in La *Torche* and had come to the conclusion that what he'd been praying for, for years, had come to pass: Pel had got himself into trouble and was due to be kicked off the force. Pel could hardly blame him. He had been hoping for years that Brisard would be kicked off the Magistrature Debout, that part of the judicial system which supplied juges d'instruction.

'You still on the Arri case?' Brisard said.

'I am.'

'Have you found anyone yet who could be charged?'

'We've only just identified the body. We're trying to discover how he got to where he was found. You're a little late in the field.'

'Of course I am.' Brisard's eyes glowed with triumph. 'Because when I arrived at Suchey the body had been removed. I didn't see it.'

'You've still plenty of time. He's in the mortuary. He's not going anywhere.'

'I should have seen the body in situ.'

'Then', Pel snapped, 'you should have taken notice of the message passed to your department by Inspector Darcy.' He was in no mood to bandy words with an old enemy. At that moment, he was ready to do battle with anybody – the President of France, if necessary.

Brisard's eyes gleamed. 'I hear you've been taken off the Barclay kidnapping.'

'You've heard correctly.'

'I'm going to insist that you're taken off this case, too. There have been too many occasions in the past when my department's been ignored, too many times when things have happened and I've not been informed, too many witnesses questioned without me being present.'

'You don't *have* to be present. And if we had to wait for your department, we'd never make an arrest.'

'I insist that… '

Pel rose to his full height. It wasn't much and, with his balding dome and the spectacles on his forehead, he wasn't a lot to look at. But in his anger he was something to beware of. And he detested Brisard – quite unashamedly, feeling that a good hearty detestation kept the adrenalin flowing. 'You do not insist on *anything* in this office,' he said.

Brisard was a little taken aback. Arguing with Pel in this mood was like questioning with Moses as he came down from the mountain. Nevertheless, he didn't give up without a struggle.

'I've had too much of your waiving the rules.' he said. 'I'm going now to the Procureur. I've also talked to Lamiel, the man from Paris. I gather he's also not satisfied with the way you behave.'

Darcy was next to appear. He looked upset, which was unusual because Darcy normally was never upset.

'Patron,' he said. 'I'm damned sorry. I'd like to set fire to the whole of the bloody press for this. What's more, I wouldn't mind setting fire to Lamiel or Thomas. It was one of those two bastards who put that story out. The Chief didn't tell the press, I know. Nobody in our department did either.'

'Could it have been Misset?' Pel asked. Misset had been suspected for a long time of passing information to the press.

'It wasn't Misset, Patron,' Darcy said. 'I'd swear to it. He was the first to come into my mind, of course, and I had him in my office and put him through the hoop good and proper. I think I frightened him to death. Enough, in fact, if he *has* been leaking stuff to Sarrazin, to stop him dead. But it wasn't Misset. It could only have been Lamiel or Thomas, or whoever looks after their press statements.' He paused, still indignant. 'What's happening to you, Patron? They say you're off the case.'

'Yes.' Pel lit a cigarette. 'I'm still to continue with Arri. You're to co-operate to the best of your ability with Lamiel.'

'I'm damned if I will!'

'I think you'd better, Daniel. I don't think this will destroy my career. It's no more than a hiccup. But if you refuse to co-operate it could destroy *your* career. Do what they ask –

all they ask. You've got everybody but Claudie, Lagé and young Didier.'

Darcy drew a deep breath. 'Merde alors,' he said bitterly. 'All right, Patron. I'll do as you say. But I'll keep in touch.'

'I'm still interested in Barclay.'

'Why, Patron? Think there's more to it than we realise?'

Pel shrugged. 'Not really,' he said. 'I'd just like to know what made him tick. The all-gold hero. The man who got a decoration at Dien Bien Phu. The man who saved the life of Sergeant Jules Arri. The junior minister at the Department of Health. The do-gooder. The art collector. The man who works so hard for charity. The popular, handsome, silver-tongued Member for Yorinne.'

'He's all of that, Patron.'

Pel frowned. 'So why was he kidnapped?' he asked.

Pel was still brooding on his demotion when he received a request to call on Leguyader at the Lab. For a while he was tempted not to bother because Leguyader was the last person he wished to see just then. Nobody would enjoy gloating over Pel's downfall more than Leguyader. Then he decided that perhaps Leguyader who, after all, it had to be admitted, was good at his job, had discovered something important.

Leguyader was busy at his bench as he arrived and as he looked round Pel went into the attack at once.

'Well?' he snapped. 'What do you want?'

Leguyader feigned surprise. 'What do you imagine?' he said. 'Have no fear. I haven't asked you here to sneer at the fact that you've been removed from the Barclay case – though I must say, it's the sort of thing I've been half-expecting for years… '

'What do you want?' Pel snarled.

Leguyader looked smug. 'I've found something you might be interested in,' he said. He placed a plastic sack on the bench and gestured at it. 'Take a look at that,' he suggested.

'What is it?'

'Clothes. Belonging to one Jules Arri.'

For a moment, Pel forgot his dislike of Leguyader in his curiosity. 'You've found something on them?'

'Yes.'

'How? Under the microscope?'

'Not really. There's nothing to see.'

Pel glared. 'Are you having me on?'

'No.' Leguyader opened the mouth of the sack. 'Just stick your nose in there and sniff.'

Pel stared at him suspiciously. The only thing he expected to smell was the odour of decomposition, decay, damp soil and leaves.

'Got it?' Leguyader asked.

At first Pel missed it, then he sniffed again and it came, faint but quite distinct.

'Perfume,' he said.

'Perfume,' Leguyader agreed. 'Exactly. And by the smell of it, fairly expensive perfume. I've tried to establish what it is. Probably Yves Saint Laurent, L'Air du Temps or Chanel. We have samples of them all here. I can't be sure, of course, because there are too many other smells in there besides, not all of them pleasant.' He looked at Pel triumphantly. 'What was Jules Arri who, from what I can learn, was an old soldier, doing with perfume on him? Was he a poof or something?'

Pel frowned, his interest caught. 'That's something I doubt very much. How come this perfume appears now? It wasn't there before.'

Leguyader shrugged. 'Before, the clothes had just come from the earth and from a decomposing body. When they first appeared they were cold and damp and there was no trace of perfume. But, since then, they've been here in the laboratory, which is warm. They should have been put in the cold room but one of the idiots I'm supposed to work with forgot.'

Pel was frowning. 'Perfume?' he said again.

'Indicate something to you?'

'What does it indicate to *you*?'

'That the man might, as I say, be a poof. A pervert. A homo. A fag. A pederast. He was a soldier and had served in the Far East and there's been more than one man disgraced for the tastes he picked up there – in the days, that is, before we started believing it was nothing but another social bad habit like smoking or bad breath. Statistics show that pederasty's always been common in the Middle East and more than common in places like Indo-China where the men are small and delicately-boned. I was there for a time and you could find them at it behind every bush if you looked hard enough. The ancient Greeks accepted homosexuality.'

'So do we – now.'

'Indeed. A report in the USA in 1948 found that thirty per cent of adult US males had engaged in some homosexual activity and ten per cent were committed to primarily homosexual behaviour patterns. About half as many women were predominantly homosexual.' Leguyader looked smug, as if the fact that *he* wasn't was a triumph of skill and judgement. 'Kinsey doesn't identify people as exclusively homosexual or heterosexual,' he went on. 'He observed a whole spectrum of sexual activity of which exclusive orientations of either type make up the extremes.'

He had obviously been at *Larousse* again. Because of his enjoyment in airing his knowledge on every subject under the sun, it was said in the Hôtel de Police that his favourite off-duty reading matter was the encyclopaedia and that the subjects he read up in the evenings were always worked into the conversation next day so he could trot out as knowledge the facts he'd learned overnight.

All the same, it was an idea. *Had* Arri been a homosexual? Had there been a lovers' quarrel? As Leguyader said, it had happened before.

Leguyader hadn't finished. 'Homosexual activity increases, of course, in environments where there are no heterosexual outlets for sexual desires.'

'Such, for instance,' Pel said, 'as in an army posting to a foreign country where they're cut off from female company.'

Sitting at the end of the dining table, Professor Grandjean looked a little like an elderly stork.

'I was suspicious from the start,' he was saying. 'I'd never heard of a *Landscape with Houses* by Vlaminck. It hasn't appeared in any of the catalogues, though that's not important because there's never a complete record of any painter's output. After all, before they start making money, they exchange paintings with friends or sell them to buy food, so we lose track of them. But this one is different.'

Nosjean glanced across the table at the Professor's niece, Mijo Lehmann. They had been invited to lunch because the Professor was bursting to tell someone what he'd discovered. Mijo Lehmann was occupied in conversation with the Professor's wife so that the Professor could concentrate on Nosjean, but she couldn't help sneaking glances at Nosjean from time to time, all pink and proud and possessive. She had waited a long time and with incredible patience and not a little heart-ache for him to throw off all the other Charlotte Ramplings.

'The Collège Privé de l'Est gave me permission to examine the painting,' the Professor was saying.

'Didn't they mind?' Nosjean asked.

'Not at all. They were so confident I would be proved wrong. But I'm not. I've examined the painting carefully now. And I'm certain it's a copy. Most oils have a degree of spontaneity where some mistake has been painted over or the artist has changed his mind. You never find it in a forgery, though, because the forger copies with great care. Corrections indicate authenticity.' The professor gestured. 'The brushwork's like Vlaminck's brush-work, of course, but it isn't Vlaminck's.'

'What if provenance is produced, or a letter from an original owner or a gallery operator of the period?'

Grandjean was unmoved. 'You could always check the handwriting. Even handwriting can be faked.'

Nosjean frowned as an idea occurred to him. 'Can you buy a painting, have it copied, sell the original in, say, Japan or the States – especially if it's unlikely to go to a public gallery – and then sell the copy in France?'

'Without the slightest doubt.'

'But it would be necessary, of course, to have the provenance or such a letter as I suggest?'

'Absolutely.'

Nosjean frowned. 'Have you told the college what you think?'

'Not yet.'

'Then, sir, if you don't mind, I'd rather you didn't. Not just yet.'

'They'll want to know.'

'Play them along for a few days.' Nosjean needed a little time and it seemed to require a visit to Professor Solecin.

Professor Solecin lived in a small house on the outskirts of Lyons. It was shabby-looking and, Nosjean noticed, there was no sign of a car's wheels in the muddy drive, while the garage seemed to be full of junk. The professor seemed to have hit hard times.

The door was opened by a small bent old man with a club foot, a parchment-like face and grey lips. Faded wet eyes stared at Nosjean.

'Have you come about the gas?' he asked.

'No, I haven't.' Nosjean presented his identity card. 'I'd like to talk to you.'

He thought he saw a flicker of alarm cross the old man's face but he backed away and Nosjean pushed into the house. It smelled of mustiness and stale food and the rooms were shabby and littered with rubbish, with unwashed plates containing the remains of meals on chairs and tables and window ledges.

Nosjean didn't waste time, and started off by asking the old man's profession.

'I'm a writer.'

'What have you written.'

'Books.'

'What on?'

'Anything you want. All non-fiction. I get an idea, read it up at the library and write a book. About Marconi. The discovery of electricity. Napoleon's campaigns. The French railway system. Anything.'

'Make much at it?'

'Not much. They're not very good books really.'

'Ever written about art?'

'Oh, yes. Lots about art. That's easy. There are a lot of books written about paintings so it's easy to look up. I always make sure first that there's plenty of material before I suggest the idea to a publisher.'

'Know anything about art?'

'If I read it up first.'

'Ever owned a painting?'

'Never had enough money.'

'But you once ran the Musée Fervier?'

Solecin's eyes flickered. 'Yes,' he agreed. 'I did.'

'I can't find anything about it in any of the directories.'

'Ah – ' the old man's eyes gleamed ' – no! It no longer exists.'

'Did it ever?'

'Oh, most certainly.'

'Where exactly?'

The old man hesitated. 'Well,' he blurted out, 'it didn't exactly exist. Not as a museum. It was an art gallery.'

'What size?'

'It had a few pictures.'

'A few?'

'Yes, a few.'

'When was this?'

'It would be around the end of the war.'

'How old are you?'

'Eighty-nine.'

'Well, the end of the war's a long time ago. Do you have much to do with art these days?'

'Not a great deal.'

'Have you had for a long time?'

'Not for a long time. I'm getting old.'

'Have you always worked with paintings?'

The old man hesitated. 'Well, not always,' he admitted.

'You've done other work?'

'I told you. I'm a writer. I started as a newspaperman.' The old man seemed to consider he was now so old it no longer mattered what he'd done and seemed unconcerned with the fact that he might be accused of misrepresentation.

'*Are* you a professor of Fine Art?'

'Well, no. Not exactly. But I studied. In Lyons. Before I became a newspaperman. From the age of sixteen.'

'Until when?'

'Well – eighteen. Actually, that stuff on the letterheads is a mistake. My brother – he's dead now – had those things printed. Years ago. You can't get paper like that these days. And he was a bit over-enthusiastic. I didn't like it but when I found it brought work I decided to leave it.'

Nosjean produced the authentications of Chevrier's painting. 'This one values it at 200,000 francs. This one three months later at 750,000 francs. Cubescu didn't think it was worth that much. Nor did Chevrier when he bought it. There's a lot of difference. Why did it go up more than twice in three months?'

The old man seemed quite untroubled. 'Second thoughts,' he said. 'I changed my mind.'

Nosjean produced the written provenance. 'You wrote this?'

'Yes. I got it from an art book.'

'It states the work has also been verified by Jerôme Sède, of Metz. Is he a friend of yours?'

'I've never heard of him.'

'He's supposed to be a professor of Fine Art, too.'

'I don't think he is.'

'Does he know anything about art?'

'I shouldn't think so. My brother found him. He was also a reporter. On a Marseilles paper. He wasn't very good. I was told to put that bit about him in.'

'Who by?'

'A type called Riault. He said it would add weight.'

'Where did you examine this painting of Chevrier's?'

'At the home of a painter. His name's Ugo Luca. He lives at Fougerolles. I did several.'

'Have you done this sort of thing before?'

'Oh, yes. Several times.'

'Who got you into this? Who first introduced you to people like Luca?'

'This type called Riault.'

'And you verified the painting as original?'

'Yes.'

Nosjean studied the old man out of the corner of his eyes. 'Pay well?' he asked.

'Not really.'

'How much?'

'Two hundred francs.'

'Not a lot for expertise of this nature.'

Solecin shrugged. 'I'm an old man now. I can't expect as much as I used to.'

For lack of other news and because people were already bored with the election, the newspapers were still going to town over Barclay and their pages were plastered with instances of his good deeds, his wisdom, his charitable pursuits. Perhaps, Pel thought cynically, their sycophancy was due to a hope that he would buy them up out of gratitude when he turned up again. Newspapers were having a rough time these days and it was well known that Barclay had a great deal more money than he needed.

He still felt vaguely like an outcast. Nobody in the Hôtel de Police was saying much. With their jobs to consider, he could not, he realised, expect open support there but he had rather hoped his relations might have rallied round. His wife was firmly behind him, of course, as – to his surprise – was Madame Routy and Yves Pasquier through the hole in the hedge. But he had hoped that his sister in Chatillon might have written to say 'Take heart, we're on your side,' or that Madame's relations might have telephoned to indicate their faith in him. There was, however, only a deafening silence.

That lunchtime, gloomy with a feeling of martyrdom, Pel met Darcy in the Bar du Palais des Ducs. It had once been the Bar Transvaal but there was so much ill-feeling these days about South Africa and apartheid that the proprietor had changed the name to that of the venerable pile that stood opposite across the circular parking lot. It didn't make much difference. Everybody still called it the Bar Transvaal.

Pel and Darcy had not arranged the meeting. It had been carefully fixed up for them by Claudie Darel, so that they could honestly say, hand on heart, if Lamiel accused them of anything, that they weren't acting in collusion. They hadn't said a word to each other about meeting – the fact that Claudie had was different and, having met quite by chance, old colleagues for years, surely they could exchange the time of day with each other.

His mouth full of bread and ham, Darcy informed Pel of the progress they were making with the kidnapping.

'There's been no ransom demand', he went on, 'and nobody's claiming to have done it. Lamiel's boys are going through every group of dissidents and terrorists they can think of and thinking up reasons why not.' He gestured with the remains of his sandwich. 'They're running round, in fact, like a lot of cockerels with their heads chopped off.'

A telephone exchange had been set up in the basement of the Hôtel de Police expressly to deal with the kidnapping, and extra men had been drafted in to take calls from the drunks, practical jokers and mentally sick who usually tried to climb on the bandwagon, and it was now fully manned. A demand for information had been put into the papers and flashed on to TV screens, requesting help from anyone who had seen anything suspicious, and there were already plenty of people willing to help. Unfortunately, there were also plenty of nuts, and those who were foolish enough to give their addresses had had them marked down and would in due course, if their information were flippant, be arrested for wasting police time.

'Do they still think it's a political kidnap?' Pel asked.

'Yes.' Darcy shrugged. 'But no photograph's arrived, Patron. And these days there's a pattern to these things and kidnappers usually send a photograph of their victim holding up a copy of *Le Monde* or *Figaro,* with the date prominently displayed, to prove they've got him and he's still alive. But there's been nothing. Just the usual lunatics who claim they know where he is. There's always someone willing to join in the fun. Self-importance. Twisted mind. What have you. But we can't pass them by.'

'Have you told Lamiel?'

'I can't pin him down long enough. He's flying about like a misdirected rocket.'

'Have they found out who it was who knew Ennaert's car would be in the garage?'

'I've got Brochard on that. It could be any of a dozen people round there. I also checked Barclay's office but nobody could think *why* he should be kidnapped. I reckon his secretary's half in love with him. She produced his papers and later the keys to his safe. It contained bearer bonds which could be exchanged anywhere for cash and 500,000 francs in notes.'

'That's a lot of money. Have you informed Lamiel?'

'I've made out a report. So far I haven't heard anything.'

'Did he usually keep that sort of sum in his safe?'

'His secretary thought not, but she couldn't be certain. She'd opened it from time to time but had normally only seen plans and documents. Never large sums of money. She had no idea why there was so much and could only assume it was for some project he had in mind.' Darcy finished his sandwich and licked his fingers. 'How about the Arri business?'

Pel shrugged and explained what Leguyader had found. 'He suggested Arri might be one of those.'

'I bet he wasn't.'

'So do I. I telephoned your friend, the historian of the 179th Regiment, and he also refused to believe it. He admitted that it did happen from time to time with people who'd served in the East, but not with Arri.'

'Perhaps he'd just come from seeing a poule, Patron. Some woman he knew. You say Leguyader claimed it was an expensive perfume?'

'That's what he says.'

'I have to admit the bastard's usually right.' Darcy took a final swig of beer. 'Well, in that case it suggests a woman rather than another man. Men go in for perfume these days, of course, but they're not the same perfumes as women use.'

'You know, of course?'

Darcy grinned. 'But of course. Women's perfumes are more subtle. Men's are like men – lacking in finesse. Arri either had an expensive girl friend or he'd visited an expensive whorehouse.'

'So how did he afford that on an army pension?'

'Moonlighting, Patron? He was doing a job somewhere at night. He was getting money from somewhere to add to his pension. How else would he afford to put away all that champagne and pay for all those bottles of expensive wine we found empty at his house? If you ask me, our friend Arri was a bit of a dark horse. Think he was pimping? Think he had a stable of whores he was running? If he had, he'd be visiting them from time to time and, if he did, he probably had an occasional romp between the sheets with the favourite. They do, you know.'

'Fully clothed?'

Darcy frowned. 'He could have tossed his clothes down on hers. That would pick up her perfume. Even just clutching her might.'

'You have experience?'

Darcy grinned. 'I was once kicked out of a bedroom – that redhead from Normandy – because I'd had a little necking session with somebody else and the perfume was on my clothes. Many a wife's grown suspicious of her husband because she's found another woman's hair on his collar or because she's smelled perfume.'

Homosexual? Pimp? Brothel owner? Pel frowned. Somehow none of them seemed to fit what they knew of Jules Arri. But they were worth considering all the same, and that afternoon, he collected Lagé and headed out to Valoreille where Jules Arri had lived.

The Ponsardin sisters were in the house hard on their heels to find out what had happened.

'Have you caught him?' Yvonne demanded.

'Not yet, Mademoiselle,' Pel said. 'Give us a chance.'

He stared about him, frowning. What sort of man was this ex-Sergeant Jules Arri, of the 179th Regiment of the Line? What sort of man came home smelling of expensive perfume and made a habit of knocking back the finest wines?

'Did he get drunk much?' he asked.

Yvonne shook her head. 'I never saw him the worse for drink.'

'Did he *look* as if he drank a lot?'

'No,' Yvette said. 'He looked fit and healthy.'

'But he ate well. We came across portions of duck à l'orange. Once it was roast sucking pig. That's what he told us. He didn't often say much but I remember him saying that. He seemed proud. Do you think he'd come into an inheritance?'

'It wouldn't last long if he spent it on fast women and costly wines,' Pel pointed out. As he spoke, he was fishing in the cupboards and he produced one of the expensive-looking plates they'd found and a cut glass goblet. 'Or, for that matter,' he ended, 'these.'

Holding the goblet in his hand, he ran his finger along the edge. 'Where did it come from? Not from the pension of an ex-sergeant, I'll bet. It's chipped but it must have cost a bit originally.' Watched by the two old ladies, he had his head in a cupboard now and was examining a small cream jug of bone china. 'Perhaps he *didn't* drink all that wine,' he said slowly. 'Perhaps he didn't even pay for it. Perhaps even he didn't choose them.'

'What's on your mind, Patron?' Lagé asked.

Pel turned and showed the cream jug to him. 'Take a look at that. Same standard as the plates. First quality, I'd say. The very best.' He fished out a small side plate in green and gold. 'And that. Much the same. Both slightly chipped, though. I dare bet he didn't inherit them, though I suppose anything's possible. No, I think these came from a restaurant.'

Lagé looked doubtful. 'Surely not the sort of restaurant an ex-sergeant could afford to run, Patron? *They* go in more for routiers – transport cafés. The old red and blue circle. Faux filets and pommes frites. That sort of thing. Good substantial stuff. On good substantial plates. With table wine out of good substantial glasses.'

'Perhaps he didn't own it,' Yvonne Ponsardin suggested.

'Perhaps he just worked there,' Yvette agreed.

Pel fished out several of the plates and ran his finger along the edges. 'All chipped,' he pointed out. 'Like the glasses. Only a little, but chipped, all the same. These came from a place where they're careful to throw out any damaged glasses or plates. Customers paying a lot of money expect perfect chinaware. So, when something gets cracked or chipped, it's tossed out. Perhaps even smashed. But I dare bet the people who work in places like that help themselves to them when they can. The same sort of thing applies to the booze. People who eat in restaurants of that quality are generous with what they order. "A second bottle, waiter." You know the stuff. Showing off a bit. And then the lady friend finds she's had enough and, unlike you and me, the chap who's paying doesn't demand the cork and walk out with what's left. He leaves it, and the waiter puts it on one side and takes it home when he goes off duty.'

Lagé's frown deepened. 'Think he worked as a waiter somewhere?'

'He didn't work during the day, so our restaurant or whatever it was opened only in the evening. Perhaps we can find it by the day it closed. Most restaurants close on Monday.' Pel turned to the two old ladies. 'Did his?'

'No,' Yvonne said firmly. 'He was out seven nights a week.'

Pel frowned. 'It must be a pretty select restaurant, all the same,' he said.

'Well,' Lagé pointed out, 'it isn't one of those in the Rue de Bourg area where I was searching. They mostly serve cheap grub.'

Pel was deep in thought. 'Perhaps it wasn't round there at all,' he said. 'Perhaps when he left his car he was picked up. Perhaps several of them were picked up. By minibus. Something like that. If it were in the country, it's possible. He was probably just adding to his pension with some sort of job in this restaurant. And he didn't buy food because he ate there, probably brought food home – in those plastic boxes we've heard about – and helped himself to the leavings of the wine. And when there were any going and he needed them, he also helped himself to the chipped plates.'

'I'd say he was the doorkeeper,' Mademoiselle Yvonne decided. 'In one of those uniforms like an Albanian field-marshal.'

'Something of that sort,' Yvette agreed.

'The parking attendant perhaps.'

'Or the handyman.'

Pel studied them. It was a pity, he decided, that he couldn't recruit the Ponsardin sisters to his team. They seemed to have plenty of bright ideas.

ten

Nosjean had been frowning hard as he drove away from Solecin's house. He had a feeling that the old man had acquired his knowledge of art solely through reading and had been committing frauds on people ever since.

Luca's home turned out to be an old farmhouse in the Forest of Fougerolles, not far to the north. Luca's wife let Nosjean in and the first thing he saw among the paintings hanging on the wall was a *Soldier with Helmet,* exactly as Roth had described it to him, exactly like the painting he had sold to Chevrier who had given it to the bank as security for a loan.

Luca was not at home and, in answer to Nosjean's questioning, his wife claimed he had given up painting.

'He had a bad car accident', she said, 'and he's never been able to paint since.'

Nosjean stared about him. 'You've got some nice paintings here,' he said. 'Do you collect them?'

'Oh, yes. My husband's quite wealthy and a painter himself. He's always enjoyed paintings.'

'They must be worth a lot of money.' Nosjean carefully kept his eyes away from the *Soldier with Helmet.* 'The one over there. That's a Van Gogh.' Nosjean turned slowly. 'I wouldn't mind owning so many paintings myself.'

Remembering that Roth, the gallery owner, had said he had seen a *Soldier With Helmet* at the home of Raoul Riault, the lawyer who dealt in paintings as a sideline, Nosjean set out for Riault's home.

Riault was on the telephone when he arrived and he could hear him talking as Riault's wife let him in. As she showed him into a long sitting room, the first thing he noticed was another *Soldier With Helmet* hanging over the fireplace. The house itself didn't seem to go with the painting, however. It had no pretensions to grandeur, as if Riault didn't make a lot of money from law.

Riault himself appeared a few moments later. He was a myopic fat man in a creased suit. He had a large moustache, several chins, and glasses so thick they looked like the bottoms of wine bottles.

'Sorry to keep you,' he apologised. 'Business.'

Nosjean got down to things quickly. He was becoming quite adept at side-stepping extraneous matters.

'That painting,' he said gesturing at the *Soldier With Helmet*. 'I'm interested in it. I'm investigating another one like it which is obviously a fraud. What do you consider it's worth?'

Riault looked passably modest. 'Nearly two million francs,' he said.

'That's a lot of money.'

Riault smiled. 'My one little indulgence.'

'It's genuine, of course?'

'Oh, mais oui. Of course it is.'

'Are you a wealthy man, Monsjeur Riault?'

Riault shrugged. 'No. Not really.'

'I was thinking it's a very valuable painting for a man in your circumstances.'

'The strangest people collect,' Riault said. 'I know a plumber who has a Van Gogh. He saved all his life for it. As I did for that.'

'Do you have any security? Alarms? Anything like that?'

'Just good locks.'

'Aren't you taking a chance?'

Riault smiled. 'Who'd expect to find a Rembrandt in a house like this?'

Not me, Nosjean thought. 'We've become very concerned about art frauds,' he went on. 'Would you mind if we had our experts examine your painting? To confirm that it's genuine.'

'It *is* genuine.'

'Merely to confirm?'

Riault looked nervous and Nosjean pressed on. 'There's a machine that identifies the age of the pigments exactly.' As far as he knew, there wasn't such a thing within hundreds of kilometres but Riault didn't know that. 'It won't take long,' he urged.

Suddenly Riault seemed to lose his affability. 'Well,' he said, 'I think I'm going to have to say no. I've heard those things damage the paint and ruin the picture.'

'I'm assured they don't.'

'I couldn't risk it.'

Riault was now in a hurry to get rid of Nosjean and his smile became a grin that was so fixed it looked as if it were wired to his back teeth. 'Look,' he said, almost throwing Nosjean out of the house, 'I'm in a hurry just now. It's a bit inconvenient, and this needs some thought. You'll have to forgive me. Some other time. I've got an appointment. A man who's in a bit of trouble over selling his house. A mix-up about the deeds and I'm having to sort it out. It can't wait.'

Nosjean didn't worry. Riault wasn't going far. Returning to the Roth gallery, he found Jean-Philippe Roth still pondering the supposed Steen.

'Having doubts?' Nosjean asked with a grin.

Roth managed a smile. 'Have you come to arrest me?' he queried. 'Because, I assure you, you haven't a case.'

'I haven't a case,' Nosjean agreed. 'In fact, I've come to ask a question or two, that's all.'

'Such as?'

'Have you ever seen two identical paintings?'

'Never.' Roth frowned. 'What's behind this? Vacchi asked me that question not long ago.'

'Did Vacchi buy from you?'

'Occasionally. But this time he was just picking my brains. I know he was.'

'What about?'

'He'd seen a painting exactly like one he possessed and it had him worried.'

'Did he buy it from you?'

'Not this one.'

'*Had* he seen one?'

'He might have.'

'Which was genuine?'

'He said *his* was. I had a look at it.' Roth indicated the Steen. 'In my opinion it was like that. Possible.'

'A fake?'

Roth shrugged. 'Is it a fake? I don't know. I bought it feeling it wasn't a genuine Steen because there was no provenance, but that it was near enough for someone to take it for a Steen. You saw it happen. Vacchi's paintings were that kind. He fancies himself – as our fat friend did with the Steen. He bought them thinking they were what he felt they were.'

'What did he think they were?'

'One might have passed for a Vermeer.'

'But it wasn't?'

'I wouldn't have touched it.'

'What about the rest of Vacchi's paintings?'

'Some are sound. But not all. A genuine painting has resonance. A feel. Call it what you like. You can measure things in laboratories and look at things with ultra-violet rays; but really they only confirm what the experts have already decided. Vacchi's Vermeer wasn't a Vermeer. He thought it was, though. Or, at least, that it could pass as one.'

'Would a painter ever paint the same picture twice?'

'Never. Sometimes he'd paint the same subject. But there would always be a difference. Light, colour, positioning. That sort of thing. I think Vacchi thought someone had copied his. He said he'd seen an exact replica hanging in a gallery. I told him it wasn't possible. But he wouldn't agree.'

'Did he mention who sold him these so-called originals?'

'Yes, he did. It was a man called Riault.'

Nosjean rubbed his nose. The case was growing more convoluted but, oddly, clearer as it progressed. 'Do you know whether Riault uses an art restorer?'

'Yes.'

'Name?'

'I don't know what I'm getting into.'

'Nothing you need worry about.'

'It was Ugo Luca.'

Nosjean nodded. 'I thought it might be,' he said.

When he returned to Luca's house, Luca had turned up. A small plump dark-skinned man with spaniel eyes, he was sitting outside in the sunshine drinking coffee with his wife. He was wearing a paint-marked overall and his fingers were stained with colour. As Nosjean stepped from his car, he saw Luca's wife nudge him. As Luca rose to meet him he seemed nervous.

'I thought you'd given up painting,' Nosjean said.

'Painting,' Luca said. 'Not restoring. That's different. I also repair canvases and frames, sometimes for major art galleries.'

'Do you know Raoul Riault? He's a lawyer.'

'Yes,' Luca said warily. 'I know him.'

'What about a man called Vacchi?'

'I restored paintings in his collection.'

'He seems to have what he thinks are original old masters. But some of these seem to be identical with paintings that are hanging elsewhere.'

Luca licked his lips. 'What are you suggesting?'

'That somebody made copies. As far as I can make out, Vacchi left his paintings with Riault, who left them with you for cleaning and restoration. Soon afterwards, it seems, identical paintings appeared on the market.'

Luca licked his lips again, glanced at his wife, lit a cigarette and finally gave in.

'Vacchi's pictures aren't genuine', he said. 'I made them for him because he said he wanted something expensive-looking for his office. He told me what he had in mind and offered a lot of money. He's a bit of a bully and it's not easy to refuse him. It would be just like him to claim them as original works of art.'

'Why did he create such a fuss when he found there were other pictures like his? Wouldn't it have been better to say nothing?'

Luca shrugged. 'Perhaps he was trying to convince people his were the genuine ones.' He managed a small smile. 'Perhaps even he was trying to convince himself.'

'Was one a painting known as *Soldier with Helmet.*' Nosjean gestured at the wall. 'That one.'

'Yes.'

'Which is the original?'

'Neither. I copied the original for my own enjoyment when Riault sent it to me for an American client of his to have it cleaned, appraised and verified. I did the others from that. It's been done before. When the *Mona Lisa* was taken from the Louvre, it turned up some months later unharmed. But by then there were half a dozen copies in existence in America. The people who stole it had no need to keep it. They'd more than made its value with the copies.'

So Nosjean had heard. 'Was the *Soldier with Helmet* one of the paintings Riault sold to Vacchi?'

'Probably. There's another Riault's house.'

'So I noticed. How many are there altogether?'

Luca looked on the verge of tears. 'Several,' he said.

The situation at the Hôtel de Police was still difficult. There was no doubt that of the two major cases on their hands, the murder of Jules Arri and the kidnapping of the Deputy for Yorinne, the kidnapping was considered the more serious. Both newspapers and television were constantly harping on the case, decrying the absence of any momement by the police but failing to notice that it was impossible to move very far when the kidnappers had not yet bothered to get in touch with anyone in authority.

Every possible hiding place had been searched, and had been searched within a few hours of the kidnapping. But by this time the victim could have been at the other end of France and, without any demand from the kidnappers, it was impossible to tell where.

Policemen had been drafted in from every district within reach and were working all hours so that many of their wives were beginning to wonder what they looked like and why they'd bothered to get married. Every available man was on the streets, checking on every likely suspect. Officers in plain clothes appeared in the strangest places and anyone who was reported by neighbours to be behaving oddly, or not where he ought to be, was brought in and questioned. The request to the public had turned up a few likely suspects but they were none of them the right ones.

An emergency telephone number was announced and the pressure was kept up. Information continued to come in but it was never the information that was wanted and there was never anything positive to go on. Tracker dogs and men with walkie-talkies were still searching and a large reward had been offered.

The whole area was stood on its head and messages were sent to all forces to check everyone who was brought in for theft, because the kidnappers, alarmed at the enormous search they had caused, might have gone into hiding and been forced to steal to stay alive until the uproar died down.

By this time Lamiel was arguing even that they must be hidden somewhere with a woman's assistance, and a search was made of all small hotels and apartments. Most of the sightings that were reported were made in good faith but a few jokers found themselves in 72 Rue d'Auxonne. Every postbag brought letters and they all had to be checked – so much so that normal crime in the area virtually came to a stop.

'There's not much point in anything else,' Darcy was told by a man he'd brought in more than once for burglary. 'There are too many flics about.'

Still nothing happened. There were no ransom notes and no arrests were made and the streamer headline in *France Soir* seemed to indicate what the country thought of the police's efforts. 'VIVE L'ENNUI,' it declared.

With the Hôtel de Police in a state of controlled panic, Pel's position was difficult. There he was, sitting in his office – suitable in size for a chief inspector, choice of colour for carpet, hat-stand instead of a hook on the door, and a Goya print, which he detested, on the wall – taken off the case, which was being handled locally at police level by his deputy, Darcy.

Everybody in the Hôtel de Police was aware what had happened and Judge Brisard had made sure that everyone at the Palais de Justice had heard, too, so that people meeting Pel in the corridor gave him nervous 'Bonjours' or disappeared into offices so they could avoid saying anything at all. Nobody quite knew what he'd been accused of but there was a feeling around that he'd been taking bribes or something from Deputy Barclay. Fortunately, among his own team there was still a lot of loyalty and they were solidly behind him. Didier Darras punched one of the other cadets on the nose and Bardolle promised to take apart anybody he heard taking the name of his boss in vain. Since Bardolle was built like a carthorse and had fists like sacks of coal this was very effective at shutting people up.

But it didn't halt the feeling that Pel had been caught with his hand in the till or something, and Lamiel made no attempt to alter this view.

Madame Pel watched her husband carefully. He was quiet, subdued and thoughtful and she was concerned for the effect the ban was having on him, feeling he was depressed and low in spirits. In fact, he was anything but, and was brooding chiefly on vengeance on people like Lamiel and Judge Brisard. Pel was no saint and enjoyed thoughts of vengeance as much as anyone. And having long harboured the hope that Judge Brisard might one day break out in warts all down one side, he could see no harm in Lamiel doing the same.

His silence worried his wife, though. She knew her Evariste Clovis Désiré well by this time and, while she was aware of his faults, the fact that he could well at times be a subject for a psychiatrist and was likely in his old age to descend into bigoted eccentricity, she loved him nevertheless. Despite his confidence as a policeman, in his private life he was a mass of doubts, permanently concerned that he didn't come up to the high standards he assumed his wife expected of him, humble in his attitudes to her, and grateful that she, a successful businesswoman, had taken him, a poverty-stricken, ageing policeman with what must by this time be incipient lung cancer – Pel's opinion of himself – and seemed prepared to cherish him.

'Are you worried?' she asked.

'No,' he said.

But he was. He knew a thing like this could ruin his career. Policemen these days were far more vulnerable than they used to be. A small incident on his file could turn his future from success to disaster. He pretended it didn't matter but it did, and his wife tried to make it clear that she was right behind him whatever happened.

There were other allies, too. Surprising ones. Madame Routy had become astonishingly quiet and, these days, when she handed Pel his briefcase as he set off for the Hôtel de

Police in the mornings, she never did it with the sort of expression that suggested she hoped it would blow up in his face. Yves Pasquier also made his position clear. 'I'm on your side, Monsieur Pel,' he announced gravely as they shook hands through the fence before breakfast. 'Whatever they say about you, I'm on your side.'

'My side?'

'Maman said you'd been taken off the kidnapping.'

Pel gestured. 'Nothing,' he insisted. 'It's nothing.'

'All the same,' Yves Pasquier insisted, 'I'm loyal.'

'I'm deeply touched,' Pel said. He was, too.

Finally a letter arrived from Cousin Roger, who, though he might enjoy his wine a little too much, obviously had his heart in the right place.

'It's rubbish,' he wrote about the newspaper reports. 'Half-wits writing rubbish to be read by more half-wits.'

There was more in the same vein and it was pungent stuff that helped to smooth Pel's ruffled feathers. He seemed to have been accepted by one member of Madame's family, at least.

Lamiel had turned up again. From time to time he could be seen at the Hôtel de Police, usually heading for the office of the Chief who, these days, was wearing a hangdog expression, as if he were finding it all a little too much and was longing to call in Pel and toss the whole thing in his lap.

But Lamiel had power behind him and the Chief could do little. And Lamiel was still baffled that there had been no ransom demand, no demand for an exchange of hostages. There were always hostages, he knew, usually from half a dozen countries, languishing in French prisons, so surely *someone* must be interested. He seemed loath to regard the kidnapping as a straightforward moneymaking affair.

'All right,' he informed the Chief. 'They're not demanding anything from the government. So eventually they'll demand money. What's the point of it, otherwise? If it's not political, it's a fund-raising exercise. It must be. They need to fund their activities and this method's been used before. We shall get the ransom note all right.'

But it showed no sign of coming and Lamiel was still keeping an eye on Kiczmyrczik and his friends in case they made any suspicious moves, and had his men out checking the movements of Furet's Right Wing Groupe Revanche Française. So far, he had not turned up Furet himself, who was believed to be in Corsica endeavouring to recruit followers, so he occupied himself with delivering regular lectures on terrorism to bored policemen to keep them on their toes.

'There's one other thing,' Darcy said, 'that we might look into. Madame Pouyet. Huguette Pouyet. She was at Barclay's house the night he gave the party there, I've discovered. She was one of his girl-friends.'

'Mistress?'

'Yes.'

'Then say so.'

Darcy shrugged and pressed on. 'She's since left her husband and gone to Italy.'

'You're suggesting it's a crime of passion?'

Darcy gave Lamiel a cold look. 'French people go in for crimes of passion. That's why our knives are always sharp. So they can be snatched up to deal with an unfaithful wife or husband. The English never have sharp knives. They don't believe in passion.'

Lamiel didn't appreciate Darcy's kind of humour. *'You're suggesting this has happened to someone as important as Barclay?'* he asked.

'Pierre Chevallier', Darcy pointed out slowly, 'was shot by his wife in 1951 when he was a minister in the government of René Pleven. In 1914, Madame Caillaux shot the editor of *Figaro*. In 1946 a sixty-six-year-old former Minister of Justice in New Zealand was found guilty in London of the murder of an innocent man he thought was making eyes at his woman friend, who was also sixty-six years old. There are other cases I can find if you want them.'

Lamiel was effectively silenced for a moment. 'Go on,' he said sharply.

'Could Pouyet have got Barclay somewhere and be holding him until he promises to leave his wife alone?'

Lamiel looked at Thomas. 'Get hold of this Pouyet,' he snapped.

'He goes over the top a bit, Patron,' Darcy said in the Bar Transvaal. 'He sees a Russian spy behind every lamp-post. He's found a little cell out near the Industrial Zone now. It's Kiczmyrczik and Michelowski. We stopped watching them years ago. Kiczmyrczik is sixty-nine and Michelowski's sixty-five, and their only supporters are more old socks like themselves.'

Pel managed a dry smile. 'Is he going to arrest them?'

'I think he feels they're a direct line to the Kremlin.'

Pel decided it was worth having a cigarette on the strength of it. He dragged the smoke down to his shoes and felt better at once. 'Kiczmyrczik's been wanting to be a martyr to the Cause all his life,' he said.

'Martyrdom gets you nowhere,' Darcy said flatly. 'Look at Joan of Arc. The English burned her.'

'They didn't make a very good job of it.'

Darcy shrugged. 'They never did know how to cook.'

They discussed possibilities for a while.

'What about the offices overlooking the kidnapping?' Pel asked. 'Anybody in there who might be interested?'

'Nobody at all. We've checked. Nobody seems to have had much interest in Barclay, though he seems to have been liked by those who knew him. That's understandable, of course, because he's good-looking, wealthy, approachable, has a voice like a trumpet and a politician's flair for putting people at ease.'

When Pel returned to his office, Claudie Darel was waiting for him. 'I've checked with Central Computer, Patron,' she said. 'Our friend Arri seems to have a record.'

Pel looked up sharply. 'He has?' Perhaps he'd been involved in major crime and this could lead to who had killed him. He was due for a disappointment.

'A break-in at a supermarket.'

'Not the one at Talant, for God's sake?'

Claudie smiled. The supermarket at Talant was a standing joke at the Hôtel de Police. 'In Dole, Patron,' she said. '1961. Mitigating circumstances. He was badly wounded at Dien Bien Phu – as we know. Stomach and arm. Hadn't been able to work and he'd gone down the drain a little. Good army record, though. I checked the reports on the case. Claude Barclay spoke up for him. You'll remember he was also at Dien Bien Phu.'

'Go on.'

'Arri mentioned that Barclay was his officer, somebody contacted him and he turned up in court. He spoke up for Arri and even offered to find him a job. Arri was let off with a suspended sentence. Touching pictures in the press of him and Barclay shaking hands. I went through the files.'

Pel nodded and even managed a smile. Claudie drew a smile from most people, even Pel, and besides she was efficient and didn't miss much. It was typical of her that she'd not only checked the court and police reports but had also checked the newspapers.

He frowned. 'It's a pity Barclay's not available,' he said. 'This job he obtained for Arri might well be the one that kept him occupied at night.'

eleven

Lamiel was beginning to grow a little desperate.

'A strategy session held in Teheran last year was attended by the Foreign Ministers of Libya and Syria,' he announced to the cops assembled in the lecture room at the Hôtel de Police. 'And the Israelis maintain that they agreed to a joint strategy for terrorist operations on targets in Western Europe. It's a hundred per cent certainty, they insist, not speculation, and they say they decided to divide responsibilities and territories so they could operate separately or in close co-operation. It could be anybody who grabbed Barclay.'

'Suppose it's not terrorism?' the Chief said.

'What else could it be? Anything might have happened to delay the ransom demand or the claim for responsibility.'

The Chief sighed. 'What about this Pouyet?'

'He swears he wasn't responsible.'

'Have we let him go then?'

'No,' Lamiel said firmly. 'We're holding him.'

It was a long session and Darcy was feeling weary as he returned to his office. As he sat down the telephone rang. It was the front office to say Henriot of *Le Bien Public* was asking for him. Going downstairs, he found Henriot by the front desk, looking nervous and holding a brown envelope.

'I've got this for you,' he said.

'What is it?'

'It's a ransom demand.'

Darcy stiffened. So Lamiel had been right. It had come at last. 'It's *what?*' he said carefully.

'A ransom demand. It says… '

'Hold it!' Darcy knew exactly what had to be done and he was determined to protect his tail. 'Hang on! Let's do this thing properly. We'll need to have this thing recorded and witnessed. Come upstairs to my office.'

Leading Henriot upstairs, he yelled for assistance and sent Didier Darras to contact Lamiel. When the shorthand writer arrived and De Troq' was present as a witness, Darcy looked across his desk at Henriot. 'Right. Let's have it. You're Joseph Henriot, of *Le Bien Public.*'

'You know I am.'

'Of course I do. But let's have it down.' Darcy glanced at the shorthand writer and gestured. 'And this ransom note? It's in the envelope, is it?'

'Yes.'

'Well, put it down. And don't touch it again. It may have fingerprints on it.' Darcy studied the envelope. 'Note that, De Troq'. One brown envelope. Creased and a bit grubby. Grease stains and what have you.' He frowned and looked at Henriot. 'How did it come?'

'I found it stuck in my door.'

'At the office?'

'No. At my home.'

'Why at your home?'

'I suppose whoever wrote it had seen my name in the paper. They've read La *Bien Public.* Something like that.'

Darcy frowned. 'Which indicates he's a local, and that doesn't sound like some international organisation to me. What did you do with it?'

'I opened it, read it and took it to the office. There's obviously a story.'

'Maybe. What happened then?'

'The editor told me to bring it here.'

'Did he handle it?'

'Yes.'

'Anybody else?'

'His secretary. I had to show it to her first. The editor was in conference.'

'Go on. Anybody else.'

'The chief sub-editor. He looked at it. To decide... '

'So every con in the office had his maulers on it?'

Henriot looked put out. 'We didn't realise.'

'No, of course not.'

'We're not in the habit of handling ransom demands every day.' Henriot was beginning to sound faintly indignant now.

'That's all right,' Darcy soothed. 'I understand. Right. Let's have a look at it.' He took a pair of tweezers from a drawer, carefully removed a single sheet of paper from the envelope and examined it, speaking all the time to the shorthand writer. 'Single sheet of paper. Looks as if it's been torn from a school exercise book. Grease stain top right hand corner. Could be a fingerprint. Writing unformed. Spelling indifferent. Several words are wrong. It's headed "Leftist Freedom Movement". It reads, "We have the missing politician, Claude Barclay, Junior Minister for Welfare. He will be executed unless a million francs are handed over immediately." It goes on to say the money should be placed in a poste restante box at the general post office where it will be picked up by one of their members.' Darcy paused, gave a deep sigh and laid the sheet of paper on the desk. 'I think I should stop worrying,' he said.

Henriot looked startled. 'Why?'

'It's a fraud.'

'What?'

'It's a fraud. No self-respecting terrorist organisation would have its ransom left in a poste restante box. It's too dangerous. The post office would be full of cops. Besides, they've got Barclay's title wrong. He's not Junior Minister for

Welfare. He's known as Under-Minister for Health. They'd surely know that.'

'Oh!'

'What's more, I suspect they'd run to a clean envelope and a decent sheet of paper not marked by greasy fingers. If only to indicate they were a responsible organisation, something they're always keen to show. They'd have used a typewriter and they'd have sent it via the ordinary post, not stuck it in the door of a reporter of La *Bien Public*. At the outside, they'd have addressed it to the editor. Besides – ' Darcy wondered how he could put it ' – if the people who sent this note really were some Leftist Freedom Movement and they were serious, they'd have sent the letter to *Le Monde* or one of the big Paris dailies, not to an unknown provincial paper like... '

'Oh, would they?' Henriot sounded piqued. 'Thanks for the compliment.'

'I'm sorry. But you must surely realise that.'

There was a long silence 'So what do we do?' Henriot asked.

'We'll have it checked, of course. There may be the odd dab on it – in fact, it looks as if there is – and, if there is, whoever sent it is going to be in trouble if we can find out who it was.'

'Can we use it? As a story?'

'No, you can't! Not without the permission of the DST. You can ask them, of course, but I'd advise you not to. They're not the easiest people in the world to deal with. They might slap *you* in Number 72, Rue d'Auxonne, for being an accessory after the fact or something.'

Lamiel arrived two hours later when the message was safely in the hands of Prélat of Fingerprints. He had just come back from Paris and was inclined to take the ransom note more seriously than Darcy, but even more seriously the fact that Darcy had acted on his own initiative.

'You had no right to make decisions,' he said.

'I merely told him my opinion.'

'You don't offer opinions.'

'All right,' Darcy retorted angrily. '*You* offer one. Is it genuine?' Lamiel frowned. 'I doubt it.'

Pel was thoughtful as he listened to Darcy in the Bar Transvaal. 'It claimed to be from the Leftist Freedom Movement.'

'I've never heard of it.'

'Neither have I,' Darcy agreed. 'Neither, I suspect, has Lamiel. But he's getting the computers red hot trying to place it.'

'Who's it addressed to?'

'Henriot of Le *Bien Public.*'

'Nobody else?'

'Who else would they negotiate with? Barclay's got no family and I'd hardly imagine a provincial architect's office was worth much, even if Barclay is. I'm sure it's a fraud. There's always someone trying to jump on the bandwagon. Give too much publicity to a crime and there's always someone who'll have a go. There was that case in Corsica where half a million francs were paid out in a hurry and then the real demand came in for a million. There were a few red faces around after that.'

'What's Lamiel doing?'

'Sweating on what Fingerprints find. Prélat's found an incomplete dab and Lamiel's hoping we'll be able to place it.'

They did.

It wasn't easy because the print was poor, but there was enough of it to identify the author and he ended up, nervous and on the verge of tears, sitting at Darcy's desk facing Lamiel, his fingers twitching at the knees of his trousers.

'Who's behind you?' Lamiel was demanding.

'Nobody.'

'What organisation do you belong to?'

'I don't belong to any organisation.'

'I don't believe you.'

'I would if I were you,' Darcy said flatly. 'That's Henri Guillon – Henri à Mi-Mât. Half-mast Harry. He wears his trousers above his ankles and jumps on every bandwagon that comes along. He did two months two years ago for claiming to have murdered a woman.'

Lamiel glared at Guillon. 'Is that true?'

Guillon was frightened to death now. 'Yes, yes,' he gabbled. 'I swear it on my mother's grave.'

'Name of God!' Lamiel's voice was bitter. 'Take him away. Charge him with wasting police time.'

As Guillon vanished, Lamiel scowled and decided they were even going to have to let Georges Pouyet go, too. His alibi seemed to be sound – though alibis were sometimes not as sound as they seemed – and there was still Deputy Furet who had finally been found and was now under house arrest at Bourg-en-Bresse where he lived, because his alibi didn't stand up. He claimed to have been driving from Marseilles north at the time of the kidnapping, but there was no proof and Lamiel was taking no chances.

He had done his homework, however, and it turned out that, in addition to other insults, Barclay had once accused the Groupe Revanche Française of supporting terrorism. It was enough for Lamiel. He had all the officials rounded up and, although he had to release them all almost immediately, he had them all placed under surveillance in the hope that they might lead him to someone.

The newspapers loved it. According to the opinion polls, the government had even gained a few prospective votes from the kidnapping. The rest of the news was much as usual – a murder in Marseilles of three men, which seemed to be a gang killing; a disaster relief organisation at Grenoble which had suddenly discovered it was a million francs short in its funds and was looking for someone to accuse; a hospital in Lyons which had reported 5000 sheets, 5000 pillowslips and 5000 towels missing; a wine scandal on the Rhône – but now basically the editors were directing all their attention to Barclay's wealth. Perhaps, Pel thought in a burst of cynicism, the tax inspectors had him locked in the cellars of the tax office for non-payment of revenues. As the thought crossed his mind, he sat up, because people *had* been known to disappear because they were in difficulties financially. But that wasn't all, because someone had discovered an entirely new angle to the case.

'Missing Minister Wanted Out,' was *France Soir's* headline.

'World Weary Minister's Plea,' said *Figaro*.

It was a trivial story hinging on the fact that someone had heard Barclay proclaim his wish to put things aside, though no one knew why he had said it or to whom. It was enough, however, to set the press speculating. Barclay had been overheard saying 'I've had enough' at a reception in Paris and they'd decided he was finding politics too much for him. But was it politics, Pel wondered, or was it something else entirely?

Despite Lamiel's warnings, he was still unconsciously brooding on the kidnapping. Though Lamiel was still baffled by the absence of any claim from any terrorist organisation, it still *remained* a kidnap. *It had been seen to be a kidnap.* Barclay had been snatched from his car, bundled into another car and driven away. Lamiel's opinion was still that they were bound to hear something before long, and despite the fact that the only ransom note that had arrived was a fraud, it was still possible that a genuine one might yet arrive.

But, if it did, who paid it? The government? Pel couldn't see that happening and Barclay had no family because he wasn't married and his parents were dead. So who *was* going to cough up? His firm? Barclay was the firm. His other interests? It would take some doing to get all the people concerned with his financial affairs to come to some agreement to raise the sort of money kidnappers demanded. And, anyway, since Barday's interest in those other affairs was largely only financial, though his presence wasn't necessary, his money certainly was, and nobody was going to hand it over in a hurry. It looked to Pel as if the kidnappers had picked a very sticky subject.

twelve

Pel was still frowning when Lagé appeared. He looked puzzled.

'Patron,' he said, 'I've found something that's got me a bit baffled. I've discovered Arri's car was in Courtois-Saint-Seine the night before he's supposed to have died.'

'Courtois?' Pel looked up. 'That's where Barclay has a house.'

'That's right, Patron. There's an old touch there called Boileau who used to be on the stage. Sous-Brigadier Linais who runs Courtois says she's a bit of a character. Everybody knows her because they can always hear her singing.'

'I suspect I heard her myself that night I was there. What about her?'

'She told Linais she saw Arri's car arrive in a hurry just before dark and Arri get out of it. At least, she assumes it was Arri because it seems to have been Arri's car.'

'Where did it stop?'

'Barclay's house, Patron. It's opposite hers.'

Pel sat up with a jerk. This was one for the book. Immediately, he realised it was the very thing he needed to enable him to stick his nose into the Barclay kidnapping.

'I think we ought to go out there,' he said.

The Chief listened carefully but he was inclined to be wary.

'There seems to be some connection between the two cases,' Pel pointed out, silkily determined to get his way. 'I think I ought to see this woman and see what she knows.'

The Chief was none too happy. Paris could be spiteful with provincials, but he was anxious to keep his diocese clear of mysteries and it seemed a lead in the Arri case. 'Put a note in,' he said. 'I'll pass it on to Lamiel. I don't suppose he'll read it but it'll cover you and it'll cover me.'

Courtois looked different in the midday sunshine, glaring white instead of the yellow-bronze it had been when Pel had visited the place with the family group from Bois Haut. The brooding bulk of Barclay's twelfth century mansion dwarfed everything else around.

Madame Boileau was at her piano as they arrived. The window was open and the music was clear. They were shown in by a maid, a village girl in a grey dress and a pink apron. Behind her, a small dog with a bark like a tin trumpet went on yapping until she gave it a discreet kick up the backside that sent it scurrying to the rear of the house.

The voice that had once been able to reach the back of a theatre gallery still had sufficient power to make the glass rattle in the windows. Madame Boileau turned out to be a plump sixty-year-old with ash-blond hair, a pink and white complexion that came out of a make-up jar, and enough mascara on her lashes to make them a public peril.

> L'amour est un oiseau rebelle
> Que nul ne peut apprivoiser,
> Et c'est bien en vain qu'on l'appelle
> S'il lui convient de refuser...

'*Carmen,*' she announced. 'The *Habanera* from Act I. It was thought up originally for Zulma Bouffar, whom Offenbach discovered singing risqué songs in a Cologne café, but it was eventually introduced by Marie Galli-Marié. Always one of my favourites.'

She gestured to them to sit down and they found places in an over-decorated salon full of lace drapings, feathers, flowers, miniatures and what appeared to be acres of photographs of long-vanished singers.

'My music salon,' Madame Boileau said. 'Here I feel at home.'

She launched into a long spiel about her career, sang them a couple of songs from the Auvergne – 'I'm an Auvergnat, of course,' she said – and was about to launch into another long diatribe about her career when Pel decided it was time to get down to the nitty-gritty.

'The car, Madame,' he said. 'The car you said you saw.'

None too willingly she tore herself away from contemplation of her former glory. 'Of course,' she said. '1111-AR-41.'

Pel's eyebrows rose. 'You remember the number?'

'Of course. A small Peugeot. Grey. With a dent in the back.'

'That sounds very much like the one we're interested in. Can you tell us what happened exactly?'

She was more than anxious to do so. 'I was here,' she said. 'Practising. I like to keep my voice pliant… '

'The car, Madame,' Pel urged.

'Of course. The car. I saw it appear in the village street.'

'What time was this?'

'Late in the evening. The sun was still out but it was just going down.'

'You're absolutely certain it was the car we're interested in?'

'I wrote the number down.'

She pushed across a sheet of music and there on the corner in pencil was the number, 1111-AR-41.

'Why did you write it down, Madame? Surely you don't normally write down the numbers of strange cars on your music?'

She gave a tinkling laugh. 'No, of course not. But I wished to show it to my husband. I was expecting him home. I have a similar car and my husband was using it to go to his office that day because his own had been involved in an accident and was at the garage. And, you see, there is an extraordinary coincidence. My car number is 1111-AP-45. It's a Doubs number. We bought it in Besançon. I saw the car arrive and, as it was about the time my husband was due home, I assumed from the colour that it was him. Especially as I could only make out the first part of the number. And when it drove into the drive of the house opposite – Monsieur Barclay's house – I wondered what on earth he was doing and why he didn't drive immediately into our own drive as he usually does.'

'What, in fact, did the car do?'

'It arrived very fast – which is another reason I thought it was my husband. He always drives far too fast – and turned into the drive there. If you look carefully, you can still see the wheelmarks where it swung round.'

There were a lot of wheelmarks on the gravel opposite, but it was true one set seemed to have disturbed the surface more than the others.

'When the driver got out and I saw it wasn't my husband, I lost interest, though I wrote down the number to show him when he came home.'

'Did you notice what this driver did?'

'Yes, of course. He ran round to the back of the house, where the entrance is. He just left the car door open and vanished. I became intrigued again because he seemed in such a hurry. He came back almost immediately – still in a hurry so that I assumed there was no one in the house – climbed into the car and drove away.'

'Nothing else?'

'Nothing.'

'Have you ever seen him since?'

'No.'

'Had you ever seen him before?'

'Never.'

Pel gestured at Lagé who produced from his briefcase the blown-up copy of the photograph Darcy had obtained of Arri from the regimental museum of the 179th of the Line.

'Would that be him, Madame?'

Madame Boileau stared at the picture. 'It might be,' she agreed. 'But he looks younger.'

'He is younger, Madame. This was taken some time ago, when he was in the army.'

Madame Boileau nodded. 'He had the look of a soldier,' she agreed.

Leaving Madame Boileau thrashing away again at the piano, Pel got Lagé to drive down the street to the bar. The two old men he had seen before were still there, arguing fiercely in the heat about some triviality, and a third sat with his eyes closed and his chin on his chest, asleep or dead. Either way, no one seemed very interested. In the alley alongside, two more old men were playing boules.

Pel ordered beers and tried the photograph on the landlord. It didn't work.

'He's not from here,' the landlord said.

'No, he's not,' Pel said. 'He's from Valoreille. But it seems he paid a visit to Monsieur Barclay's house the night before he was found dead at Suchey.'

'Is that the type all that stuff was about in the paper?' the landlord asked eagerly.

'That's the one. Do you know him?'

'Never seen him before in my life.'

The landlord's wife, fetched from the kitchen and still wiping her hands on her apron, studied the picture gravely for a long time.

'Know him?' Lagé asked.

'No,' she said.

They were making a lot of headway.

The two old men playing boules and the old men arguing felt the same as the landlord: he was not from Courtois. It didn't help much, because undoubtedly Jules Arri, ex-sergeant of the 179th Regiment, wounded at Dien Bien Phu and rescued by one Sous-Lieutenant Claude Barclay, who had received a gong for his bravery on that day, had undoubtedly been trying to see his benefactor, the man who saved his life and who had probably been responsible for the mysterious job that puzzled them so. And, by the look of it, it had been a matter of extreme urgency, though it had got him nowhere because at the time, it seemed, the house had been empty.

Pel was deep in thought, debating what to do. The obvious thing was to go to Barclay's house and check up there, to ask if they knew Arri and if so, to find out what had been so urgent about his visit. But he knew he was treading on dangerous ground. Barclay belonged to Lamiel and Pel had been warned off that case. He could well imagine Lamiel making a lot of song and dance about it, too, if he found Pel had been shoving his nose in. On the other hand, Pel *was* involved with Jules Arri and certain aspects of Jules Arri's behaviour seemed to require explanation.

'This is between you and me, Lagé,' he pointed out. 'Have you got that?'

'Yes, Patron, I've got it.'

Pel studied the old detective. Lagé looked a little like a bloodhound and he had some of the same qualities. He wasn't likely to talk.

Remembering how, on the occasion of his visit with the party from Bois Haut, they had entered the old house by a small door at the bottom of the turret, they left the car where it was outside the bar and walked back to try the bell. At first there was no answer, then eventually they heard the bolts being withdrawn and found themselves facing the handsome young manservant, Gefray.

'Monsieur Pel,' he said at once.

'I wish to come in,' Pel said quickly, anxious to be off the street where he might be seen.

Gefray stepped back and, as they slipped inside, he pushed the door to and slid the bolts home.

'Are you still locking the door?' Pel asked.

'I was advised to do so, Monsieur.'

'By whom?'

'By a gentleman by the name of Lamiel.'

'Did he say why?'

'He seemed to think there might be a break-in. Forgive me, Monsieur.' Gefray was wiping his mouth on a striped apron. 'I was just taking my meal.'

'Where?'

'In the kitchen.'

'Let's go there.'

The kitchen fitted in with all that Pel had seen about the house on his visit from Bois Haut. It was revamped, rebuilt and repainted to look like a medieval kitchen with modern accoutrements. The table stretched almost its full length and there were half a dozen chairs round it where the staff obviously ate. Gefray indicated that they should sit down and seated himself at the head of the table. Alongside him was another place setting.

'Who's that for?' Pel asked.

'The maid,' Gefray said. 'Annette Gilbert.'

Pel remembered the pretty maid. 'Are you alone here?' he asked.

'At the moment, Monsieur. There's a gardener and a cook. But it's the cook's night off and the gardener only comes during the day.'

'You'd better carry on eating.'

Gefray shrugged. 'It can wait, Monsieur. It's only a cold collation.' He produced a bottle of wine and three glasses. It was good wine, Pel noticed, without doubt one of Barclay's best.

'Have you news of Monsieur Barclay?' Gefray asked.

'Not yet.'

'I trust it won't be long before there's something. At the moment, we're still running the house as if he were about to appear. But there's a rumour in the village that he's dead.'

As Gefray spoke, the maid appeared. She was wearing yellow trousers and a flowered shirt and didn't seem to be dressed for work.

'Lolo,' she began. 'I saw two men prowling round... '

Then she saw Pel and Lagé and blushed. 'I'm sorry, Messieurs. I didn't see you there.'

Gefray gestured at the girl. 'This is Chief Inspector Pel of the Police Judiciare,' he said. 'You'd better leave us alone for a moment. I'll let you know when you can eat.'

The girl nodded, eyed Pel for a moment, then retreated through the door, closing it softly after her.

'Lolo,' Pel said. 'That your name?'

Gefray blushed. 'Short for Louis, Monsieur.'

'Does everyone call you Lolo?'

'Just friends, Monsieur. We're all good friends here.'

Pel nodded. 'What hours do you work here?'

Gefray shrugged and took a sip of his wine. 'All hours, Monsieur. I know that these days there are supposed to be rigid hours for workers but running a house for a man as busy as Monsieur Barclay puts you in a rather different category. We are on duty whenever he's here and off duty when he's not.'

'Isn't that rather an arduous routine?'

'No, Monsieur. He's often away.'

'What about Monsieur Barclay? Did you like him?'

'He paid good wages.'

'That isn't what I asked.'

Gefray paused. 'Then, yes, Monsieur. I did.'

'The 15th. Were you here then?'

Gefray didn't bother to consider. 'Yes, we were.'

'All the time?'

'Yes, Monsieur.'

'That was a Wednesday like today. Was that the cook's night off, also?'

'It must have been, Monsieur.'

Pel fished out the picture of Arri and laid it on the table.

'Ever seen him before?' he asked.

Gefray looked puzzled. 'No, Monsieur. Should I have? It's the man who was found murdered at Suchey, isn't it? I've seen the picture in the papers.'

Pel next fished out the photograph of Arri's car and laid it alongside the picture of its owner.

'Ever seen that car before?'

'No, sir.'

'It was here late on the evening of the 15th.'

Gefray frowned.

'The owner arrived in a hurry, ran round the back of the house, obviously trying to see someone, then ran back to the car, climbed in and drove away. Are you sure you didn't see him?'

Gefray was frowning heavily. 'Quite sure.'

'Then why did he run back to his car and drive off in a hurry? I think he tried the bell but nobody answered, so he decided there was no one at home. He seemed to be on urgent business, perhaps concerning Monsieur Barclay. In fact, he was an old comrade of Monsieur Barclay from Dien Bien Phu, the man Monsieur Barclay rescued when he was wounded, and for whom Monsieur Barclay received a decoration. It seems to me he arrived with something important to give to Monsieur Barclay but, apparently finding no one at home, he left again. Some time the following day, we believe, he was murdered. I'm interested to know why he came here?'

Gefray looked a little confused. 'I know nothing about it, Monsieur.'

'Nothing?'

'No.'

'And you never saw him?'

'No.'

Pel gestured to Lagé. 'Go and ring the bell, Lagé,' he said.

Lagé rose and lumbered off. They heard the door open and shut. There was a long pause. Lagé was obviously making the most of the dramatic moment. The bell jarred in the silence. Pel said nothing until Lagé returned and sat down.

'It makes a loud noise,' he observed and Gefray swallowed. 'But you didn't hear it?'

'No.'

'Why not?'

Gefray's glance flew to the door where the maid had disappeared. 'Perhaps I had gone to bed.'

'The sun was still out. The man was seen to arrive and disappear. Where was Barclay that night?'

Gefray glanced at a diary on the bench near his arm. 'He had been to Paris. He wasn't expected back for two days.'

'So you were alone?'

'Yes.'

'With the cook taking her night off.'

'What are you getting at?'

'You know what I'm getting at. You were in the house but you didn't hear the bell. This man, Arri, arrived in a panic, obviously anxious to get in touch with Monsieur Barclay. He must have rung the bell, which is loud. But you didn't hear it.'

'I've told you, I must have been in bed.'

'With the girl who appeared just now?'

'That's none of your business.'

'No. Your morals are your own affair. I'm only concerned with what that man wanted when he arrived in such a hurry. You *were* in bed with her, weren't you? And you'd locked the door and chose not to answer the bell.'

Gefray nodded silently.

Pel wondered how much further to pursue the enquiry. Could the incident have been connected with the kidnapping? He had to remember he was there only to investigate Arri's murder, not Barclay's disappearance. That was Lamiel's business and Lamiel had decided he didn't like Pel.

He was silent for a moment. 'The women who came here,' he asked eventually. 'I know there were women. I saw one the night I came. Her name was Huguette Pouyet. There were others, too, weren't there?'

'Yes. They came, stayed the night and left the next day. Most of them I never saw again. But there was one who came more often. She never stayed and I got the impression she wasn't a – er – a friend, but a business associate. They seemed to discuss money most of the time.'

'Do you know her name?'

'Monsieur Barclay was careful to avoid mentioning it when I was around, but I once heard him call her Dédé.'

'Dédé? That sounds like a nickname. Or a special name between lovers. What was she like?'

'She was very beautiful. Will that be all?'

'Not quite.' Pel gestured at the plates on the table. 'I've seen plates like that before,' he went on slowly.

Gefray stared at the plates. They were green and gold and of fine china.

'The man who called here on the 15th,' Pel said, 'Jules Arri. He had one or two plates like that.'

Gefray shrugged. 'I've never heard his name mentioned. Except... ' he paused. 'Perhaps – one night when I came into the salon. Monsieur Barclay was on the telephone and I heard him say "Thanks, Jules. Still the good sergeant." '

' "*Thanks Jules. Still the good sergeant.*" That was all?'

'Yes. Then he put the telephone down.'

'Jules Arri was Monsieur Barclay's sergeant when he was in Indo-China in the Fifties. What do you think he meant?'

'I have no idea, Monsieur.'

'And you have no idea how it is that Jules Arri, who apparently didn't make a habit of coming here, had plates identical to the plates Monsieur Barclay uses.'

'None at all, Monsieur.'

'Do you know where Monsieur Barclay bought his china?'

'I have no idea, Monsieur. None's been bought while I've been here.'

Pel picked up one of the plates and examined it. It was exactly like the chipped plates they had found at Arri's cottage.

'Do you normally use Monsieur Barclay's best plates to eat from in the kitchen?'

Gefray flushed. 'It has a crack, Monsieur, you'll notice. It would never be used for a dinner party so it had been relegated to the kitchen.'

'Are there many?'

'Of course, Monsieur. There is a full dinner service. Fifty-four pieces. With matching coffee cups.'

'What about glasses?'

'Monsieur Barclay used only the best.'

Pel was thinking of the wines found at Arri's cottage. Had Barclay been in the habit of visiting Arri? 'Was he much of a drinker?' he asked.

'Not particularly. He kept good wines, of course.'

'I'd like to see them.'

Gefray didn't argue. He took a key from a hook on the wall and gestured to the door.

The cellar was off the living room, down a few stone steps close to the fireplace. It was neat and clean, with the wine racks along one wall. Pel moved along them, noticing the names. To his surprise, because he had been expecting them, there were none of the names he had found at Arri's cottage.

He was silent and thoughtful as they returned to the salon.

'Had Barclay ever received visits from other men? Men you know about. Men who didn't arrive when you were in bed with the girl. Men you let in.'

Gefray was flushing. 'Not normally. But there was a visit from a man about a month ago. Late in the evening.'

'What did he want?'

'I don't know.'

'Didn't you hear anything?'

'He was careful to shut the door. But he seemed angry.'

'Did you hear his name?'

'No. Monsieur Barclay received a telephone call, then he told me the man was coming and that I was to let him in and go to bed. It was late.'

'So you went to bed?'

'Yes.'

'And you've no idea what the visit was about?'

'I got the impression that the man was a colleague of Monsieur Barclay and that he had some sort of business disagreement to discuss. I heard him say "What are you up to, Claude?" '

'That's all?'

'No. Then he said "You'll not get away with it." '

It didn't sound like a terrorist kidnap organisation. Terrorists didn't make a habit of warning first.

'No other visits?'

'None I know about.' Gefray frowned. 'There were letters, though.'

'What sort of letters?'

'Some of them seemed to worry Monsieur Barclay?' 'Blackmail letters perhaps?'

'I suppose they could have been.'

Could it have been a jilted woman, Pel wondered. But a woman could hardly have done the kidnapping on her own and they knew several men had been involved. Even a jilted girl could usually round up a few friends, though – brothers or assorted cousins – to grab a wayward boyfriend, imprison him, threaten him, blackmail him, beat him up even, to let it be known her affections were not to be trifled with. Pel knew all about that sort of thing. As a young cop he had once spent a whole week using unfamiliar bars because a girl he had dropped rather too suddenly had threatened to set her family on him.

It was all very puzzling. For some reason Arri's murder seemed to be connected to Barclay's disappearance. But why? Were they involved in something together? Did Barclay get rid of Arri because he was troublesome? It didn't seem so. 'Well done, Jules,' he had said. 'Always the good sergeant.' That sounded approving. But could it have been to give Arri a sense of false security? After all, hadn't Delilah made love to Samson before cutting off his hair? Hadn't Judas kissed Christ to identify him to his enemies? Hadn't Ney sworn his loyalty to the throne before going over to Napoleon? History was full of treacheries.

If that were the case then, had Barclay killed Arri and staged his own kidnapping to divert suspicion? But, if that were so, *why* had he removed Arri from the scene? Could Arri be some part of the terrorist scene? It didn't seem to make much sense.

thirteen

Suddenly they began to make headway – in both the Arri and the Barclay cases.

'Pomereu's found a farmer,' Darcy told Pel, 'who saw what might well have been some sort of rehearsal for the kidnapping. He was driving cattle on a hill out towards Villers-Chenaudin when he noticed several cars on the road below him. It must have been interesting because it seems he lost one of his cows among the trees.'

As usual, the report was coming over the top of a bock of beer in the Bar Transvaal.

'They were going through a set of movements that seem to have been the same as the ones Jacqueline Duhamel saw when Barclay was snatched. There was even a motor cyclist who set the thing going. We're trying to find out more but we already know one of the cars was a yellow Passat. We've also found a type who could have known Ennaert's Citroën was in its garage the night it was needed. In fact, there could be a whole bunch of them. It's a nosey neighbourhood.'

The habits of Ennaert and his girl friends were well known, it seemed, and everybody in the street, even in the bar opposite, seemed to know what went on, though none of them seemed to deserve a second glance except a man called Henri Journais.

'He was in the army,' Darcy said.

'179th Regiment?'

Darcy shrugged. 'His neighbours think he knows all about karate, and, what's more, he seems to be tall enough to drive a car with the seat pushed right back. He's done his time in the army but he worked for a while with a security firm until the job fell through. Now nobody's quite sure what he does.'

'Have you brought him in?'

'No. He's disappeared with his wife. The neighbours think he's gone to Blois to do some fishing in the Loire. I've got the uniformed boys here to keep an eye on his apartment and asked Blois to pick him up if they spot him. But you know what it'll be like there. Give a Frenchman a fine day and he'll have his rod over the nearest stretch of river before you can breathe.'

That evening, Darcy was on the telephone to say they'd taken another step forward.

'We've found the owner of the yellow Passat,' he said. 'A Madame Danton-Criot. Dominique Danton-Criot. She has a big house near Vallefrie. She says the car was parked in the drive overnight with the keys in it, and the gates were left open, and it had disappeared when she went out to it the next morning. It was found the same evening at Arbaçay, the next village.'

'Who found it?'

'She did. She was driving through Arbaçay in another of her cars – she seems to have three – and there it was. In the square. She had someone with her, who took over the car she was driving and she simply got in the Passat and drove it away. It was unlocked and the keys were on a shelf under the dashboard.'

'Did she report it?'

'No. It was undamaged and nothing was missing, so she decided it had been taken by kids who'd been drinking in Vallefrie.'

Pel frowned. 'But it wasn't kids, was it?' he said slowly. 'It was somebody who used the car to rehearse a kidnapping. This Madame Danton: Has Lamiel seen her?'

'Yes, Patron. He seemed very happy to accept her word.' Darcy chuckled. 'I think he was influenced a bit by the way she looked.'

'How did she look?'

'Well, you've seen Brigitte Bardot. And Sophia Loren. Maybe even Marie-France Pisier. She's a bit like all three. Only better.'

Pel frowned. 'What in God's name are you trying to say?'

'She was one of the most beautiful women I've ever seen, Patron. Not young any more, but then neither am I. I can't think how I've never managed to meet her. As tall as me. Superb figure. Dark hair and the most enormous blue eyes I've ever seen. She managed to project considerable voltage into the occasion.'

Pel gave a contemptuous sniff. 'I think you should go home and take a cold bath.'

Darcy chuckled. 'A little sex is what makes the flowers grow. Cops always have dreams about damsels.'

'Some cops just have bad feet. Who is she?'

'I don't know, Patron. I've never seen her before and apparently neither has anyone else.'

'Wealthy?'

'Judging by her house, yes. Manoir de Varas it's called. Near to Vallefrie.'

'Which is where?'

'Next village to Arbaçay. It's a big house. Long drive. Outbuildings. Stables. It's even got a couple of statues in front. You can smell money.'

Pel frowned. 'What does she do for a living? Is she a female gangster? Only gangsters can afford that sort of set-up.'

'Nothing known either in Arbaçay *or* Vallefrie. I made a point of asking. Apparently she took the place over about five years ago.'

'Don't they know *anything* about her?'

'She doesn't trade in the villages.'

'She sounds as if you'd be out of your league.'

Darcy laughed. 'With her, maybe. But not with the girl who drove the car. She'd do me any time. Dark-haired, petite, deux jolies lolos, figure like a gazelle. Patron, I've found that beautiful women don't normally have beautiful companions, in case they draw attention away from themselves. But this one has, and the companion comes a good second to the boss. Lamiel was swept off his feet. All apologies and promises not to trouble them again.'

Pel frowned. 'What about *Monsieur* Danton-Criot? Is there one?'

Darcy paused. 'We asked. Seems he's a financier of some sort. Films. That sort of thing. Spends three-quarters of the year abroad. In America.'

'So does she have boy-friends? Beautiful women usually have to fight them off.'

Darcy laughed. 'I wouldn't mind being one, Patron,' he said.

'That's not the point,' Pel said coldly. 'Was Barclay one?'

Sitting at his desk, insulated from all the tension, Nosjean studied his notes. Before him was a list of names – the cast of characters in the investigation in which he was involved: the Rumanian, Cubescu, who had sold Chevrier, the fabric designer, what was believed to be a Rembrandt, but wasn't. Riault, the lawyer who sold dubious paintings on the side. Jean-Philippe Roth, a gallery owner who was honest most of the time but was by no means above encouraging people, without using so many words, to believe that the paintings they bought from him were more valuable than their prices suggested. There was Vacchi, who liked to project his image with the works of art he bought. And Ugo Luca who, whatever his wife claimed, was a painter as well as an art restorer, and had worked for all the others at some time or other. It was Nosjean's opinion that he could take any old painting out of any old attic and, according to the subject, make it into a Rembrandt or a Cézanne or a Utrillo or a Vlaminck.

Then, of course, there was an eighty-nine year old man called Solecin who claimed, quite falsely, to have been the curator of an art museum and was prepared to write provenances for pictures for money – provenances which, in the absence of an authentication, were a great help in increasing the value of the works in question.

Somewhere in the background there also had to be an organiser. So who was it? Wondering if other police forces had come up with similar cases, Nosjean got in touch with a few and found, not entirely to his surprise, that there had indeed been other instances. There was a Degas, a couple of Gauguins, several Toulouse Lautrec chalk sketches and a number of Cézannes. They had all changed hands some time before, however, and it was going to be difficult to trace them back. But then he came across a businessman called Moncy who had come into possession of a Utrillo. With it went an authentication written on the back of a photograph of the painting and signed by Matisse, who was a contemporary. Since Utrillo had always been a good target for forgers because at times he couldn't tell his own work from a copy, Moncy had decided to investigate a little further and had sent the photograph with the authentication to a handwriting expert, together with a photograph of a genuine letter written by Matisse.

A second authentication signed by – guess who! – that same professor of Fine Art, Yves-Pol Solecin, made the Matisse authentication very suspicious and, finding Moncy's address, Nosjean went to see him. He wasn't prepared to stand up in court because the painting had been a gift but he enjoyed art and was willing to help Nosjean, and promptly put him on to a friend of his who had acquired an early Renoir, authenticated this time by a letter apparently written by Arline Charigot, who had married the artist and lived with him happily for the rest of her life. Since this was also accompanied by an authentication from Yves-Pol Solecin, however, Nosjean assumed it wasn't worth the paper it was written on.

'It's obvious what they're doing,' Mijo Lehmann said as she and Nosjean clutched each other that night in the big bed in her flat. 'They're choosing paintings that are easy to copy.'

'Easy?' To Nosjean, for whom painting a door was difficult, the meaning wasn't clear, and Mijo paused long enough to nuzzle his ear with her lips.

'Impressionists, most of them,' she explained. 'And all painters with a heavy style of laying on colour. Dégas, for instance. Not too difficult so long as you can produce his special blue. Gauguin. His Tahitian studies wouldn't be hard to produce. Vlaminck. Van Gogh. All that whirly paint.'

They were a little preoccupied for a while but when they resurfaced she went on enthusiastically. 'Manet, no,' she said. 'Toulouse Lautrec? Very definitely. Especially his cartoons and chalk drawings. I once had copies of *A First Communion* and *Riding to the Bois* knocked off for me in a couple of hours by an art student as a present. With a letter from Yvette Guilbert, who was a friend of Lautrec's, you'd have provenance enough.'

Nosjean held her tight. He was beginning to see himself directed to Paris to run the art fraud squad.

The following morning Nosjean was at his desk pondering on what Mijo had said when the telephone rang. It was Moncy, the man with the fake Utrillo.

'My expert took about two minutes to compare the handwriting,' he announced. 'He said it was impossible that the same hand could have written both letters. The authentication was a deliberate fraud.'

'Where did you get the picture?'

'It was given to me by a business acquaintance. He collects pictures. I put some work his way and he probably felt grateful.'

'An odd way of showing his gratitude – giving you a dud picture.'

'He likes to pretend he knows a lot about it and he probably thinks I don't.'

'Who was it?'

'Man called Vacchi.'

'I thought it might be. I'd like to talk to your handwriting expert. Who is he?'

'Name of De Lavigny. Lives at Auxerre.'

It took Nosjean no more than a couple of hours to reach De Lavigny. He was a small dark intense man but he had a relaxed manner that belied his appearance.

'Someone had tried to copy Matisse's handwriting,' he said. 'But forging isn't that easy and under a magnifying glass it didn't even compare with the real thing. Mind you, they'd done their homework. The picture's a view of a bridge under a sky of racing storm clouds and it's signed Maurice U Valadon, which was how Utrillo signed himself in the early days. Also, the message's addressed to him at the Rue du Poteau, Montmartre, where his mother lived. But anybody could look all that up in a book about him, so it doesn't really have much value.'

By this time, Nosjean was deeply involved and was very much intrigued to learn that the lines he had established all seemed to lead firmly back to Raoul Riault. Which, in a way, brought him back to Claude Barclay's Vlaminck, which had started it all when it had been stolen under the noses of visitors at the opening of the Hôtel du Grand Cerf at Lorne.

The manager of the hotel wasn't so easily convinced. 'If Monsieur Barclay says it's genuine', he said with a sniff, 'then as far as I'm concerned, it *is* genuine.'

He seemed to regard policemen making enquiries as if they were asking for free meals in his best dining room, and the drink he gave Nosjean was in a glass so small it looked like the bulb of a thermometer.

'If you have any doubt, you'd better enquire at the Collège Privé de l'Est,' he suggested. 'Monsieur Barclay gave *them* a picture and I'm sure that, with the experts they have on their staff, *they* wouldn't make a mistake.'

When he checked on the background of the staff of the college, however, Nosjean wasn't so sure. The man who taught art – very essential for the indulged sons and daughters of wealthy fathers, who couldn't be relied on to get a qualification in anything more technical – was simply a teacher of art with a minor qualification from the Ecole des Arts Décoratifs in Paris and no more. It seemed it might be worth a visit to the college, as the manager of the Grand Cerf had suggested.

The college was a splendid place deep in the countryside near Chaux. It was an old manor house covered with ivy, on to which a new complex of matching buildings – designed by Deputy Barclay – had been added with a great deal of taste. Several smartly-dressed young ladies were exercising horses in a paddock alongside the drive, watched by a groom. It was that sort of college.

Outside the entrance was an expensive-looking Porsche whose windscreen was being wiped by a ravishing blonde who looked like Catherine Deneuve and immediately made Nosjean wonder if he'd been too precipitate in finally giving his heart to Mijo Lehmann. As he halted his car, she turned towards him with a smile that made his heart skid about under his shirt like aspic on a hot plate.

'Hello,' she said. 'I'm Francie Lejaune. I run the office. Can I help you?'

Francie Lejaune didn't seem to do much work and Nosjean could only assume her duties were chiefly to put at ease parents – especially fathers – who called to see their children at work and play. She was chattily amusing, making Nosjean, who blushed easily when faced with beautiful women, completely at ease. She seemed able to talk about anything without really having a lot of knowledge about anything, and Nosjean wondered if she were the product of some sort of charm school.

The college principal, a tall distinguished man with a shock of white hair, seemed proud of her. 'Francie's not a typist,' he admitted. 'Though she can type a little. But she's such an asset in that she puts people entirely at their ease. She turned up a week or two ago and said she'd worked for Monsieur Barclay, and that seemed good enough for us, because he's a director of the college and has a splendid reputation. We decided to take a chance and Francie turned out to be perfect for the job. She has taste, a great ability to please people and, as I'm sure you've observed – a great natural beauty.'

Though Nosjean found the delectable Francie a fascinating subject, she wasn't the reason for his visit and he worked the conversation round to the subject of the Vlaminck which had first started his enquiries.

The principal shrugged. 'Well, I've heard that Professor Grandjean's expressed doubts about it,' he admitted. '*We* have none, of course.'

Nosjean was about to say it might be better if they had when the principal gestured. 'Monsieur Barclay's word was good enough for us,' he said.

'*He* assessed it?'

'He sold it.'

'He *sold* it? I thought it was his.'

'It was until we bought it. People thought it was still his but, in fact, it belongs to the college. He owns a large share of the place and was keen to improve it. We felt the same way. We consider we got a very valuable painting very cheaply.'

'How much was paid for it?'

'Five hundred thousand francs. We have large funds at our disposal. Many well-known people back us, including Claude Barclay himself, of course.' The principal paused. 'We sincerely hope that he'll be found unharmed.'

Nosjean murmured his agreement but he was intrigued and pushed on. 'Who organised the sale?' he asked.

'The college bursar. He's an old army friend of Monsieur Barclay. An excellent man.'

'Do you have other paintings?'

'Oh, yes. We have another Vlaminck, for instance, two Van Goghs, a Cézanne.'

Nothing difficult, Nosjean noticed, and he knew Mijo Lehmann would have agreed.

'This Vlaminck,' he said. 'The disputed one. When Monsieur Barclay sold it, he was, in fact, in a way selling it to himself, wasn't he? Transferring it from one collection in which he had an interest to another of the same nature.'

'Not quite that.' The principal smiled. 'The collection at his home is personal. This one is owned by the college.'

'But the money that was paid for it went into Monsieur Barclay's private account?'

'But of course.'

'Did you have an expert examine it when you bought it?'

'It wasn't necessary. Monsieur Barclay produced provenance and we accepted his word. As we did with the Utrillo.'

'Which Utrillo?'

'The *Narrow Street in Montmartre*. It's hanging in the great hall. You must look at it as you leave.'

'Did Monsieur Barclay sell you *that*, too?'

'Yes.'

'How much?'

'The same price.'

Which, Nosjean thought, made a cool million francs. And if neither of the pictures was genuine and they were worth only around a thousand francs for the two – five hundred was what Mijo Lehmann had suggested might be reasonable for a fake – that made a clear profit of nine hundred and ninety-nine thousand!

As Nosjean moved forward, so did Lagé, and the following day, armed with one of the plates from Arri's cottage, he headed down the motorway towards Beaune, where he turned off for Montluçon and finally Limoges. He was back the same evening, bursting with excitement.

'Patron,' he said. 'That china! It was ordered by Barclay!'

'Barclay!' Pel sat up sharply. What in God's name had they got into?

'The order was for four hundred pieces,' Lagé said. 'Varying colours. Blue, pink, green, yellow and red. All trimmed with gilt.'

'Four hundred pieces!' Pel stared. 'In the name of God, what would he want with four hundred pieces?'

fourteen

The Chief's attitude to the problem was unambiguous. He simply tossed it back at Pel. 'Handle it in your own way,' he said. He was growing tired of intrigue.

'What about Lamiel?' Pel asked.

'Well, it could sour relations a bit there,' the Chief admitted. 'But it's a case of Man proposes, God disposes.'

'Which', Pel agreed, 'is a fair distribution of effort.'

'And since he tells you nothing, it would seem très fairplay if you told *him* nothing.'

The Chief had great faith in Pel's ability and he liked to see the crime statistics in his favour. If Pel sorted out one or both cases, that was all to the good and would look splendid under 'Crimes solved'. Self-interest was wrestling with the need to co-operate with Paris, and self-interest was winning hands down. But Pel was satisfied. Though the Chief's logic seemed to need overhauling by a man with a full set of tools, it was good enough for him.

As polling day in the election drew nearer the newspapers began to whip up the details of the Barclay kidnapping again. On one side there was sympathy for the government for losing one of its greatest assets, the handsome, clever, silver-tongued Claude Barclay of the sonorous speeches. At the other extreme there were suggestions that the kidnapping was because Barclay had got himself into trouble and been removed by 'friends'. There had been a rash of so-called financiers disappearing in recent years, so it wasn't all that unbelievable.

France Soir was now on yet another tack and had produced a picture showing Barclay in a bathing costume with his arm round a girl, which it claimed was a repudiation of the suggestion that had been made by *La Torche* that the unmarried Minister was a homosexual. There was beginning now to be a feeling that somewhere behind the disappearance there must be a scandal of some sort and Paris was buzzing with ideas, and the magazine, *L'Heure,* had even dug out the fact that in his youth Barclay had made a habit of frequenting the Marseilles brothels. It was not all that exciting and the French, of all people, were unlikely to be bothered by such a story. Many men were known to have visited brothels in their unmarried youth, though it was not really considered the thing for a junior minister, who was a friend of the Premier, to have done and Barclay's lawyers had applied for an injunction to prevent the sale of any copies of the magazine containing the story.

The government seemed to be making some effort, in fact, in the face of the disaster of Barclay's disappearance and the growing suspicion that he'd been up to something fishy, to rescue a little of its reputation. It was clearly embarrassed and had put it out that his disappearance was simply that he had probably gone abroad to invest money in foreign holdings. The idea rebounded a little because *Le Monde* immediately asked why a junior minister would *wish* to invest abroad. Besides, it asked, where had Barclay acquired such large sums of money – the sum of several million francs had been mentioned – and, come to that, were his investments of greater importance than the people of Yorinne whom he represented and who had a right to expect him to be around at election time?

Pel read the stories carefully, intrigued by the implications. For a while he sat thinking, then he sent Didier Darras to borrow the file on Barclay. There were several floating round the Hôtel de Police by this time and Darcy was not unwilling to lend his for a while.

Pel studied it, making notes on a pad by his elbow. It was fairly complete and the main details leapt out at him.

Claude Barclay. Under-Minister for Health. Politician, architect, art enthusiast, worker for charity. Born Mulhouse, Department of Haut-Rhin. Educated locally and at University of Nancy. Served as sous-lieutenant, Indo-China. Croix de Guerre, 1954. Prisoner of war but escaped. Completed education University of Aix-Marseilles, 1960-1963. Articled with Thomas-Georges Giraud, architect, of Toulon,1971-1974. Entered politics 1975: elected for district of Yorinne, Department of Rhone, 1976. Unmarried. Parents dead.

When he'd finished, he sent the file back and called Claudie Darel in. She arrived, spruce and spotless and looking like a young Mireille Mathieu.

'Claudie, look up Barclay,' he said.

'What am I looking for, Patron?'

'I don't know. But I suspect there's something. It's going to be difficult, so take your time. There seems to be a blank in his life. After he left school he went into the army and did well at Dien Bien Phu. But when he came out of the army, there seems to be a gap when we don't know what he's doing. There's a lot of detail, but for seven years between 1963 and 1971 we know nothing of him.'

As Claudie disappeared, Didier put his head round the door. 'Sous-Brigadier Foulet from Valoreille on the telephone, sir.'

Sous-Brigadier Foulet had a soft voice and sounded like a conspirator. 'Sir,' he said. 'I've just had a couple of seventeen-year-old kids in to see me. Name of Léon Paty and Colette Rousseau. They say they overheard Arri talking with someone outside his cottage around the time he disappeared.'

'What did he say?'

'It doesn't appear to amount to anything at all really. I was all for gettting rid of them because the boy's not the brightest. Come to that, neither is the girl. But I thought I'd better let you know.'

'Where are they now?'

'They're sitting on a bench in my office.'

'Keep them there I'll be out in less than an hour.'

Snatching up notebook and pencil and enough cigarettes to give lung cancer to the whole province, just in case he was delayed somewhere and couldn't get to a tabac, Pel called for Claudie Darel.

'Leave what you're doing,' he said. 'The sous-brigadier at Valoreille's got a couple of kids wanting to talk to us. One of them's a girl, so you'd better come with me.'

The two youngsters sat opposite Sous-Brigadier Foulet's desk. Pel eyed them quietly, and Sous-Brigadier Foulet reached out and gave Léon Paty's shoulder a shove. The boy woke up with a start. He had a portable radio beside him, with a wire leading to headphones which hung round his neck.

'We didn't come forward before', he said, 'because we didn't see the notice in the papers. We don't read the papers. We heard something. Outside Monsieur Arri's house.' He looked at the girl. 'We were in the alley just alongside. It was dark.'

'Which is why you were there, I suppose?'

Paty shifted uncomfortably and the girl gave an embarrassed giggle. 'Yes, Monsieur. There aren't many places where you can be alone.'

'Go on.'

'Two men stopped outside the house. I recognised Monsieur Arri's voice. I sometimes work at the garage at weekends and I'd often served him petrol. I couldn't see who was with him because we kept back in the shadows.'

'Of course.'

'They came from down the street somewhere. I heard Monsieur Arri say "He wouldn't do that." '

'Do what? Did he say?'

'No, Monsieur. He just said "He wouldn't do that". And the other man said "But he *did* do it". Then Monsieur Arri said "Are you sure?" And the other man said "Yes" and Monsieur Arri said "I'll ask him". Then the other man said "You'd better not".'

'Is that all?'

'Yes, Monsieur. It's not much, is it?'

'It helps. What happened then?'

'Nothing. Monsieur Arri went into his house and we heard the other man walk away. Then a car started up and we saw lights come on and a car went down the street past us. It was small. Something like a Citroën Visa. That size.' Paty frowned and the girl's hand slipped into his. 'Will there be a reward?' he asked.

Pel's eyebrows shot up. 'You were expecting one, maybe?'

Paty blushed. 'We thought it would be useful. We'd like to get married.'

Pel gazed at the two earnest young faces. 'I'd advise you to wait a little while, mon brave,' he suggested.

Climbing into the car again to return to the Hôtel de Police, Pel sat silently as Claudie let in the clutch. The following night, as they now knew, Arri had turned up at Barclay's house at Courtois where Madame Boileau had seen him. Had he gone, not to give something to Barclay, but to tell him something, to warn him? Was Barclay the man who was being threatened? It began to seem likely.

So why *had* Arri gone to Barclay's house? Pel remembered Yves Pasquier's words. 'I'm on your side. No matter what they say about you, I'm on your side.' That was loyalty, undisguised and unqualified. Had Arri felt the same about Barclay? Barclay had saved his life, and had later rescued him when he was on his uppers by finding him a job – this mysterious job they were still trying to identify – and probably he had never forgotten it. Whatever it was that Barclay was up to, had Arri's loyalty remained with him and had he attempted to warn him of the kidnap attempt, only to lose his own life?

It seemed to slot together.

The following morning, there was a report on the radio of a bomb exploding at Saint-Etienne, the responsibility claimed by some Arab organisation Pel had never heard of. Saint-Etienne could be considered important because it was an arms manufacturing town and it was a great deal nearer to home than Paris, and he could well imagine Lamiel being uptight about it.

Sure enough, when he arrived at the Hôtel de Police he found himself in the middle of a panic. As he entered, he met Darcy heading for the lecture room Lamiel was using for his talks.

'Some old dear's reported men going in and out of a house at 47, Rue des Closeries, near the Industrial Zone,' he said as he shot past.

Pel knew the Rue des Closeries. He even knew Number 47.

'One of them had a gun, she said,' Darcy went on. 'We've all been called in. Briefing in five minutes. Everybody's got to attend. Even young Darras.'

'What about me?'

Darcy managed a grin. 'I dare say he wouldn't say no this time, Patron,' he agreed.

In the lecture room, Lamiel was deep in conversation with Thomas and as soon as they separated Darcy spoke up.

'I know this address we have,' he said. 'It's where Taddeus Kiczmyrczik's sister lives.'

Lamiel clearly wasn't impressed. 'He's a dissident,' he rapped.

'He's always been a dissident,' Darcy agreed. 'Give him exactly what he wants and he'd still be a dissident.'

'This isn't a laughing matter,' Lamiel snapped.

'I'm not laughing,' Darcy snapped back.

'Then don't treat it lightly. Who're the people who visit him?'

'Other men like him. I've given you their names. But he also surrounds himself with anybody who has a grievance. Anti-Bomb people. Anti-government people. Anti-left people. Preserve the countryside people. Anti-vivisectionists. Take your pick. Half the time they don't have a thing in common beyond the fact that they're anti.'

'How do you know there aren't young activists among them? – younger terrorists?'

'I don't. I'm guessing from long experience.'

Lamiel turned to Thomas. 'We'll pick them up,' he said. 'Are they dangerous?' he asked Darcy.

'Of course they aren't.'

'We'll take no chances. Get going, Thomas. You know what to do.'

The telephone exchange set up in the basement of the Hôtel de Police was fully manned and Lamiel's men were in the house next door to Number 47, Rue des Closeries. The owners were a little startled but had been warned to behave as normally as possible and were busy making coffee for everybody. They had no idea what was going on but they suspected that the old man who visited next door had been up to his tricks again. He was always causing trouble in one way or another, always being run in for acting the goat, and they could only suppose that it was the mixture as before.

There were more men in the houses opposite and a disgusted Darcy was standing in the doorway of a laundrette listening to his personal radio. He had tried to get out of taking part in the raid but he had been unable to and was now watching the windows of Number 47. As he concentrated the owner of the laundrette appeared. She was fat and hostile.

'Those citizen band things should be banned,' she said, indicating Darcy's radio.

'It's not a citizen band thing,' Darcy said.

'Well, whatever it is, they affect the television.' She indicated the set placed above the washing machines for the entertainment of her customers.

Darcy smiled. 'They also have a nasty effect on people,' he said cheerfully. 'They do things to their chromosomes. Especially women. Makes them lose interest in sex.'

The woman stared at him and, not sure whether to believe him, decided to play safe and backed away.

Upstairs in the house next to Number 47, Lamiel's men had clamped microphones to the adjoining walls and were sitting over their equipment, their faces blank, headphones on, listening.

'I think there are four of them', one of them was saying. 'And a woman.'

Lamiel frowned. 'Get Darcy.'

A message on his radio brought Darcy to the back door of the house.

'There are four there now', Lamiel said. 'And a woman.'

'That's normal enough. She lives there. She's Kiczmyrczik's sister.'

'How do we know it isn't the two old types you mentioned joined by two younger ones and a woman activist?'

'We don't,' Darcy said. 'That's what *you* say. But I'll go along with it.'

'You're not being very helpful.'

'I'm doing exactly as I'm told.'

'The television's on.' The voice came in a flat monotone from the back of the room. 'It's the news.'

'They're trying to find out if anything's happened,' Lamiel said. 'Or else it's to drown their voices.'

Perhaps, Darcy thought, they were just hoping to learn that the Russians had taken over. Or the Fascists. Or the Liberals. Or the Social Democrats. Or the Wets. Or the Dries. Or the Hawks. Or the Doves. It wouldn't matter much to Kiczmyrczik. Perhaps they were just wanting to know what had won the 2.30.

On the other hand, with a bomb in Paris and another in Saint-Etienne – that one doubtless a protest against the manufacture of arms, or the sale of arms to the wrong people, or the non-sale of arms to those the makers of the bomb considered the right people – he could see why Lamiel was nervous and not prepared to take any chances. And if Kiczmyrczik had been stupid enough to introduce a weapon into his sister's house at this highly sensitive moment, then he deserved all he got. Kiczmyrczik had never been popular with the police and Darcy could well imagine him, if he had a weapon, being a great deal less popular.

Lamiel listened to the reports. He seemed to be on edge and looked as if he hadn't slept for some time, his mouth tight, his face drawn, his eyes ringed with shadow. Eventually, it seemed he could stand it no longer, as if the tension had built up so much he would burst if he didn't do something to relieve it.

'We're going in,' he said.

Darcy eyed the equipment they had stacked up. The rifles, revolvers, stun grenades and smoke bombs. It would be God help Kiczmyrczik if that lot started going off, he decided, and he tried to put in a word of caution.

'You won't need all those,' he said.

'We usually do.'

Darcy looked alarmed. 'For the love of God,' he said, 'don't start shooting unless they shoot first.'

'Why not?'

'They're old men. You might find you've made a mistake and they might drop dead.'

Lamiel gave him a contemptuous look, the look of the ruthless Paris operator for the weak-minded provincial. 'We'll do it whichever way we have to,' he announced. Nevertheless, he made a point of telling Thomas not to shoot first.

As they left, Darcy sat down at the kitchen table and waited. For a long time there was silence.

'What's happening?' the owner of the house asked.

Darcy shrugged. 'I think', he said, 'that somebody's trying to commit career suicide.'

As they waited, almost holding their breath, there was a sudden outbreak of shouting, a couple of shots and a dull thud.

'Mother of God!' Darcy said, jumping up and heading for the street.

He arrived just in time to see one of Lamiel's men burst out of the house next door. 'We've got them,' he announced as Lamiel appeared round the corner.

He was followed by billowing clouds of smoke, then an elderly woman and four elderly men appeared, all looking dazed, their hands in the air, coughing and spluttering, the last one, Kiczmyrczik, cursing bitterly. Behind them came two more of Lamiel's men holding machine pistols and wearing gas masks.

Lamiel stepped forward. 'What were they doing?' he demanded.

The men with the machine pistols looked puzzled. 'Playing cards,' one of them said.

'What in God's name was the shooting then?'

'One of them reached under the table. Georges thought he'd got a gun there and fired a couple of rounds into the ceiling.'

'*Was* there a gun?'

'No. Just a bottle of brandy.'

'A gun was seen being carried in.'

The man with the machine pistol pulled a face. 'It wasn't a gun. It was a metal rod for a curtain runner. They put it up, hung the curtains, got out the brandy bottle and started playing piquet.'

Darcy was hardly able to contain his delight. He had suffered a lot at the hands of Lamiel.

'Old revolutionaries nobody takes any notice of,' he crowed to Pel. 'Old men dead as mutton. Lamiel's gone to Paris. I think he's none too keen to show his face at the moment. Thomas has gone up there, too, and there are only their stooges left here at the moment, sitting around with their thumbs in their bums, wondering what to do.'

It was worth celebrating with a beer at the Bar Transvaal.

When Pel returned to his office, Lagé was waiting in the sergeants' room with a short thickset man who was screwing his cap in his hands.

'Jean Clenot, Patron,' he said. 'He's a taxi driver. He's just come in.'

'And?'

'He's been away for a few days and just returned. He's heard of our enquiries and he thinks he picked up our friend, Jules Arri, one evening just off the Rue de la Liberté.'

Pel sat up. 'He did *what!*'

'Seven-thirty, he says, so it must have been just after he'd parked his car in the Place de la Liberation.'

Pel pushed a chair forward and Clenot sat nervously. Noticing his fingers were stained yellow, Pel pushed forward a packet of Gauloises. 'Smoke?'

Clenot took one gratefully and lit up. Pel followed him, glad of an excuse.

'Go on,' he said. 'Inform me.'

'Well,' Clenot said. 'I saw this photograph of this guy in the newspaper and I decided it was this type I picked up last month.'

'Where did you pick him up?'

'On the Rue de Bourg. Just off the Rue de la Liberté. He was waiting and waved me down.'

'Where did you take him?'

'Out Arbaçay way.'

'You're sure of this?'

'Dead sure. It was a good long drive and worth a bit. You remember that sort of thing. He paid and gave me this good tip.'

'Did he mention how he was getting back?'

'He said he'd be able to get a lift. I asked him if it was where he lived and if his car had broken down. He said, no, he worked out that way and normally was picked up but that night this type who picked him up hadn't been able to make it. I got the impression he did the journey regularly and was going to work or something.'

'Where did you drop him?'

'Outside Arbaçay.'

'Where exactly?'

'About five hundred metres outside the village.'

'This side?'

'No. The other. The Vallefrie side.'

'No address?'

'No. I asked him what address he wanted and he said, "No address. I'll tell you when to stop". He didn't have much to say and eventually he said "Stop". So I did. He paid me and I turned round and set off back.'

'Did you see where he went?'

'No. He just set off walking from Arbaçay to Vallefrie. He was still walking when I turned the corner and lost him.'

'How was he dressed?'

Clenot shrugged. 'Normal. He wore this suit. You know – not smart, but clean and tidy. Tie. He was well shaved. In fact, he looked as if he'd only recently shaved.'

'As if he were going to work? At some place where he was expected to look clean and reasonably smart?'

'I suppose so. I didn't think of it at the time but, yes, I reckon that's how he was.'

'And he gave no hint of where he was going?'

'None at all.'

When Clenot had gone, Pel sat staring at his blotter until Lagé came back after showing the taxi driver out.

'Vallefrie,' he said slowly. 'Know it, Lagé?'

'Sure, Patron. I've been there often.'

'Anything special about it?'

'Not that I know.'

'How about hotels or restaurants?'

'There's just the Hôtel de la Poste. Nothing special. Used to be good but it changed hands and they say the grub's terrible now.'

'Nothing else? Nothing classy?'

'Nothing I know of, Patron.'

'But Arri was going out there. Regularly, that type said. What was he doing then? Moonlighting? Working in a restaurant we don't know about? Is that where those wine bottles at his house came from?' Pel frowned. 'Somewhere between Arbaçay and Vallefrie, Clenot said.' He began stuffing cigarettes into his pocket. 'Perhaps we should go and have a look, Lagé. We might find something interesting.'

The road between Arbaçay and Vallefrie was long and straight and ran between extensive woods on either side for a matter of eight or nine kilometres. There were no villages in between, hardly a house in fact. Just an occasional farm, shabby-looking and ramshackle because it didn't seem to be good farming country. They didn't see many people. Just an old woman on a bicycle with a couple of loaves stuck into her saddle pannier. A symbol of France, Pel decided. If France ever had a new coat of arms, it would be crossed baguettes with a ficelle rampant and the motto 'Let them eat bread'.

Eventually, Lagé stopped the car and gestured. Set at the end of a short sanded drive among the trees were a set of gates, large, decorative, cast-iron gates, secured with a heavy padlock, with the sign alongside them 'Manoir de Varas' and underneath another sign 'Propriété privée'. The grounds seemed to be surrounded by a double-strand barbed wire fence and there were notices every fifty yards, 'Propriété privée', 'Chasse gardée' and warnings that trespassers would be prosecuted.

'They seem to like their privacy, Patron,' Lagé observed dryly. Vallefrie lay in the fold of the hills, a small village clustered round a church with an overdecorated tower and a tall spire, set at the side of a dusty village square where half a dozen men were playing boules, watched by several children and two old women. Lagé halted the car and they produced a photograph of Arri. None of the men playing boules had ever seen him before. Nor had the old women. The children insisted on getting in on the act, too, but they also had never seen Arri. They tried the three bars, the one hotel the village boasted, and finally the police station. The sous-brigadier in charge, like everyone else, had never seen Arri but he promised to show the picture around and let them know if anything turned up.

'You'd better let that lot at Arbaçay have one as well,' he said to Lagé. 'But you'd better mark it in big letters. They're a bit slow on the uptake.'

'Well,' Pel said, as they climbed back into the car, 'it doesn't look as if Arri worked *there*. If he had, someone would surely remember him. He'd apparently been doing the job for around five years and if he'd been doing it in Vallefrie, he'd have been noticed. Let's try Arbaçay.'

Arbaçay was almost a copy of Vallefrie except that the church looked more careworn, and the village square, instead of being surrounded by horse chestnuts, was surrounded by clubbed acacias. The result was the same. Nobody had ever noticed Arri.

'Have you tried Vallefrie?' the sous-brigadier in charge asked. 'Not that they'd notice, of course. That lot never notice anything.'

It seemed there wasn't a lot of love lost between the constabulary of the two villages.

Pel was frowning as he returned to the car. 'Well, nobody saw him in Vallefrie *or* Arbaçay,' he said. 'But he was dropped by Clenot's cab somewhere between and, according to what he told Clenot, he went nightly. He was picked up in the city and brought out here. So where did he go? If it wasn't Vallefrie and it wasn't Arbaçay it must be somewhere between. Let's have a look around.'

It took them a long time but no one at the few scattered farms had ever seen Arri.

'That only leaves the Manoir de Varas,' Pel said. 'So what could he have been doing there?'

The sous-brigadier at Vallefrie couldn't imagine. 'They keep themselves to themselves,' he said. 'They don't seem to employ anyone from the village.'

'The place's closed up at the moment. Where are they?'

The sous-brigadier shrugged. 'I heard they'd gone to the States. Someone telephoned to inform us it would be empty from the 20th of last month. We can't get in but we take a look at the gates as we pass. That's all we can do. They don't seem to expect more.'

'This Madame Danton-Criot who owns the place: where does she get her money? Do you know?'

The sous-brigadier shrugged. 'She's a bit of a mystery. But she seems to have plenty. They entertain occasionally. Cars have been seen going in there. Big ones, as though their friends have money, as I suppose they must have, to be friendly with a set-up like that. But nobody from here visits them.'

'What about food? Don't they have deliveries?'

'They've got an estate wagon. It goes into the city.'

'What about vegetables?'

'They're not supplied from here. I've heard they have a few interests in the food trade so perhaps they supply themselves from their own sources.'

'Ever been in there?'

'Never.'

'Know anything about it?'

'I've heard they've got a pitch and putt golf course, a tennis court, saunas, a squash court, a solarium, a swimming pool. They must have a lot of money.'

'What about Monsieur Danton-Criot? What does he do?'

'Nobody's ever met him. Our people have noticed a man driving in there occasionally. Other men, too. *And* women. But only as they were passing, so they never got a good look at them.'

'Families?'

'They didn't seem like families.'

'When was the last time cars were seen going in there?'

The sous-brigadier shrugged. He couldn't be certain but he thought about three weeks before. Since then the gates had been kept closed.

'Can you fix the exact day?'

The sous-brigadier couldn't but he thought it was around the time the body had been found in the woods at Suchey.

'That's odd, don't you think?' Pel asked. 'Because the body was that of a man who seemed to come regularly to this area and then vanished. I'm interested in this Madame Danton. I'd like to know who she bought the house from?'

'It belonged to the Baron de Lisé,' the sous-brigadier said. 'It was open to the public for a while but he was old and he ended up gaga and had to go into a nursing home, so the family sold the place to pay for it. He's dead now.'

'And the family?'

'Emigrated to the States. Toumelins', the estate agents, might be able to tell you something about it. I remember seeing their board outside when the place was being sold. They're in the city so you'll know them better than I do. Perhaps you could try them.'

Toumelins' didn't know a great deal.

'We only acted as local agents,' Alain Toumelin, the owner of the firm, said. 'We're not big enough to handle a place like that. It was sold through us for a firm in Paris.' He sent for files and pawed through them on his desk. 'Firm called Garniers'. They might help, though not much more than we can, I imagine. We knew everything that went on. It's owned by a Madame Danton-Criot.'

'What about Monsieur Danton?'

Toumelin shrugged. 'I never heard of Monsieur Danton.'

'So who paid the money over? There was a lot, surely.'

'Oh, sure. It was an expensive property, and they've spent a lot of money on it since. Put in tennis courts and saunas and a swimming pool and so on.'

'*Who* spent a lot of money on it?'

'Madame Danton, I suppose.'

'She must have a lot.'

Toumelin frowned and pawed among the files again. 'Come to think of it,' he said thoughtfully, 'I don't think it *was* Madame Danton who actually paid the money over. It seemed to be a consortium of some sort.'

. 'Names?'

'We have only one. A man called Dupont. Edmonde Dupont. He's a Belgian, I believe. Millionaire, I was told by Madame Danton.'

'So why did he buy it for Madame Danton?'

Toumelin shrugged. 'Well, all the cheques were signed by this Edmonde Dupont. And they were honoured all right. The money was there and it was properly paid over. From the

Banque Française du Commerce in Paris. But I was worried until it was, because I felt that Dupont wasn't his name.'

'Why?'

'Because when Madame Danton was here, she let slip the name Rykx. She called him Bernard Rykx. Twice. It made me wonder if he were hiding his identity. Naturally, I was concerned about the money, but it was properly paid over and went into the estate of the Baron de Lisé, so I never thought about it again. Perhaps at the back of my mind I thought she'd confused him with someone else. But now – well, you've started me thinking about it again.'

'So why did this Edmonde Dupont or Bernard Rykx buy the house for Madame Danton? Is she his mistress?'

Toumelin smiled. 'I wouldn't mind having her for my mistress. She's very beautiful.' He smiled again. 'But, no. I'm happily married to a small plump woman who makes me very content. I'm not serious. I don't know. It's none of our business and millionaires can afford to indulge their fancies, can't they?'

'Do you have a key?'

'Not now. We handled them, of course, and showed people round. Most of them took one look and backed off. It was in a pretty poor state. I gather it isn't any longer.'

'And this Monsieur Dupont-Rykx. Did you ever see him?'

'Only once. Madame Danton did all the inspecting.'

'What was he like?'

'Short. Squarish. A lot of curly black hair. Big moustache. Wore dark glasses all the time as if his eyes were bad.'

Or, Pel thought, because he didn't want to be recognised. It seemed a good idea to check up on Monsieur Dupont-Rykx. It might even be a good idea to check up on Madame Danton.

Returning to the Hôtel de Police, Pel telephoned the sous-brigadier at Vallefrie and Arbaçay and told them that between them he expected them to keep an eye on the Manoir de Varas.

'Discreetly,' he pointed out. 'Don't stop outside and try the gates. I just want to know when there's someone in residence. As soon as you see signs of life there, let me know.' He paused, remembering the obvious rivalry between the two places. 'And no non-co-operation,' he added. 'I expect intelligence.'

fifteen

When they returned to the Hôtel de Police, they found that Claudie Darel had taken another step forward.

'Barclay,' she said. 'I think I've found something, Patron. He seems to have been involved in a bit of dirty work in Marseilles as a student. With a girl called Denise Darnand. She was on the streets. Came from a good family but went wrong somewhere along the line. It's not in the main files. I found it in the supplementary files, which are much briefer. A man found himself in her bedroom and was approached for money.'

'Blackmail? Photographed without his trousers?'

Claudie smiled. 'It looks like it, Patron.'

Pel's eyebrows rose. 'Barclay was involved in *that?*'

Claudie shrugged. 'Well, I'm not certain, Patron. It made me wonder, when I found it wasn't in the main files – and if it *is* Barclay of course – if he somehow managed to have it extracted.' She made a gesture with her thumb and forefinger.

'Bribed some cop?'

'Or the civilian employee running the records department. It was before computers so there'd be a human element involved. Marseilles dug out the facts for me. A civilian employee by the name of Auguste Loget was sacked for passing information from police files. He was working with a blackmailer called Risse. The note in the supplementary files dealt with a student called Achille Barclay, aged nineteen, which would be the right age. There was only one entry and I could find no other reference to Achille Barclay. But it seemed interesting so I went to the Registrar of Births, Deaths and Marriages in Mulhouse, where Barclay was born. There it was, Patron: Achille Claude Barclay. If it was our Barclay, when he was questioned either he deliberately gave only one name or the cop who looked at his identity card was lazy enough to write down only one.'

'What happened? Were they charged?'

'They got away with it. The man who accused them said he'd paid over 20,000 francs for the photographs, but they'd kept the negatives and when they tried again he went to the police. The police got nowhere. No negative or camera was found and the photographs didn't even match the girl's room. The police thought they'd changed the decor and furniture. When Claude Barclay first stood for the House of Assembly it was just about the time when the civilian employee, Loget, was arrested for selling information from the files.'

'As if Barclay had dropped the "Achille" and had realised his misdemeanour could be an embarrassment to him as a politician.'

'And paid to have it removed from the files, but forgot the entry in the supplementaries.' Claudie shrugged. 'I can't be certain of any of it, though, Patron.'

The touch of pitch. Here it was again. Had Barclay got his finger in an unwholesome pie? But Marseilles was renowned not only for its bouillabaisse and vociferous fishwives. The old Phoenician city teemed with jobless immigrants, drug traffickers, white slavers, gang bosses, prostitutes, and the castaways from other countries. It had long been a crossroads of crime, and if a man wanted to get involved with under-the-counter dealings, Marseilles was just the place to find an opening.

'If Risse was Rykx,' Pel said slowly 'as he might well have been, a lot connects up.' He paused. 'I wonder what happened to the girl – Denise Darnand. Dig a bit deeper, Claudie. And while you're in touch with Marseilles, I've another job for you. I want a list of brothels and the madames who run them. The police will know them. I want the name of the most respectable and intelligent and preferably the one with the longest memory.'

Claudie looked puzzled. 'Right, Patron. And what do I do with them?'

Pel had the grace to look sheepish. 'Give them to me. I'm going down there to pay a visit.'

'Patron,' it was Darcy's voice on the telephone from the set of offices Lamiel had set up, 'we've picked up that type, Journais, who we think reported on Ennaert's car.'

'Can I see him?' Pel asked. 'He might be involved with Arri.'

'Slip down, Patron. I've got him with me now.'

Journais looked very much as Arri must have looked. He was very tall, Pel noticed immediately, tall enough to be responsible for the pushed-back seat in the Citroën used in the kidnap of Barclay. He also looked strong and seemed to possess a degree of pride in himself.

He admitted at once that he had been on the Loire fishing. He had a pension from the army, he said, and had worked for a while with a security firm, but the job had fallen through and he was now entirely dependent on his pension until he could get another job.

'Which', he added, 'isn't going to be easy at my age.'

He seemed frank and cheerful but he refused point-blank to agree that it was he who had passed on the information about Ennaert's car. 'It could have been anyone round there,' he insisted. 'Everybody knew what he got up to. When we saw him arrive on Friday with a girl and put his car away, we all knew we shouldn't be seeing him again until Monday morning. They always arrived with a box full of groceries, a few bottles of wine and a bottle of whisky. We called them Ennaert's weekends.'

'Ever meet a man called Barclay?' Darcy asked.

'The politician?' Journais shrugged. 'I've seen his picture in the paper, that's all.'

Sure, he said, he knew all about unarmed combat, because he'd been taught it in the army but he'd never met Jules Arri.

'Same background as yourself,' Pel pointed out quietly. 'Soldier, 179th Regiment.'

Did he detect a flicker of the eyes?

'I was in the Paras,' Journais said. 'We didn't have much to do with the Line regiments. We thought we were a superior lot. We were, of course.'

'Arri was at Dien Bien Phu. Were you in Indo-China during the trouble there with the Vietcong?'

'Half the French army served there at some time or other.'

'But you never met Arri or Barclay? They were both out there.'

'I wasn't at Dien Bien Phu. I'd served my time by then and I was home.'

Pel nodded. 'Karate,' he said. 'You were good at it?'

'We all were.'

'Ever heard of a blow across the throat. Something that would destroy the voice box, damage the larynx and flood the throat with blood?'

Journais' eyes had narrowed. 'Of course. It was a standard blow in unarmed combat.'

'Your army experience got you a job in security?'

'Yes.' Journais had visibly relaxed as the subject of karate was dropped.

'With whom?' Pel rapped.

Journais was at a loss for a moment. 'Well,' he said, 'Sécurité de Bourgogne.' He paused. 'Yes,' he went on. 'That's the firm.'

'You don't seem very sure.'

'Oh, yes, I'm sure.'

'Then why did you hesitate? I'd have thought a man would know at once whom he worked for.'

For the first time Journais showed signs of agitation. 'I did know. It was the way you tossed the question at me. It was just that I wasn't ready for it, that's all.'

'Right. Daniel, telephone Sécurité de Bourgogne. We can soon check.'

Journais suddenly seemed worried. 'Hang on a minute,' he said.

'You didn't work for Sécurité de Bourgogne?'

'No. Well, you see, it was a sort of secret.'

'So where did you work?'

Journais now had a desperate look. 'Actually I didn't work at all.'

'You didn't?'

'No. I didn't have a job. But I pretended to. For the wife's sake. I didn't like to tell her I was unemployed. So I pretended I had a security job and used to drive off.'

'Night or day?'

'Well – night.'

'Where did you go?'

'I drove into the country and slept in the car.'

'Funny you were never noticed. Where did you drive?'

'Just around.'

'Out Arbaçay way?'

Journais looked scared, then angry and Darcy rose and put his hand on his shoulder. 'Take it easy,' he said. 'Just answer the question.'

Journais drew a deep breath. 'Sometimes,' he said.

'Did you ever give a lift to this man?' Pel pushed Arri's photograph across the desk.

Journais stared at it for a moment; his mind seemed to be seething. 'No,' he said at last.

'I think you did,' Pel said. 'I think you picked him up.'

'No.'

Darcy leaned forward. 'We have a truth serum,' he said. 'Would you like a shot? They say it does things to your balls.'

They hadn't got any such thing but it was enough to make Journais look alarmed.

'You did know him, didn't you?' Pel asked.

Journais swallowed. 'No,' he insisted.

'Then why were you so interested in Ennaert's car?' Darcy asked.

'I wasn't.'

'You passed on the information to someone that it would be available in its garage the weekend Barclay was kidnapped.'

'I didn't.'

'I think you did. Who to?'

But that was the end. Journais refused to say any more. 'Take him away,' Pel said. 'You'd better lock him up, Daniel. He's already said too much for his own safety and if we want him as a witness, it'll be best not to turn him loose.' He paused. 'I suppose you'd better inform Lamiel.'

Darcy shrugged. 'Lamiel isn't available,' he said. 'He's still in Paris and Thomas is with him. The rest of his mob seem to be scattered half-way across Burgundy.'

sixteen

The news that there was someone in residence at the Manoir de Varas came sooner than they expected. It was the brigadier from Arbaçay who supplied the information.

'There's someone there at the moment, sir,' he said. 'I saw a car turn into the drive as I went past on the way to Vallefrie. I turned round and went back but it had disappeared, so it must be inside. The gates are closed but I tried them and they're not locked. I don't suppose that clot from Vallefrie noticed anything, did he?'

Slamming down the telephone, Pel yelled for Lagé, then changed his mind and started yelling for Claudie Darel instead. He wasn't sure what he expected to find at the Manoir de Varas but, if it were Madame Danton-Criot, he had a feeling that Claudie might be a better bet than Lagé, with his slow movements and big feet.

Sure enough, the gates were closed but not secured and Pel opened them enough for Claudie to drive in, then closed them behind them. A big Volvo was parked outside the front door as they halted and climbed the steps to ring the bell. There was a long silence then the door was opened by a girl. Pel's mouth dropped open because she *was* beautiful. Darcy had been right.

She looked startled, though. 'How did you get in?' she demanded sharply.

Pel gestured. 'The gates were unlocked.'

'That doesn't mean they're open to everybody.'

Pel produced his identity card. 'We're not everybody,' he said. 'We're the police.'

For a moment she seemed nonplussed, then a smile came, a flashing smile like a searchlight that warmed the heart and took the chill out of the interview. 'Oh, well,' she said. 'I suppose it's our own fault. I'm Domino. Domino Doignat.'

Domino, for God's sake, Pel thought. Perhaps he'd no cause to complain about Evariste Clovis Désiré. On the other hand, Domino was probably her own choice, which was different.

'I wish to see Madame Danton-Criot,' he said.

The girl looked slightly disconcerted. 'I think Madame Dédé's busy just at this moment,' she said.

'Who?'

'Madame Dédé. That's what I call Madame Danton.'

'You are on warm terms with her?'

'Of course. She likes to be friendly.'

'Then I hope she'll be friendly enough not to be too busy to see me.'

There was a long wait in the hall as the girl vanished, and Pel sat on a stiff-backed chair so high his toes barely touched the floor. His eyes were all over the place and his nose was twitching.

'Perfume,' he said. 'What is it, Claudie?'

Claudie sniffed. 'Chanel? Rochas? Dior? Whatever it is, it's expensive.'

After a while, they heard doors slamming and the girl reappeared, to lead them down a short corridor. All the doors they passed were firmly closed, Pel noticed, and the few articles of furniture in the corridor were all covered with dust sheets.

'Madame Danton's only just returned from the United States,' the girl said. 'And she's off to her villa on the south coast tomorrow for a rest.'

The room into which they were shown looked like an office. There were metal filing cabinets, shelves full of ledgers and what looked like a card index system. There were also several deep leather armchairs, a painting by Toulouse-Lautrec on the wall and a huge desk behind which sat a woman Pel assumed was Madame Danton-Criot. Once again, Darcy had been right.

She *was* beautiful, with huge eyes and a cloud of dark hair. She rose as they entered, tall and stately with perfect features and a superb figure that was clothed in a blue dress that matched her eyes and showed her shape to perfection. Yet, somehow, there seemed to be something missing. She was a woman who wore her sex like a badge of office but her face remained that of a businesswoman and there was no innocence there.

'Chief Inspector Pel,' she said. 'Please do sit down. Domino, how about some tea?' She smiled at Pel. 'You're lucky. Officially, I'm not here. I'm just between trips. I've just returned from the States and I'm due to leave on Sunday for the south for a week. I have a villa at Saint-Tropez. Normally the gates would be locked but today, because we weren't staying long, we decided not to bother and you found them unsecured.' She gestured at the girl. 'Domino is my companion.'

'Doesn't she find it lonely here, Madame?' Pel asked. 'Without other young people around.'

Madame Danton shrugged. 'Oh, it's not that lonely. And she always goes away with me when I go. She'll be with me at St Trop'. She looks after tickets and luggage and hotels and hire cars and that sort of thing and when we're here we have a lot of guests. Young men among them. She enjoys herself, I think.'

They chatted about the weather for a while, then the girl appeared with a tray and proceeded to pour tea and hand it round. Pel took his with a nod of thanks, sipped it, then produced the picture of Arri.

'We're trying to identify this man, Madame,' he pointed out. 'We have his name. Jules Arri. An ex-soldier. He had a job somewhere round here – possibly in Arbaçay, possibly in Vallefrie. We can't find out where and I'm wondering if perhaps you know him.'

Madame Danton studied the picture. 'Should I?'

'He was dropped every night somewhere between Arbaçay and Vallefrie and there's nothing between them except isolated farms who certainly didn't employ him and don't know him. That only leaves this place. Could he perhaps have been employed here in some capacity?'

She shook her head and offered the photograph to the girl who also shook her head.

Pel kept his face straight. 'He's not on your staff?' he asked.

She smiled, the picture of graciousness. 'We have a very small staff. They all live in.'

'Where are they now?'

'They're all on holiday. When I go away, so do the staff. It's an arrangement that suits them well. There are only three and I've sent them all on splendid holidays. The cook's gone to Majorca, the housemaid to Corfu.'

'And you paid for them? That must be expensive.'

'It's also a good way to keep your staff. They have a pretty good life. When I entertain, I do so in style. But when I'm not here, I close the place up.'

'It's a fine house,' Pel said.

She smiled. 'We've transformed it,' she agreed. 'It's now become quite a show-piece.'

'Have you thought, Madame, of making it a château classé and having people visit it? There's a lot of money in it.'

Madame Danton smiled again. 'We haven't reached that stage yet. It might come to that, but at the moment it's just a home. We're always trying to improve. We're building a new swimming pool at the moment. A smaller one. Some of our friends have children and, as they're too small to be in the big pool, we decided to build a new one especially for them. We started a day or two ago. We got a firm from Dijon. They sent a digger. It was working near Vallefrie so we contacted them and they sent it over at once. It's important to get it finished quickly. We'll get Piscines Myrtha from Dijon to concrete and tile it when we return from St Trop'.'

'Is the house safe to leave?'

'I think so.'

'I hope you have a good burglar alarm system?'

She laughed. 'We have good shutters.'

'Guard dogs?'

'No guard dogs. They frighten my friends.'

'No gardien?'

'My friends don't like to be regarded as security risks.'

Pel slipped his coffee and examined the cup. 'Pretty china,' he commented.

'I like nice things.'

'I've seen the pattern before somewhere.'

'It's not uncommon.

Pel gestured. 'Don't you find this place large for one person, Madame?'

She smiled. 'Not really. I was brought up in a place like this. My father was very wealthy and had a small château in Provence. You've probably heard of him. The Baron de Mahieu.'

Pel hadn't.

'And the house is yours?'

'Oh, yes.'

'But I understand the cheque for it was paid for by a Belgian gentleman by the name of Edmonde Dupont.'

She looked startled that he knew the name but she recovered quickly. 'Well, yes,' she said. 'He's my cousin. He's a very wealthy man. But he's a bachelor and he does a lot of travelling on business. He has an apartment in Paris but he felt he wanted a pied-à-terre in the country. He likes shooting. He bought this place.'

'So it isn't really yours?'

She shrugged. 'Well, yes, it is. He wanted a country home and someone to look after it. He installed the swimming pool and the tennis and squash courts. He's very keen on keeping fit. The house was then made over to me. It's as simple as that.'

Pel spoke, blank-faced. 'And what does he get in return, Madame?'

She studied Pel for a moment then she laughed. 'I know what you're thinking, Monsieur,' she said. 'But it isn't *that*. I look after it, that's all. We have an arrangement that if he should ever wish to marry, then the house reverts to him and I receive compensation in the form of another house of equal quality.'

'Think she's this type Dupont's mistress?' Pel asked as they drove down the long winding drive.

'She's *something* a bit odd,' Claudie decided.

'There's some connection between her and Arri. Those plates we had our biscuits on were the same as the ones at Arri's cottage – *and* at Barclay's house at Courtois.'

As they closed the big iron gates at the bottom of the drive a car drew up. It was a large and expensive-looking Mercedes and the driver was a young man very smartly dressed in a blazer, grey flannels and a pink shirt with a blue polka dot silk scarf at his throat. He glanced out of the car window at Claudie, who was just pulling the gates into place.

'Hello,' he said cheerfully. 'I haven't met you, have I? Are you new?'

'No,' Claudie said. 'I've been around for quite a while.'

'Really? How about turning round then? I'm just going in.'

Claudie smiled sweetly as she climbed into the car alongside Pel. 'Afraid you can't,' she pointed out. 'The place's closed.'

He looked started. 'What do you mean? Closed?'

'What I said – closed.'

'It can't be. It's never closed.'

'It is now.'

'Who's closed it?'

'The police, for a start.' Claudie beamed. 'I'm police!'

The man's jaw dropped and he promptly put his car into reverse. 'I've obviously got the wrong place,' he said. 'Place I was looking for was a hotel.'

He did the fastest three-point turn Pel had ever seen and, since the car was powerful, he was half a kilometre away before they could do anything to stop him.

Pel stared after it for a moment. 'It makes you think, doesn't it?' he said slowly.

'Yes, Patron,' Claudie agreed. 'And I expect that what you're thinking is the same as what I'm thinking.'

Pel nodded. 'I'd be very interested to get inside this place when there's nobody around,' he said. 'Sunday evening, for instance, after she's left for St Trop'. Meantime, Claudie, get in touch with the Quai des Orfèvres. Ask them if they've ever heard of this type, Bernard Rykx. If necessary, try Interpol. You could also look up the *Repertoire des Administrateurs, Directeurs et Gérants Français*. He should be in there.'

Claudie didn't take long.

'Bernard Rykx, Patron,' she said. 'The only Rykx they know in Paris is a Georges Rykx. Also known as Dupont. A Belgian who's lived in France for thirty years. He seems to be a very dubious piece of goods.'

'In what way?'

'They aren't sure. They've never been able to pin anything on him, but they think he's mixed up with the gangs. I also had a long session with the *Directory of Directors*,

Administrators and Managers. It gave a lot of Georges Rykx's interests. It also gave a lot of Barclay's, too, Patron, and I noticed that some of them were the same.'

'And Rykx is involved with the gangs?' Pel frowned. 'So: Is Barclay also?' The case seemed to grow more confused with every enquiry they made.

'Could they be working together somehow, Patron?'

'I've known stranger things in politics.'

'Could they have been ever since they were young men? Could Rykx – who *must* be that Risse type in Marseilles, Patron – could he have found out about that little peccadillo we unearthed that could have been Barclay, learned more about him from Loget, the civilian in the records department who sold information, tried to blackmail him and in the end decided to work with him?'

'It's pure supposition,' Pel said.

'Yes, of course, Patron. But a man like Rykx could use Barclay's political influence to good value. Perhaps Barclay couldn't refuse in case Rykx brought out what he knew about him and the girl, Denise Darnand.'

Pel studied his fingers for a moment, pushed his spectacles up on to his forehead, lit a cigarette slowly and deliberately, drew several deep satisfying drags at it, then looked up.

'Could Denise Darnand be Dominique Danton-Criot?' he asked.

It was worth thinking about.

Pierre Lamotte, known to the police as Pépé le Cornet, had crossed Pel's path on more than one occasion, the last time when Pel had put his second-in-command away for a long time for organising a big jewel haul. His home was on the outskirts of Paris near Meudon, a large house in its own grounds and surrounded by iron railings. As Pel – by arrangement made on the telephone – drove in, he noticed men prowling about and what looked like large and fierce Dobermanns wandering around loose.

He was shown in by a square dark man who looked as if he might be a Corsican and led down a corridor. Pépé le Cornet was sitting in a deep armchair, stroking a very small lapdog. Alongside him was a woman who seemed to be dripping diamonds and looked as if she'd just stepped out of the *Folies Bergère*. While policemen struggled along in old cars, in small houses, with wives in clothes they'd had for years, crooks had magnificent houses, drove Citroën CXs, Cadillacs, even Rolls Royces, had pads in the Seychelles and the South of France, and women as beautiful as goddesses.

'Chief Inspector Pel!' Pépé didn't rise. Indeed, he was so fat these days, Pel noticed, he would probably have found it an effort. 'This is a bit unexpected. Sit down. Drink?' He gestured at the woman. 'Cherie, a drink for the Chief.' He stroked the Pekinese on his lap and looked at Pel. 'My little favourite,' he said.

'I hope you don't let it out unaccompanied,' Pel said dryly. 'The Dobermanns look as though they'd eat it for breakfast.'

Pépé frowned, then he managed a grin. 'I'm very careful, Chief' he said. 'Especially these days. What can I do for you?'

Pel decided to come straight to the point. 'Know a man called Claude Barclay?' he asked.

Pépé's eyebrows shot up. 'Deputy Barclay?' he asked. 'Look here, Chief, don't come here accusing me… '

'I'm not accusing you,' Pel snapped. 'I asked if you knew him.' Pépé calmed down. 'Well, yes, I know him. Half France knows him. Especially since he was kidnapped.'

'What about him?'

'I've heard a few things.'

'Such as what?'

'Such as that he's not all he's cracked up to be.'

'In what way?'

'He has his finger in a few pies.'

'What sort of pies?'

Pépé clammed up. 'Look, Chief, you shouldn't be asking me these questions.'

Pel acknowledged the fact. He was touching pitch again with a vengeance and could land up in a lot of trouble. But it had to be done.

'We're on different sides of the fence, Chief,' Pépé pointed out.

'Sometimes even enemies arrange an armistice,' Pel said.

'That's true enough, Chief. But I'm not telling you anything. I've said all I'm going to say. Have another drink?'

Pel declined and shifted the course of the conversation.

'Bernard Rykx,' he said. 'Ever heard of him?'

Pépé's face suddenly closed up and the hand that was stroking the Pekinese stopped. He gestured at the woman and she rose and left the room.

'What are you after, Chief?'

'Who is he?'

'I don't know anybody called Bernard Rykx. But I know a little shit called Georges Rykx who's trying to muscle in on things. Is he the one?'

'More than likely. Is he interested in the things you're interested in, Pépé?'

Pépé managed to compose himself. 'I'm not interested in anything these days,' he said. 'I'm too old. I've gone legitimate. You can inspect my books, if you like.'

'So what about Rykx? Why does he worry you?'

'He doesn't worry me, Chief. But he worries a few people round here and in Marseilles.

'Such as Maurice Tagliatti?'

'Maurice wouldn't mind seeing him off.'

'What sort of things is he in?'

'You name it, he's in it.'

'Drugs?'

'Drugs. Booze. Nightspots. Protection. Pimping. Brothels. He tried to muscle in on the Nice casino business but Maurice saw him off.'

'How come he's never been picked up?'

Pépé scowled. 'Because he's too clever,' he growled. 'He fronts everything with a legitimate business. He runs a wholesale meat distribution business and was right at the front when the Rosbifs in England tried to flood the country with their rotten lamb. He's also got a string of small businesses. Wholesale vegetables. Restaurants. Grocery chains. You name it, he's in it. He's into finance, too. He started work as an accountant so he knows the ins and outs. I dare bet he fiddles his tax.'

'Don't you?'

Pépé gave a weak smile. 'It's only the tax people, and everybody likes to have a go at those sharks. They don't have a sense of humour, Chief.'

Pel had noticed it himself. They certainly showed none where *his* salary was concerned.

'Did this Rykx know Barclay?'

Pépé shrugged and started stroking the Pekinese again. 'Chief, I don't know. These days I don't want to know. I'm sixty-two now and I've got an ulcer. I thought it was a cancer at first, in fact. All I want is a quiet life. I don't go shoving my nose into other people's affairs. On the other hand...'

'On the other hand, what?'

'On the other hand, there are a few people round here who wouldn't mind seeing Monsieur Rykx removed from the scene for a bit. It would enable them to get in on his territory. If they did, he'd never get it back.'

Pel nodded. 'I'll do my best to oblige,' he said and tried the newspaper story about Barclay being weary of politics.

'Barclay was heard saying he was wanting to get out,' he said. 'Was it politics, as they suggested, or something a bit more dubious?'

'It wasn't politics. He was talking to Rykx.'

'How do you know?'

'I heard.'

'When was it?'

'Several days before he disappeared.'

'Was he trying to pull out of whatever it was Rykx had involved him in?'

Pépé shrugged and Pel didn't press the point. Pépé had a strange kind of reliability, he'd found. Provided you didn't ask too many questions about his sources.

Claudie was waiting for him when he returned. 'Risse, Patron,' she said. 'He *was* a Belgian and he might very well be Rykx. The age is right and the description fits. Marseilles thinks that they couldn't have got his correct name. They have now, though, because he was one of those who tried to muscle in on Maurice Tagliatti's territory over the casinos.'

Pel nodded his approval. 'What about the Darnand girl?'

'Age right. Description right. Said to be very beautiful. Tall. Striking. Moved north after the affair involving Barclay.'

'Perhaps she never lost touch with him. Perhaps Rykx didn't either. What happened to her?'

'Operated in Paris for a while. Then some man took her under his wing and set her up in a house outside Lille. Wealthy industrialist called Videlle. That lasted about eight years. Then he died and his family moved in and claimed everything and, as there was no will, she was out on the streets again. She disappeared. Then, if she's Dominique Danton, she turned up in our diocese about five years ago. It all seems to fit very neatly.'

She had also prepared a long list of Rykx's interests and Pel decided it was time he visited the ones in their area. It seemed pointless getting involved with the wholesale meat trade or the wholesale vegetable trade or any financial affairs, but there were a lot of other small businesses – a chain of grocery shops called Epicéries de l'Est, an estate agent's office, a restaurant – just the sort of things for a man wanting to make his profits disappear from the sight of the tax inspector. Hé, presto! Now you see it, now you don't! There were plenty of people at it, which made taxation a bit of a fraud, really, because, while a poor man couldn't hide a damn thing because he had nowhere to hide it, a wealthy man could always find a corner or two where he could stuff money out of sight.

The nearest of Rykx's interests was at Maillay, a large employment agency with branches in other places. Pretending she was interested in finding a job, Claudie went in and a girl appeared from a door behind the counter. Through the window, Pel was startled by her looks and svelte clothing. She wore a name tag on her shirt, with the word Din-Din on it, but she didn't seem very sure of herself and fetched an older woman to answer Claudie's questions.

'There's something very odd in there, Patron,' Claudie said as she returned to the car. 'The first one who appeared – that Din-Din, or whatever she calls herself – claims to be running the show, but she didn't know the first thing about it and had to call the other woman. It's my bet the second one runs it really and the one with the looks is the owner. Or some sort of front. She didn't even know her way round the card index system.'

Their next call was in Gervigny, where a flashy-looking estate agency fronted the town square. A girl was sitting at a desk, smoking. She was smartly dressed and had endless legs and bright red hair that looked as if it were dyed. Her eyes were green and she wore green earrings that matched. Never in his life had Pel seen a clerk in an estate agent's office who looked like that.

It seemed to be part of the Rykx policy to establish personal contact with customers and clients, and the girl wore the same sort of name tag on her dress that the girl in the employment agency in Maillay had worn, this time with the name Reggie emblazoned across it. She made little attempt to answer Pel's questions when he said he was interested in houses in the area, and called over a young man with long hair from a neighbouring desk who supplied the answers they didn't really want.

Finally, for lunch, they decided to try another of Rykx's interests, the Relais de Chanzy, a restaurant on the main road to Dijon. It was set back among the trees and wasn't as expensive as it looked. Outside were several cars, including a large red Jaguar. The maître d' was a girl, and she seemed to fit into the same category as all the others they'd met that morning. On her breast was a small badge with the name, Nenette. Since her job consisted of no more than showing people to their tables and taking bookings, she seemed well able to do it, but she made no attempt to take orders for food or advise on wine, and once again they had the impression that she was new to the job.

'Another one,' Pel whispered as they ordered. 'All beautiful. They could have come from the Crazy Horse. And all with cozy names. Domino, Nenette, Reggie. What happened to all the Marie-Frances, the Madeleines, the Sophies, the Michelles? Where have they all come from all of a sudden?'

seventeen

The last publications before the election flung out their final flurry of insults so that it began to seem there wasn't an honest politician in the whole of France.

Opinion polls showed that the government had slipped back several points, something that was attributed to the mystery surrounding Barclay. There were still references to him in the newspapers: in his own party's press with words of deep sympathy and a suggestion that his disappearance had been engineered by the opposition; in the opposition's with a suggestion that there was something pretty shifty behind it all. *France Dimanche* tried to imply he'd gone off with a woman, but nobody believed it, of course. *France Dimanche* was not aimed at intellectuals, anyway, and didn't really expect to be believed.

On the Sunday which had been designated as polling day, because nothing much was moving Pel rose in leisurely fashion. 'Leisurely fashion' was something of a misnomer because there was nothing about Pel that had ever been leisurely. The minute he was on his feet, his nervous energy drove him like a bee possessed. However, he was aware that there were times when he owed it to his wife to *appear* to be leisurely and this was one of them. One couldn't vote for the next government of France with a rush, after all. The fact that he had already made up his mind made no difference. France had always contained millions of political parties – one for every voter – and no good Frenchman, and certainly no good Burgundian, to whom things were always more important than they were to flippant Parisians, would ever dream of showing haste in indicating his choice. Even the method of voting had a certain amount of ceremony, which the French enjoyed, unlike the British who were casual enough to make jokes about theirs.

After a long slow breakfast, which had Pel wriggling on his chair with impatience, he waited for his wife to disappear upstairs to dress, then headed for the garden. Inevitably Yves Pasquier was waiting by the hole in the hedge and the shaggy dog standing beside him wagged its far end to indicate it was facing Pel and not away from him. It wasn't always easy to tell.

'Elections today,' the boy said. 'Who're you voting for?'

'It's supposed to be secret, so I never tell anyone.'

'My Mother and Father do. They argue about it. They want to vote for different people. My father said my mother should vote the same way he does, and she said. "Haven't you ever heard of Women's Lib?" '

'I trust the dust has now settled.'

'Oh, yes. They're all right now. When I grow up I shall vote socialist.'

Pel shrugged. 'There's a saying that if you don't vote socialist before you're forty, you have no heart, but if you continue to vote socialist after you're forty, you've no head.'

'Is it true?'

Pel paused – who was he to influence the future generation? 'It's a matter of opinion,' he said.

The day's ceremonies completed, Pel returned to the house, to find his wife descending the stairs, singing quietly to herself as she often did.

> Plaisir d'amour ne dure qu'un moment,
> Chagrin d'amour dure toute la vie...

She smiled at him, picked up her handbag and called for Madame Routy, who appeared from the kitchen, girded for the fray in a square red coat like a cloth box and a hat that looked like a turban belonging to a not very particular Arab. She looked at Pel, as if daring him to vote differently from her, and headed for the car.

The village hall, where the voting was taking place, had been emptied of chairs, save for half a dozen or so ranged behind two long tables, in the centre of which was a large black box with a handle, in front of it small piles of paper containing the names of the candidates. In a long row behind sat the presiding officers, clerks, returning officers, tellers and what have you, all very solemn in their temporary authority.

Picking up their papers, Pel, his wife and Madame Routy went to the booths to ponder their decisions, then returned to the long table to hand them in. It was all very serious. After all, the future of the Republic depended on them.

As Madame Pel handed in her name, the man behind the table called out 'Geneviève Hélène Pel,' and the man handling the black box watched the paper disappear into the slot and slammed down the lever. 'A voté,' he shouted solemnly. 'Voted!'

Madame Routy followed and the same ceremony ensued. 'Annabelle Angéline Philomène Routy' – bang! – 'A voté!'

Pel was still delighting in discovering that Madame Routy's name was as daunting as his own when he noticed the officials staring hard at him and came to life with a jolt. This was the bit he dreaded. 'Evariste Clovis Désiré Pel', the man behind the table yelled and Pel cringed, certain that everybody in the hall had turned round to examine the possessor of such an outlandish name. He had always sworn never to disclose it in public until he had to report to St Peter at the Pearly Gates.

Bang went the box, 'A voté' yelled its operator, then they were safely outside again and Pel's secret was safe until next time.

'Who do you think will get in?' Madame asked as they reached the car.

Pel shrugged. 'It won't matter much. These days we don't vote for the man who can do any good. We simply vote for the one who can do least harm. It's safer.'

As a celebration, Madame had laid on a special lunch and Pel drank enough wine to drop off in a deck chair in the garden afterwards. When he woke, he realised it was later than he'd intended – that was the trouble with French meals, they *always* went on longer than intended – and he headed for the telephone to contact Lagé.

By the sound of him, Lagé had also just appeared from a deck chair in the garden and his voice seemed drowsy.

'I'm ready, Patron,' he announced.

He arrived soon afterwards, driving his own car, and they headed for Vallefrie and Arbaçay. It was almost dark and the countryside was bathed in a purple twilight as they drew to a halt under the trees on the grass verge alongside the barbed wire fence of the Manoir de Varas. They sat there for a while, smoking, until dark finally came, then climbed from the car. It didn't take them two minutes to climb through the wire and head into the trees.

'I don't like this, Patron,' Lagé said.

'Neither do I,' Pel agreed.

'French law says you can't search private premises in the hours of darkness.'

'We're not searching them. We're examining the outside. Now shut up and keep your eyes open.'

After a while, they spotted a small cottage through the trees. It looked old but it had been newly decorated, as if someone had taken a woodman's home and modernised it. Then they saw another cottage beyond it, though it was clear that both were unobtrusive and that neither could be seen from the other.

For a long time they watched until they were certain the cottages were unoccupied, then they moved towards the nearest of them. It was locked and the shutters were closed on the inside. But one of them was not properly secured and, peering in, they could see a large bed with a canopy of filmy drapings.

'Funny bed for a woodman's cottage,' Pel observed.

At the other cottage they were able to see into the bathroom where they could see rows of cosmetics, high quality bath salts, and male and female perfumes.

There were six other cottages in the forest, four of them old and renovated, two of them of recent construction. They were all attractively done, with bright paint and small gardens, and not one of them was overlooked by any of the others, because high fences had been erected and beech hedges had been planted.

Moving further among the trees, they came to a square building that was obviously a squash court. Pel knew all about squash – an hour of frenzy then a heart attack; Darcy played it regularly. There were also two tennis courts, a large swimming pool and a small pitch and putt course. Beyond them were the workings for what they assumed was the new swimming pool. It was near the trees and seemed a long way from the buildings for a children's pool. Parents weren't all that keen on being at a distance from their children.

As Pel approached it, he was surprised to see that it had been filled in again. The marks of the scoop and the caterpillar tracks of the digger were plain, but the earth had been shovelled back and was level once more. Slowly, he walked round it, deep in thought.

It looked very much as if someone had had second thoughts about it.

Driving round the lanes at Vallefrie early the following morning, eventually they heard the racket of an engine coming from behind a farm and found a digger at work. Ear muffs in place, the driver didn't hear them approach and Lagé had to risk his neck by appearing in front of the scoop with waving arms. Stopping the digger, the driver removed his earmuffs.

'You could have been killed, you stupid con!' he roared.

'Never mind that now,' Pel said. 'Were you responsible for digging out the swimming pool at the Manoir de Varas?'

The digger driver nodded. 'Yes, I dug it. But, merde, they asked us the following week to fill it up again. Said they'd made a mistake and would have to think again.'

They ate at the Hôtel de la Poste at Vallefrie. Lagé's opinion of it appeared to be correct because the meat tasted like old carpet slippers and the wine had the flavour of shellac. Returning to the city, they discovered that the party Pel had voted for had failed to get in, but he decided that the man who would now be Prime Minister was so stupid he couldn't do any harm, anyway, and felt much better.

The sergeants' room seemed to be occupied less with stamping out crime than with assessing the damage done to the Republic by the election. Inevitably, Misset was loudest in his protestations.

'That type couldn't run a crêpe stall in Brittany,' he was saying. 'In two years time we'll be a banana republic. What do *you* think of the type who's going to be running the country, Patron?'

Pel scowled. 'I'm just thankful', he growled, 'that it isn't you.'

He had just sat down in his chair when Nosjean appeared.

'Art frauds, Patron,' he said.

Pel leaned back. 'Inform me, mon brave.'

'There's been a new development.'

Pel sat up. 'Go on.'

'It's a big one. Involving the United States. I've been in touch with Paris and even with the States.'

'On the telephone?' Pel was aghast. 'For how long? The Chief will have a fit.'

Nosjean smiled. 'Not on the telephone, Patron. Paris put me on to an American cop who's in Paris checking it out.'

Pel relaxed. 'You'd better tell me.'

Nosjean drew a deep breath. 'In the States, it seems, donations to charity are considered exempt from tax, which means that anyone giving a big donation can deduct it from his income tax. People give buildings to hospitals, universities, schools and churches, and the charities benefit while the type who does the giving doesn't lose. That's fine. Only there are snags.'

Pel shifted restlessly. 'Let's get to them.'

'A type called Kaufman started a racket to make money out of it. Valuable paintings given to decorate walls, of course, come into the category of charitable donations. But, unlike buildings, carpets, etcetera, paintings can be fiddled. Duds can be offered as genuine and a few people started getting hold of fake old masters, giving them to some deserving cause and then claiming back their value from the Inland Revenue. The outlay amounted to only a few hundred dollars for the fake but, with present-day prices on old masters, the profit was considerable. The big advantage, of course, was that the recipients of the fake pictures would never admit their pictures were fakes.'

'And Kaufman?'

'He organised it. He had a middleman to contact owners of genuine paintings, and find charities who would be happy to receive gifts. There was also a type to copy the pictures and some guy who knew enough about art to write a provenance – the verification which would suggest the picture was genuine. Kaufman, of course, took a cut and, in addition, had a little sideline selling duds to eager collectors.'

Pel listened carefully, his fingers entwined, his spectacles up on his forehead.

'The racket was finally uncovered and broken up by the police,' Nosjean went on. 'But it seems Kaufman wasn't arrested and they think he came to Europe and transferred his operations here because Europe's considered safer for the production of fake works of art. It seems they're copied over here and then smuggled unframed into the States. The racket, of course, can't be operated here because we don't have this tax exemption for donations to charity in Europe. But the profit's enormous and the Americans think the same organisation exactly has been set up. There's a middleman, a copyist and a guy to write the provenance, with Kaufman beavering away behind it all. The middleman persuades an owner to have his painting restored and, while it's being restored, a copy's made, and from this other copies are made. The original's returned to the owner and nobody knows what's happening. There's a Belgian involved and a few types busy over canvas, while the whole thing's stage managed at a safe distance. It's a racket of some size and I seemed to have got into it.'

Pel was deep in thought. 'And this Kaufman, of course, has a European organiser?'

'Yes, Patron.'

'Are you on to him?'

'I'm making progress. It's not been easy but I've built up a file on art frauds and they all seem to be connected.' Nosjean outlined what he had discovered and the people involved: Chevrier, the fabric designer who bought pictures because he liked art; Macus, who bought them because he was a twister who'd been involved in insurance frauds before; Vacchi, who simply wanted to impress people. 'Barclay,' Nosjean shrugged. 'He lent the picture – several pictures, in fact – for the opening of the Hôtel du Grand Cerf at Lorne, but he also sold a picture – two, in fact, Patron – to the Collège Privé de l'Est. The college was very pleased to have them and didn't quibble about the price he put on them – 500,000 francs each. If they'd been genuine, they got a bargain, but one of them certainly isn't genuine and I think, if we got Professor Grandjean to look at the other, we'd probably find that isn't either because it seems to have come from the same source as all the others and the provenance and valuation are by the same old boy who claims to be a professor but isn't.'

'So Barclay was taken in?'

Nosjean gestured. 'If he sold two dud paintings for 500,000 francs each, Patron,' he said, 'then he *wasn't* taken in. Whoever came off badly, Patron, it wasn't Barclay.'

Was it Barclay who was working the fiddle? Had he, in fact, been working a lot of fiddles? And was that the reason why he was kidnapped? It was an interesting point but one which Pel could see quite clearly was not at the moment in his own field of play.

'Do I pass it on to Lamiel, Patron?' Nosjean asked.

'Leave it with me for a while,' Pel suggested. 'It's a tricky one. Lamiel's looking for terrorists and he's determined to find terrorists. He might not be very happy to learn this.'

He looked at Nosjean, his mind whirring away like wasps wings. 'You remember the châteaux thefts, mon brave?' he asked.

Nosjean nodded. '1980, Patron. A few types were sent down.'

'The men who did the breaking in. Got their names?'

'Sure, Patron. I picked them up. Demi-sels, small-timers, both of them. Jean-Jacques Raméai and Henri Préz. Raméai was the skilled man. Préz was the hired help. I hear they've just got out.'

Pel sniffed and rubbed his nose. 'I need your friend, Raméai,' he said.

Nosjean looked startled.

'I need to get into the Manoir de Varas,' Pel explained quietly. 'I need to get in – and out again – quickly and quietly, without anyone knowing. Could it be done?'

It took Nosjean's breath away but he was prepared to bet Pel had a good reason. 'Do we know anything about the place, Patron?'

'There's no burglar alarm. No guard dogs. No gardien. I also suspect that security's lax. Can Raméai get me in?'

'Name of God, Patron...!'

'Can he?'

Nosjean swallowed. 'I dare bet he could.'

'Can you find him?'

'I'm sure I can.'

'Then bring him him.'

Two days later Jean-Jacques Raméai appeared in Pel's office. He was understandably nervous. He hadn't mended his ways and he expected to be charged with something.

Pel didn't beat about the bush. 'I need to get into a house,' he said. 'The house is empty and there's no burglar alarm, no guard dog and no caretaker. I think you can get me in – and out again – without anyone knowing.'

Raméai looked indignant. 'You think I'm going to risk my neck on a job like that?' he bleated.

'Yes, I do,' Pel said calmly. 'I've been having a look at you and I think you're as shifty as you were when you were sent down seven years ago.'

It was only a guess but it was a good one and Raméai went pale. 'Look, Chief,' he said. 'I don't know what you know... '

'Never mind what I know. Are you prepared to do it?'

'What do I get out of it?'

'Nothing, except a promise to tear up the evidence I have in my hands about you.'

Raméai thought for a long time, gnawing at the quick on his finger. 'All right,' he said. 'I'll need a good look-out, though.'

Pel smiled. 'You'll have one. Nosjean here.'

Nosjean's head came up, startled. 'Patron... '

'Dry up, Nosjean. Is it a deal?'

Raméai shrugged. 'I've got no option, have I?'

'No,' Pel said cheerfully. 'You haven't.'

Raméai swallowed. 'I'll need to look the place over,' he said.

'You'll be given the opportunity. There's a barbed wire fence but I doubt if that will cause problems. How long do you need? There are a lot of trees. A good pair of binoculars should tell you all you want to know.'

'How long have I got?'

'Forty-eight hours.'

Raméai jeered. 'I like to take longer than that.'

'You don't have longer. We need to get on with it.'

'Suppose I just bolt?'

'I wouldn't advise you to.'

'Suppose I sell it to the newspapers?'

'I wouldn't advise that, either. Doubtless, if it comes off there'll be a small contribution from police funds.' Providing, Pel thought, he could square it with the Chief. 'It would be worth your while in more ways than one.'

He produced a map and marked the spot, and as Raméai disappeared, looking vaguely troubled, he sat back. He had been accused of touching pitch; now he was touching it with a vengeance. He just hoped it would prove worth while.

Raméai's voice came on the telephone two days later, soft, quiet, sibilant.

'It's as easy as falling off a log,' he said.

'I thought it might be.'

'There's an unfastened shutter on the first floor just above the main door. The windows are latched but I can open them. Then I can go downstairs and open a side door I saw. I expect it's only bolted. I've got a plan of the place.'

'How did you manage that miracle?'

'It used to be open to the public and I found the old gardien and got his plan off him. He says there's some good stuff in there.'

'Where,' Pel warned, 'it will remain.'

'All right, all right,' Raméai said bitterly. 'When do we do it?'

Pel glanced out of the window. 'It's a fine day and the weather forecast is good. How about tonight?'

As Nosjean's car pulled off the road among the trees, Raméai leaned forward. 'Look, suppose a cop comes by and sees the car,' he said.

'He won't,' Pel pointed out. 'The men at Vallefrie and Arbaçay have been informed that there's a suspected planned break-in at the Chateau de Chameroi-Fontaine at Praislay and they've been drafted there to keep an eye on the place. Despite their mutual dislike, they're panting with enthusiasm and excitement and expecting to get promotion by capturing the thieves.'

Raméai snorted. 'Poor bastard thieves!'

'Save your sympathy,' Pel said. 'There aren't any. It's a false alarm.'

It was dark by this time but Raméai led them unerringly into the bushes and shone his torch on the two-strand barbed wire fence. As Lagé put a foot on the bottom strand and hauled up the other, they scrambled through and pushed their way into the undergrowth, leaving Lagé behind to give a warning if anything went wrong. Once they came to a sudden stop as they heard movement in the bushes but it turned out to be a fox, and they saw its eyes glowing in the torch's beam.

Raméai found his way to a daunting cast-iron fence which had once been the original boundary, but one of the railings had been broken and it wasn't difficult to slip through. Soon they were moving across a wide lawn that led to the front of the house, then their feet were crunching on thick gravel.

Raméai indicated the three large glass doors of the terrace. 'Locked,' he said. 'And bolted from inside. I'm not touching them.' He gestured to the first floor windows. 'That's where I'm going.'

On the terrace he produced a rope from his bag. It had a three-pronged hook on the end, the spikes covered with bicycle inner tube to stop it clattering. Tossing it up, he managed to hook it on a convenient protuberance.

'I'll be seeing you,' he said. 'Wait for me by the side door.'

They watched him, a shadowy figure as he made his way along the wide ledge below the first floor windows. Then they heard the clink of tools and a faint grating sound.

'Patron,' Nosjean said, 'I don't like this.'

Pel sniffed. 'Neither do I, mon brave. But there's a lot hanging on it.'

As they waited, they heard a loud click above their heads then the creak of a rarely-used hinge.

'He's inside,' Pel said.

The hook and the rope came down on them and they gathered them up. A few minutes later, as they waited by the side door, they heard bolts withdrawn, then the door opened, gaping like a cavern into the blackness.

'Look slippy, for the love of God!'

Inside, they switched on torches. The shutters were closed and secured by iron bars. 'They don't bother with the second floor,' Raméai said. 'I drilled a thirty-millimetre hole and poked a screwdriver through to lift the latch. It was a piece of cake. Where do we go now? What are we after?'

'Nothing,' Pel said. 'I just want to look.'

There was a strong smell of perfume and the place was luxuriously furnished, while the doors, which had been closed on Pel's visit, when opened revealed luxuriously-appointed rooms. In one of them was a large bar, hardly the thing for a private house. Upstairs, the corridors were divided into a series of apartments. In each was a small salon containing a dining table, a chaise-longue, and comfortable armchairs. The drapings were in excellent taste. Each also contained a comfortable furnished bedroom containing a large double bed. There was a refrigerator containing drinks, and the bathrooms, like those of the cottages, contained cosmetics, perfumes and bath salts of the highest quality.

Each bedroom was walled with mirrors and there were more mirrors above the beds. On the walls were life-size paintings of girls – all in the nude, some of them in suggestive poses. Beside the beds were low tables and it didn't take more than a glance to see that a lot of the books they held were pornographic, but all in the best of taste, with more photographs of naked girls.

Moving down to the kitchens, they found just what Pel had expected – plates like the ones he had found at Arri's and at Barclay's house in Courtois – dozens of them. The bar revealed the finest of wines and spirits and the cellar was full of grand cru wines and champagne.

Moving to the office, they saw a string of pearls lying on the desk and, as Raméai's hand went out to it, Pel banged his fingers with the torch. Raméai said nothing but he gave Pel a pained look. The files were all locked, but it didn't take Raméai five minutes to open them. Pel glanced inside. The card indexes contained names, some of which startled him. Many of them came from his own city, but there were others that came from Paris – big names, important names, even one or two famous names. There were even names from England, Germany and Italy. Alongside each was a date and a number, which he assumed to be the number of the suite – and a girl's name: Riri, Reggie, Francie, Domino, Din-Din, Nenette – all names they'd already come across. There were other similar names – Chouchou, Rosie, Lucy, Millie, Nini – and with them were their real names – Jeanne, Regina, Bernadine, Francine, Georgette, all much more commonplace than the cozy ones they'd adopted. Mostly their names were linked with the same man's name, though occasionally they changed, and there was a cross index that indicated that sometimes parties were made up of two or more men and more girls. There was one even of four men and four girls.

Pel nodded satisfied and indicated to Raméai to close the drawers and lock them again.

Raméai was staring at him, puzzled. Nosjean looked strained and pale in the light of the torches.

'Patron... ' he tried.

Pel gestured. 'Let's go,' he said. 'I've found what I wanted to find, and it's just what I expected to find. There's nothing more to do here.'

'It's obvious,' he went on quietly. 'It's a place for men who want to do a little business, have a little exercise, eat a little good food served on splendid china, and then go to bed with a girl. This isn't a back street operation, but it's still a brothel. And, Mother of God, what a brothel!'

eighteen

'Patron,' Nosjean looked puzzled, 'it's not a crime to run a brothel. Especially one which is obviously run on good lines.'

'It's a crime if it isn't licensed,' Pel said stiffly.

'At least they kept it quiet.'

'Not quiet enough. Sécret de deux, sécret de Dieu. Sécret de trois, sécret de tous. They forgot – walls have mice and mice have ears.' But who's going to worry about who goes to a brothel?'

'Paris might not worry about who goes to a brothel,' Pel said. 'But the provinces do and, despite the fact that Paris thinks that what Paris does the whole of France is doing, the provinces don't take these things so lightly. They would certainly object to a junior member of the government being involved.'

When he reached home Madame Pel was sitting on the settee holding a small whisky and listening to Mozart. Indifferent to music, Pel poured himself a drink, and sat on a chair at the back of the room, unobtrusively reading the headlines in the newspaper until it had finished. As the machine clicked, Madame caught sight of him for the first time and reached out to touch his hand.

'You're always so good,' she said. 'Letting me listen to things you don't like.'

Pel shrugged, trying to look as if he'd behaved with true

nobility but in reality fully aware that it was always easier to read the paper than try to understand eighteenth century melodies.

'Was it a good day?' she asked.

'A very good day. And tomorrow I think we should go to see your Cousin Roger.'

Madame almost dropped her glass.

She had never known Pel enthusiastic to meet her relations before. Usually he was full of excuses but she had noticed that, though Cousin Roger was considered the black sheep of the family, somehow he and Pel had taken to each other at the party at Bois Haut.

A telephone call brought an enthusiastic response from Roger's wife. She was delighted to be seeing Madame Pel again. 'And Roger will be pleased to see Pel!' she shrieked down the telephone.

It was a noisy day. Roger had two cats, two dogs, several goldfish and a budgerigar, to say nothing of four children, all of them at the age when they made a lot of noise, got in the way and ate enough for a carthorse. Apart from the goldfish and the budgerigar, they all seemed to spend all their time fighting cheerfully with each other and when Pel and his wife arrived the two youngest children were playing at terrorists.

'If they stick splinters under your fingernails', one of them was saying, 'will you tell them who sent you?'

'I'll tell them long before that.' To Pel the reply seemed eminently sensible.

They had lunch which started with apéritifs at midday, and finally put their coffee cups down at four in the afternoon, to look round to see if anyone was interested in tea. Roger, in fact, had dropped off to sleep in the sun.

Pel nudged him. 'Show me the garden,' he said.

Roger groaned, climbed out his chair with an effort and poured the dregs from his brandy glass into the aquarium in the hall. 'I think it cheers them up,' he said.

Leaving the rest of the family squabbling over who was going to make the tea, they drifted off up the lawn towards the shrubbery.

'I suppose', Roger said, 'you've come about Barclay.'

Pel admitted the fact.

Roger offered a cigarette and sat down on a bench in the shade. 'He was a shifty type, you know,' he admitted. 'We've been his accountants for a long time but I never knew a period when he wasn't always a few steps ahead of us.' He seemed a little puzzled. 'He'd been getting stock together,' he went on. 'Negotiable bonds, money, company assets that could be sold. I think he was planning to go to America. He'd applied for a residence permit there, I know, and he'd been transferring funds for some time.'

'Did he expect to get his permit?'

Roger laughed. 'With *his* money? Of course.'

'Has he any family there?'

'None I know of.'

'He was doing well in France, wasn't he?'

'As far as I can tell.'

'Then why go to America?'

Roger shrugged. 'We were his accountants, not his advisers. He did what he fancied, and he was good enough at it to do it well, then he left us to pick up the pieces with the tax people.'

'Was he honest?'

'We never found he was dishonest. But that's not quite the same, is it? He had his fingers in a lot of pies and I'm sure he didn't tell us everything he should. Some people are straightforward with their accountants, As a rule, it's because they're honest or because they don't understand what's going on and feel it's safer. But there are also a few who are dishonest who try to pick up a little extra on the side. The ones who're dishonest and not clever usually find themselves facing a frozen-faced accountant and, if it goes on happening, they have to find another more accommodating accountant, because shifty clients usually indicate shifty accountants. We're not that sort. But there are also clever clients – some of them not always as honest as they might be – who are able to bamboozle even their accountants, because, after all, we're only human and if the client's cleverer than we are, he manages to hide things from us.'

'Which group did Barclay belong to?'

Cousin Roger scratched his nose. 'I honestly don't know. But I know he'd been shifting money about a lot lately.'

Barclay's interests were hardly on a world-wide scale, but he seemed to have a lot of them. Boutiques, perfume shops, supermarkets, restaurants, linenware, vineyards. They were none of them vast undertakings and, Pel noticed, they weren't grouped under one title like Barclay Enterprises. That in itself seemed suspicious, as if, perhaps, Barclay used the funds of one to bolster up another. Fraud in France was rising at an alarming rate – insurance companies believed that computer frauds were costing billions of francs a year – and the number of cases detected bore little relation to the total committed.

The list Cousin Roger was able to offer was far from complete – he admitted it himself – and didn't include those affairs that were not based locally. But, Pel noticed, he and his department were already familiar with several of the names.

'Of course,' Roger said, 'he was deeply involved in charities, too.'

'Which charities?'

'Children's homes for a start. Ex-servicemen's charities. As you'll know, he was a much-decorated soldier as a young man. He fought at Dien Bien Phu and was taken prisoner.'

Pel was growing a little tired of Barclay's heroism. 'I've heard of that. What else?'

'The disabled. He runs several disabled ex-soldiers' homes and collects funds for them.'

'Any more?'

'Natural disasters. The Mexican earthquake, for instance.

Africa. He took a great interest in those and raised a great deal of money. Things of that nature always captured his attention at once. He'd handled millions of francs for recovery schemes.' He paused. 'Hospitals, too. There must be a lot of hospitals grateful for the funds he's raised. Art galleries. He's given dozens of pictures and sculptures. He was always working. I don't know how he found the time. A lot of it was here, of course, but he was also in Paris a lot. He was a member of the government, after all.'

Pel nodded. 'That', he said, 'is what worries me. Was he in financial trouble?'

Roger considered. 'I think the tax inspectors had been having a few doubts about his ability to meet his responsibilities. It worried us, I have to admit.'

'You mean you think he was dodging his taxes?' Pel asked bluntly.

Cousin Roger hummed and hahed for a while. 'Well,' he said eventually, 'I wouldn't go that far.'

'How far would you go?'

'Shall we say we were investigating him a little ourselves. No firm of accountants likes to wake up and find they're mixed up in something fishy.'

'Was it fishy?'

'It was beginning to smell a bit.'

'So you did think he'd been dodging his taxes?'

'No, we didn't. But we know he was behind in his payments and the tax inspector was wanting to know why. But he's not prepared to do anything about it – not yet, anyway, because these big operators often lay well back, feeling that for reasons of their own it's best to delay paying. To have cash available for some scheme they're working. To give the impression of wealth being in the right place when it isn't really. To give confidence to investors, that sort of thing. They accept that they'll have to pay interest on their unpaid tax, but they feel that it'll be worth it for reasons of business.'

'And he *was* a big operator?'

'Oh, yes. He was a big operator. But he *had* drawn a lot out lately. And the bank contacted us a week or so ago because they'd had a request through someone who has power of attorney to draw money on his behalf. He'd been taken ill, it seems. A lot of money went out. Made out to one of his firms.'

'Which one?'

'A meat wholesaling firm. I can let you have it.'

'I don't think you need bother. I think I know it.'

Cousin Roger was silent for a while. 'Funny you should come to see me,' he said. 'I was thinking of getting in touch with you.'

'About Barclay?'

'Yes. There've been a few hints that there's something fishy going on at the hospitals here, too.'

'What sort of fishy?'

'There've been a lot of things missing.'

'Surely he wouldn't be up to that sort of thing?'

'Not him. A type called Guy Rochefort. He's administrator for three of the hospitals here. The Hôpital des Pauvres, the Hôpital Médico-Chirurgical Ballier and the Hôspital Ste Geneviève. But – and this is the point – Rochefort was given the job by Barclay. At least, Barclay was on the panel which selected him and, though the other two members weren't very impressed and wanted another type called Magny, Barclay pushed Rochefort and he got the job.'

'And now?'

'There's a belief that Rochefort's been overbuying – things like sheets, pillowslips, towels – yet the hospitals are always short of them. He handles a lot of equipment.' Roger looked uncomfortable. 'Ought I to have got in touch with you before?'

nineteen

Madame Pel had enjoyed her day. But, since Pel was rarely prepared to take time off, she was under no delusions that what had happened had been simply to please her. If it had, she thought, why had her husband disappeared for so long into the shrubbery with Cousin Roger? However, she had been very happy and it always gave Pel a cozy feeling of reassurance that her businesses in the Rue de la Liberté were so well organised that she could safely leave them unattended for twenty-four hours.

Even Madame Routy seemed happy and handed him his briefcase as he left for Hôtel de Police the next morning as if she had enjoyed *her* day too. Pel had had no doubt that she had. As soon as they'd gone out of the door, she'd have switched on the television in the salon, turning the volume control from 'Loud' to 'Unbelievable' and, pouring herself a large tot of Pel's whisky – always risky because he watched it as if it were made of uranium – would have put her feet up in the 'confort anglais' to enjoy an afternoon of good French rubbish.

He was feeling cheerful enough, however, to forget about her and, in fact, when he reached the Hôtel de Police he actually said 'Good morning' to the man on the desk before he'd even opened his mouth. It didn't last, of course – Pel's good humour never did – but Claudie followed him into his office, smiling in a way that restored a measure of cheerfulness.

'Patron,' she said. 'I heard something last night that you might like to know.'

Pel raised his eybrows. 'About Arri or Barclay?'

'Well, yes. But this is something else.'

'Inform me.'

'Judge Brisard... '

'Ah!'

'He's after you, Patron.'

'He's been after me a long time.'

'This time he means it.'

'He always did.'

'He's going to report you to the Association of Advocates and Jurists.'

Pel shrugged. 'It's taken him long enough to pluck up courage. Where did you get this gem of information?'

Claudie's cheeks grew pink. 'Well, last night,' she said. 'I went back to that restaurant where that girl, Nenette, was acting as maître d'.'

Pel couldn't resist a joke. It wasn't a very good one. Pel's jokes rarely were. 'And *she* told you?'

Claudie smiled dutifully. Pel liked to have his jokes appreciated, even when they were terrible. 'No, Patron. But that's where I heard it.'

'You were on your own?'

'Not exactly.'

'Nosjean? De Troq'?'

She smiled. 'Not these days, Patron. Jean-Luc Nosjean seems to be rather occupied at the moment and De Troq's got an eye on a girl who's got a title like him.'

'Ah.'

'He's a lawyer in Maître Polverari's office. Bruno Lucas.' Pel nodded. He'd more than once noticed a tall, good-looking young man in Claudie's office trying to look as if he'd brought documents from the Palais de Justice. He had to admire her choice.

'He was the one who passed on the information about Judge Brisard?'

'Yes, Patron.'

'I'll take note. Why were you there? Because we'd found it reasonable?'

Claudie smiled. 'It was pleasant', she admitted, 'and lawyers don't get paid a lot when they first start. As it happened, something else turned up, too. There was something wrong with Bruno's car. It's pretty old.'

Pel nodded. He understood about old cars. He'd had one for a long time before his marriage.

'He had to take it to the garage,' Claudie went on. 'So, rather than have me sitting around there, he dropped me at the restaurant until he could get it fixed enough to take us home. It took a little longer than he expected and I got talking to the girl who runs the show – that Nenette. I had an idea and said I was sick of my job and didn't meet enough people. She'd had a few drinks and she talked to me because the place was empty. She admitted her job was only temporary, then she said "You're pretty", and asked if I liked men and, after all, if I enjoyed sex.' Claudie blushed. 'I said I did. Patron, I... '

Pel's hand waved. 'Go on.'

'She said she could get me a good job, with lots of money, lots of perks and lots of holidays. Including an expensive car. You remember there was a big Jaguar outside. She said it was hers and that I could have one like it if I wanted. Patron, she's the same as all those other girls we met. I bet I'd have got the same response from all of them if I'd tried. I bet they've all got nice cars. They're tarts, Patron. Poules. Dégrafées. Horizontales. That's why they look like they do. But for some reason they're none of them working at the moment.'

Pel smiled. 'No,' he agreed 'they're not. Because whoever it is who runs the Manoir de Varas got the wind-up when Arri was found and the place was closed down until the uproar died away. But they couldn't lose track of their girls or pension them off. So those who weren't sent on holiday were found other jobs and told to keep quiet. No wonder we ran into such a plethora of beautiful women.' He looked approvingly at Claudie. 'Can you arrange for a tail to be put on this Nenette in case she decides to move? On the other girls, too, for that matter. We'll need witnesses. The local cops can do it. They might even enjoy it. It would give them a good excuse to keep calling in where they work, and there isn't a cop born who doesn't enjoy chatting to a pretty girl over a counter. You'd better also ask the boys in St Trop' to keep an eye on Madame Danton-Criot. Do we have her address there?'

'Yes, Patron. I have it.'

'Tell them we want to know if she moves. I'm going to get in touch with Pépé le Cornet about our friend, Rykx.'

Pépé le Cornet's information was that Rykx was not at home.

'Where is he?'

'Where do you think? He's a Belgian. He's in Brussels.'

As he put down the telephone, Pel sat staring at the file on the Arri case for a while. The thing had suddenly become clear – as cases always did when you got the information in the right order. Unfortunately, that was something that rarely happened and nine times out of ten the vital information that linked everything up didn't turn up until the end.

But once they'd discovered what had been happening at the Manoir de Varas, like a jigsaw puzzle everything else had clicked into place. Barclay's wealth seemed to have been founded on the 20,000 francs he'd obtained by blackmail as a student in Marseilles and, with Dominique Danton-Criot knowing exactly what wealthy men needing sex would ask for, the establishment at the Manoir de Varas had been a sure-fire success. Between them, they appeared to have made a small fortune. Danton-Criot was a good businesswoman, Barclay was a financier, and Rykx had been an accountant, and they had been careful to hide their profits in the host of small businesses they had bought for that very reason, while the Manoir de Varas had remained outwardly respectable and had even been advertised discreetly in the sort of magazines men read.

But Barclay, it seemed, had grown too greedy or too scared, and had decided to move to the States with the proceeds from his shady ventures. Unfortunately, he'd decided also to take the profits from the Manoir de Varas and Rykx had clearly found out and arranged to stop him.

Somehow, Arri had got to know what was in the wind, or had even been recruited to help. But Arri owed Barclay not only his life but the very well-paid job at the Manoir where his duties, like those of Journais and one or two others they'd turned up, were to remove anyone who drank too much or was indiscreet. It was clearly there where his clothes had picked up the perfume. In a place like that the rooms would be full of it. Probably, even, the girls gave him an occasional playful squirt.

It was a good job with a good wage – the only condition being that in return he should give nothing away, avoid company who might ask questions, and generally live a low-key life. Since he had always been a loner, it had been a good bargain and with an old soldier's loyalty – like Yves Pasquier's with Pel – he had not swerved and had attempted to tell Barclay what was being planned. But, realising what he was up to, Barclay's enemies had killed him first and the kidnapping had gone ahead as planned, the idea behind it to get Barclay to cough up his ill-gotten gains. It was doubtless Arri's disappearance that had spurred Barclay into action and he had been about to call at his office to collect the last of the swag when he was snatched.

It hadn't taken much to confirm the idea. Pel had simply picked up the telephone and asked for Barclay's office in the Place Saint-Julien. Barclay's secretary had answered.

'The money you found in the safe,' Pel said. 'The 500,000 francs and 500,000 francs in bearer bonds. Is it still there?'

The voice that came back sounded worried. 'No, it was all banked as the police instructed and put under restraint.'

'Has anyone shown any interest in it?'

'A man came. I told him what had happened. He seemed angry. He had a letter giving him power of attorney and permission to collect it. It was signed by Monsieur Barclay and the signature was genuine. I know it as I know my own.'

Unfortunately, Pel thought, Monsieur Barclay had doubtless written it with the muzzle of a gun in his ear.

'Can you describe this man?' he asked.

Thanks, in a way, to Nosjean and the misplaced pride of Vacchi whose manoeuvrings with pictures had helped to confirm a lot of what Pel had already been thinking, it had suddenly become remarkably clear, and once they knew Barclay was not the clean, bright and shining knight he had appeared to be, it hadn't been difficult to expose his other interests for what they really were.

There had been the most extraordinary corruption in the affairs of the Ex-Soldiers' Bureau, and the contracts for the building of their hospitals and homes had been let to firms which had been far from the lowest bidders, with Barclay taking a third of the profits. The three hospitals at Lyons were in the scheme, too. Invoices showed that large supplies of steroids and other drugs had been delivered, yet, within a matter of a week of their arrival, the hospitals had been complaining there were none left. Further investigations had indicated that there were even false deliveries and corruption between the suppliers and the administration, and it looked very much as if some of the missing money had gone to Barclay's election campaigns.

The scheme had been based on simple things. Floor wax had been bought in enormous quantities – enough to last for fifty years – and at high prices from Rykx-Barclay firms – and surplus equipment had been disposed of without difficulty. Eighty-four thousand brand new sheets had been sold by the group at half the price paid for them, to get rid of them without fuss at the very time when they had been buying new ones at five times the price from Barclay suppliers. Towels had gone the same way.

Drugs were involved, as were voting frauds that had helped to elect Barclay to the House of Assembly and, in addition, the vineyards of La Gratinée on the Loire, another interest of Barclay's, were among those accused of adding too much methyl alcohol to their wine; while, finally, the Mexican and African disaster funds had discovered they were short of several million francs they thought they had raised and the Collège Privé de l'Est was the proud possessor of a whole array of fake pictures it had imagined to be worth a fortune. The bursar, like the administrator of the hospital group, who – surprise, surprise! – had also turned out to be an old army friend of Barclay's, was at that moment answering questions put to him by the police. It seemed to indicate, if nothing else, that military heroes couldn't always be guaranteed to have noble intentions.

The case was coming together very nicely, thank you, Pel decided, and a list of names of businessmen – pharmaceutical suppliers and suppliers of food, furniture and linen – had been made, together with the names of a variety of hospital officials, fund raisers and the administrators of orphanages and the homes for disabled ex-servicemen and children in care. Quite a lot of people were busy biting their nails and trying to explain to their wives why they looked worried.

It seemed to be time to put it all before the Chief.

'There's no doubt at all,' Pel said. 'The woman, Dominique Danton-Criot, known as Dédé, is the girl, Denise Darnand, whom Barclay knew in Marseilles while he was at university. Dédé's short for Denise, not Dominique, and there seems little doubt that it's an old name which has stuck. She clearly knew Barclay and, with Rykx – and possibly a few others we don't know yet – she set up this business at the Manoir de Varas.

'It has splendid kitchens, and magnificent bathrooms and bedrooms. The sitting rooms aren't much but I suspect that sitting isn't something they went in for a lot. As far as I can make out from the man, Journais, he, Arri, and one or two others we've found, acted as guards – and bouncers, when necessary. This, of course, was the job Barclay found for Arri. He knew he could trust him to keep his mouth shut and Arri seems to have done just that. Whether he enjoyed the job or not is a different matter but he was loyal enough not to ask questions.'

The Chief listened quietly, studying Pel as he talked. There was a lot about Pel that irritated him – above all, his gift for always being right – but the Chief was glad he had him and was prepared to back him up all the way.

'Barclay's a public figure,' he pointed out. 'Do we bring it all to the surface?'

'Why not?' Pel said shortly. 'A shit's a shit, even if he's a politician.'

'In that case,' the Chief decided, 'since both cases are the same, they'd better be handed over to Judge Polverari who's handling the kidnapping. I'll fix it with the Procureur. So long as you're sure.'

'I'm sure. There are *no* terrorists and never have been, and there'll be no demand for a ransom. Perhaps we should rely on our own resources in future.'

The Chief glared. It was typical of Pel, he thought, to read him a lecture. 'What about Barclay? What's going to happen to him?'

Pel sniffed. 'I think it's already happened.'

'I suppose you know where they've got him.'

'Oh, yes, I know. They started building a new swimming pool but they suddenly changed their minds and filled it in again. He's underneath. I noticed, by the way, that it was surrounded by beech trees, so we'll probably find that's where they did for Arri, too.'

The Chief seemed to need to reassure himself. 'But Barclay *was* kidnapped,' he said. 'There's no doubt about that.'

'Oh, no,' Pel agreed. 'None at all. He was kidnapped all right.'

'By at least five men. Where did *they* come from?'

'Journais was one. The rest were thugs hired for the job. Rykx would know where to find them. We know he was connected with the gangs.'

'*How* do you know he was connected with the gangs?'

'I got it from Pépé le Cornet.'

The Chief gaped. 'You've been getting information from *him*?'

'I also got information from a Madame Bernadette Ké-Ath. In Marseilles. Known in the town as La Dette.'

The Chief's jaw dropped another notch. 'Who's she? Some woman from the streets?'

'She runs a house. A clean house. A respectable house. A house the police know about.'

'A brothel?'

'I believe that's what they're called.'

The Chief went red. 'You were taken off this case because Lamiel thought you'd been touching pitch,' he snorted. 'It strikes me you've been wallowing in it.'

Pel shrugged. It had not been an unpleasant experience. La Dette was a woman of the world who knew how to charm men and Pel was not immune to charm. As they had talked in a small, very feminine pink and gold salon, she had even opened a bottle of champagne.

'Champagne', she had pointed out, 'can be drunk at any time of the day and it's much better at this time of the afternoon than that awful tea the English drink.' All very proper and as respectable as a Sunday visit to Mother.

She knew Rykx all right and had filled in a lot of gaps. She even remembered Barclay and Denise Darnand. 'A very beautiful girl,' she had said. 'Très bien élevée. Very well brought up and very well educated. Unfortunately, she had no heart, and in this trade a girl needs a heart if she's to succeed. If she doesn't have one, an intelligent man can always tell. Some of them, Monsieur, don't just come to climb into bed. They're having trouble at home and they want kind words, a little warmheartedness, a little comfort. Some of my girls have married very well.'

It had seemed to make sense.

'It was necessary,' Pel said.

The Chief eyed him for a while, realising there were hidden depths to him.

'Does your wife know?' he asked.

Pel sniffed. 'Of course not.'

The Chief grinned. 'If I were you,' he said. 'I shouldn't tell her.'

twenty

Darcy was delighted to be back on Pel's team and running its affairs. 'Right,' he said as they got down to making plans. 'What's the next move?'

Pel shrugged. 'We pick up Rykx.'

'Do we know where he is?'

'He's in Brussels. He has a house there. It's being watched. I've arranged it with the Brussels police.'

The Chief glanced quickly at him. The little bugger never missed a trick, he thought.

'And the woman?' he asked.

'St Trop'. She has a villa there. She's also under surveillance.'

'We'd better arrange to have her picked up, too.'

As they talked, Claudie appeared. 'Patron,' she said, 'I think something's moving.'

'Such as what?'

'I went to the Relais de Chanzy. Nenette's disappeared. I asked where she'd gone and they said she'd given up the job. Then I wondered if any of the others had gone, too. They have. Francie, the one at the Collège de l'Est has also left. They said she'd got a job in the south. The employment exchange's being run again by the old woman who said she was running it all the time, anyway, and the estate agent's back under the old management. The girls have gone. I drove out to Vallefrie to see why and there were two cars outside the Manoir de Varas. I could see them from the road. One was the big Jag we saw outside the Relais de Chanzy – Nenette's car. The other was the red Porsche that Francie from the Collège de l'Est drove. There were others, too. I think the girls are all back there.'

'Why?' Pel asked. 'Because they've got the wind up and been told to vanish? They're probably collecting money and personal belongings. We'd better find out what Rykx and Madame Danton are up to.'

It didn't take long. Rykx had thrown off his tail in Brussels and disappeared. But the Brussels police had questioned the servants at the house he owned and been told he was due to catch the late afternoon train to Paris.

'We'll have him picked up as he arrives,' Darcy said.

'And in the meantime,' Pel reminded, 'let's have the woman picked up, too.'

But here again, they were just too late.

'She's not at the villa in St Trop',' Claudie reported. 'She's dodged them. There's nobody there.'

Pel frowned. 'Then they *are* up to something. I expect Rykx has a car waiting for him in Paris so he can drive to Vallefrie to collect what he wants. Negotiable bonds, I expect, originally belonging to Barclay. Money – probably also originally belonging to Barclay. The Danton woman's jewels and a few other things they've doubtless got locked up in the safe. Let's have Lagé out at the Manoir to let us know if anyone arrives.'

As Lagé vanished, they tried to contain their impatience, knowing there was little they could do until they were certain of the whereabouts of Rykx and the woman. Pel had no doubt they would find them, but it would be an odd experience arresting a man they'd never seen for conspiracy to murder. But that was how it was going to work out. The men who had taken part in the kidnapping would turn up, too, he knew. Someone – probably Journais, the security man, who was already in the cells at 72, Rue d'Auxonne – would talk and, if they kept quiet about the arrests they were expecting to make, they would doubtless find the kidnappers all snugly at home enjoying the money they'd received for pulling off the job.

Feeling it was necessary to keep his cool and that sitting in the office watching the clock wasn't the way to do it, Pel headed for the Bar Transvaal for a beer, leaving instructions with Cadet Darras that he was to be called back if anything happened.

He was barely half-way down the glass when the telephone went. It was Darcy.

'Paris, Patron,' he rapped. 'They report Rykx wasn't on the train from Brussels. They've decided he must have arrived by air. In which case, he must have turned up at the Manoir de Varas long since.'

When Pel reached the Hôtel de Police, Lagé had reported in.

'A car's just arrived,' Darcy said. 'Fast. From Lagé's description, Claudie says it's the Danton woman's. Nosjean's here. So's De Troq' and Aimedieu. I can get hold of Brochard.'

'We'll need Claudie, too, because of the Danton woman and the girls. Have everybody else called in, too, and inform the police at Vallefrie and Arbaçay to meet us at Arbaçay. We may need them.'

Five minutes later three cars were heading out of the city towards Arbaçay. The police from Arbaçay and Vallefrie were waiting in their little Renault vans, openly disliking each other but all hoping that after the fiasco when they'd been sent on a wild goose chase to a raid at the Chateau de Chameroi-Fontaine at Praislay that wasn't taking place, there might this time be something to do that would make it worth giving up an evening of *Dallas* on the television.

After the police had received their instructions, the two Renaults, each containing three men, began to head for the boundaries of the Manoir de Varas under the command of Nosjean, who could safely be trusted to use his head and take care of any attempts to escape in any direction but towards the front gate.

Not unexpectedly, the gates of the house were wide open and they could see all the lights were on. Lagé appeared out of the shadows.

'There's something going on, Patron,' he said. 'There are eight or nine cars there now.'

'Right. Take Brochard and go up there. Ask to see Rykx and Madame Danton. I think you'll find them there. You won't catch them, of course, but you should flush them out. Close the gates, Aimedieu.'

The police cars moved off the gravelled surface and nosed under the trees that lined the long drive. Lagé and Brochard had been gone only a matter of a minute or two when they heard shouting and screams from the house, then they heard a car start and an engine roar. Darcy fished out his gun.

'No shooting,' Pel rapped. 'Unless they start it.'

Car doors slammed and the policemen tensed. Almost at once, the beams of a set of headlights swung away from the house and into the drive, then a large Citroën appeared, black and highly polished. It was hurtling towards the road at full speed when the driver realised the gates had been closed and they saw him wrench at the wheel. The car slewed round off the gravel, the stones hissing from the tyres, the front wheels bouncing on the uneven turf at the side of the road as it ploughed through a line of saplings that twanged and thwacked against the metalwork, then there was a screech of brakes and, with a crunch, the front of the car struck one of the police cars in the shadows, rocking it on its springs and sending sparks flying from torn metal. Finally the Citroën plunged into the undergrowth, bounced off a tree and came to a full stop with steam escaping from under the bonnet.

Immediately, the driver's door flew open and a dark-haired square man they could only assume was Rykx leapt out and was about to run. As Darcy appeared, a gun was flourished but Darcy brought his own gun down across the man's wrist and, as the weapon whirled away, Darcy swung its owner round to face the car and wrenched his arms behind him to slam on the handcuffs. As he did so, the other door opened and Madame Danton-Criot appeared, shuddering with shock, to be grabbed by Claudie. Peering inside the car, Pel saw a whole pile of briefcases and suitcases.

When they reached the house, Lagé and Aimedieu had mustered the remainder of its occupants in the hall. They were sitting on settees, the girl, Domino, distinctly aggressive, the others either arrogant or nervous, one of them openly weeping. Aimedieu was staring at them in amazement.

'Who're we arresting, Patron?' he asked. 'The chorus line from the Folies Bergère?'

It was over and Lamiel had finally disappeared back to Paris, riding off into the sunset with Thomas and all his other minions. The Chief wasn't sorry to see them go.

There had been no explanations. Lamiel had simply been withdrawn and the same day a message arrived to say so. Now the Chief was busy calling in his men from the outlying districts where they had been sent by Lamiel or Thomas.

While feeling a measure of sympathy for a man who had always been driven by the need to take no chances and obviously had to work under tremendous pressure, Pel nevertheless felt satisfied as he got down to preparing the paperwork for Judge Polverari who was now handling both the Arri and the Barclay cases. The art thing had been cleared up and Barclay's body had been found exactly where Pel had said it would be found and was at that moment in the city mortuary awaiting the attentions of Leguyader and Doc Minet. As they expected, the briefcases taken from Rykx's car had contained negotiable bonds and a considerable amount of cash, most of it originally belonging to Barclay – or, to be more precise, to the hospitals, colleges, homes and other charities he had manipulated for his own ends. There had been evidence of other high-class brothels like the Manoir de Varas – one at St Trop', one, for God's sake, in the States! – and Rykx and Madame Danton were also now in Number 72, Rue d'Auxonne with Journais and five other men, all Belgians he had named, who had been rounded up in Brussels, Ghent and Liege with the aid of the Belgian police. There were also a varied collection of artists and dealers, and eight girls, Aimedieu's chorus line from the Folies Bergère – the beautiful Domino, Francie, Din-Din, Reggie and the others. The girls had been released until it could be decided whether they were to be included in the charges or not. With one or two exceptions who might have been in the conspiracy – Domino, for instance, who seemed to have been privy to all Madame Danton's secrets – Pel suspected they would eventually all go free, because they seemed to be unaware of what Rykx and Madame Danton had been up to with Barclay and were only guilty of plying their profession, the oldest in the world. Having formally arrested them, Aimedieu had managed to get the job of interviewing them with Lagé and, since Lagé was a well-married man with a wife with sharp eyes, Aimedieu was doing most of the work and thoroughly enjoying himself.

'It's like questioning a harem,' he said gleefully.

In the meantime, Pel, Claudie and Didier Darras were hard at it, putting the reports in order.

As he worked, Pel's door opened and Judge Brisard appeared. He looked pale and angry.

'I see Polverari's taken everything over,' he said. 'Both cases.'

'There's only one case,' Pel pointed out flatly. 'There always was only one case and Polverari is handling it.'

'Without doubt', Brisard snapped, 'with more help from you than I ever receive. Make no mistake, though, I still haven't forgotten that you failed to inform me when Arri was found. It's not the first time and my report has gone into the

Chief and the Procureur, and the Association of Advocates and Jurists.'

Pel said nothing. Opening a drawer, he removed a slip of paper and placed it on the desk. Slowly and deliberately, he placed two fingers on it and turned it round to face Brisard.

'It's a parking ticket,' he explained. 'Issued on the late afternoon of Sunday, the 26th of last month, the day Arri's body was found at Suchey, the day you say you were not informed. It was issued in Beaune. Your name's on it.'

Brisard stared at him for a moment, then he snatched up the ticket and studied it as if he had suddenly become myopic.

'Where did you get this?'

'Where do you think? Traffic. It was among many others that found its way to Inspector Pomereu's department.'

Pel lit a cigarette, feeling the occasion merited one, even if it was the last straw and finally did for him. 'Pomereu heard you were making a lot of song and dance about not being informed about the discovery of Arri's body and thought I might need it. It seems to indicate that, although the message *was* passed to your department, you didn't pick it up because you weren't where you should have been. You were forty kilometres away down the motorway. You were with a woman. I can even give you her name.'

Slowly Pel picked up the slip of paper and put it back in the drawer. 'Now, if you please, Maître,' he said, 'I have things to do.'

As the door closed behind the shaken Brisard, Pel sat back, satisfied. That, he thought, seemed to have disposed of the last of his enemies. He could now get on with his work.

Mark Hebden

Death Set to Music

The severely battered body of a murder victim turns up in provincial France and the sharp-tongued Chief Inspector Pel must use all his Gallic guile to understand the pile of clues building up around him, until a further murder and one small boy make the elusive truth all too apparent.

The Errant Knights

Hector and Hetty Bartlelott go to Spain for a holiday, along with their nephew Alec and his wife Sibley. All is well under a Spanish sun until Hetty befriends a Spanish boy on the run from the police and passionate Spanish Anarchists. What follows is a hard-and-fast race across Spain, hot-tailed by the police and the anarchists, some light indulging in the Semana Santa festivities of Seville to throw off the pursuers, and a near miss in Toledo where the young Spanish fugitive is almost caught.

MARK HEBDEN

PEL AND THE BOMBERS

When five murders disturb his sleepy Burgundian city on Bastille night, Chief Inspector Evariste Clovis Désiré Pel has his work cut out for him. A terrorist group is at work and the President is due shortly on a State visit. Pel's problems with his tyrannical landlady must be put aside while he catches the criminals.

"...downbeat humour and some delightful dialogue."
Financial Times

PEL AND THE PARIS MOB

In his beloved Burgundy, Chief Inspector Pel finds himself incensed by interference from Paris, but it isn't the flocking descent of rival policemen that makes Pel's blood boil – crimes are being committed by violent gangs from Paris and Marseilles. Pel unravels the riddle of the robbery on the road to Dijon airport as well as the mysterious shootings in an iron foundry. If that weren't enough, the Chief Inspector must deal with the misadventures of the delightfully handsome Sergeant Misset and his red-haired lover.

"...written with downbeat humour and some delightful dialogue which leaven the violence." *Financial Times*

Mark Hebden

Pel and the Predators

There has been a spate of sudden murders around Burgundy where Pel has just been promoted to Chief Inspector. The irascible policeman receives a letter bomb, and these combined events threaten to overturn Pel's plans to marry Mme Faivre-Perret. Can Pel keep his life, his love and his career by solving the murder mysteries? Can Pel stave off the predators?

'...impeccable French provincial ambience.' *The Times*

Pel Under Pressure

The irascible Chief Inspector Pel is hot on the trail of a crime syndicate in this fast-paced, gritty crime novel, following leads on the mysterious death of a student and the discovery of a corpse in the boot of a car. Pel uncovers a drug-smuggling ring within the walls of Burgundy's university, and more murders guide the Chief Inspector to Innsbruck where the mistress of a professor awaits him.

Made in the USA
Lexington, KY
18 January 2010